"You ~~~~ ~~~~~~ find ~~~~

Hi~~~~
exp~~~
so ~~~
she ~~~
ge~~~
We~~~
bri~~~

"No. That is, I was aware of the plan, but I didn't know that you were to be a part of it. She said that she knew the man to help put the plan into action. I hadn't the slightest notion that she meant…"

"Me?" Lord Westin also rose to his feet, the motion fluid and graceful.

She decided then that no man should be able to move with the kind of lethal grace he did. Nor, Emma continued—since she was already in a making-pronouncements-mood—should any man be quite as handsome as the earl.

Books by Mandy Goff

Love Inspired Historical

The Blackmailed Bride
Engaging the Earl

MANDY GOFF

began her foray into the literary world when just a young child. Her first masterwork, a vivid portrayal of the life and times of her stuffed animals, was met with great acclaim from her parents…and an uninterested eye roll from her sister. In spite of the mixed reviews, however, Mandy knew she had found her calling.

After graduating cum laude from North Greenville University with a bachelor's degree in English, Mandy surrendered her heart—and her pen—to fulfilling God's call on her life…to write fiction that both entertains and uplifts.

Mandy lives in Greenville, South Carolina, with her husband and three-year-old daughter. And when she is not doing laundry or scouring the house for her daughter's once-again-missing "Pup-pup," she enjoys reading good books, having incredibly long phone conversations and finding creative ways to get out of cooking.

MANDY GOFF

Engaging the Earl

Love Inspired

Recycling programs
for this product may
not exist in your area.

LOVE INSPIRED BOOKS

ISBN-13: 978-0-373-82909-5

ENGAGING THE EARL

Copyright © 2012 by Amanda Goff

www.LoveInspiredBooks.com

Printed in U.S.A.

Do not fear, for I am with you; do not anxiously look about you, for I am your God. I will strengthen you, surely I will help you, surely I will uphold you with my righteous right hand.
—*Isaiah* 41:10

To Cheryl, who has been a truer friend than I ever deserved. Considering the countless hours we spend plotting and brainstorming, our shared frustration over searching for just the right word, and your willingness to read my manuscripts again…and again…and again, I can honestly say that I would not be able to do this without you. You'll never know just how much I thank God for putting you in my life.

Acknowledgments

As always, my deepest gratitude to Daniel and Brie, for making my life not only complete, but also full. I love you both so much that I could never explain well enough to do the depth of it justice.

To Mom, Dad and Megan…
for simply being wonderful. I love you all.

And, of course, many thanks
to my editor, Elizabeth Mazer,
who offers her wisdom, insight and expertise
as I chase my dream.

Chapter One

Emma was going to be fired.

She never should have given in to her parents' entreaties to lie down and rest awhile after supper before she returned to her employers' house. But Emma had been so tired that a chance for a nap had been too tempting to resist. Opportunities for rest at the Roth residence were scarce—her young charges saw to that. But Emma had assumed her parents would wake her before the hour grew too late. It appeared that in this case, as in so many others, they hadn't employed simple common sense.

Emma bid a hasty farewell to her parents, both of whose eyes were bleary with sleep and surprise after she barged into their bedroom. The clock in the hall struck midnight—which had been the alarm to rouse Emma from her slumber—and was still chiming as she closed the front door and stepped out onto the street.

At this hour, there was little to no chance of finding a hackney cab on her parents' quiet, shabby street. Her best opportunity at hiring a hack to take her back to the Roths meant going a few streets over where there was more traffic—and rather more danger, as well.

Even this late, *that* part of the city still bustled with activity. Light, laughter and the smell of gin poured out from a pub she passed. Emma wrinkled her nose in disgust. She was leery enough passing through this area while visiting her parents during the day, and now with night bearing down on her, she was frightened.

Minutes into her walk, the feeling of something creeping along the back of her neck made Emma stop in her path and turn around. Other than some ruffians many paces behind, however, no one was there. Chiding herself for being paranoid, Emma pulled her pelisse tighter around her and quickened her step.

Footsteps on the stone walk behind her made Emma tense again. This time, however, she kept walking without turning to see what was behind her. She didn't have time for any foolishness. Her employers had been expecting her return four hours earlier. If Emma didn't find a hack soon, she would have to walk, which would add another hour or so to her journey.

And Lady Roth didn't brook such tardiness.

Possibly it was nothing but a trick of the mind, but Emma felt like when she sped up, the steps behind her sped up, as well.

Something coming from the left caught Emma's attention, and when she looked, an attractive gentleman was approaching her with all possible haste. The glint of determination in his eyes made her step falter. For a moment, all Emma could do was stand stupidly on the sidewalk, watching the man come closer.

I'm about to be robbed. Or murdered.

Emma's hesitation gave the stranger enough time to come abreast of her.

"Darling," he said, taking ahold of her arm and propelling her forward, "where have you been?"

Emma stared at him, her mouth agape. In her surprise, the stranger was able to drag her forward several steps.

"Get away from me," she said after a second's pause as she dug her heels into the sidewalk to slow the onward progression. But the command lacked any heat or force…no doubt because she was too shocked to be authoritative.

Clearly her lack of forcefulness was amusing, because the gentleman laughed, loudly…as though he was playacting for an audience. "Don't play your games, my love. Someone might think I'm trying to *abduct* you."

Did he just nudge her?

No matter how hard she pulled or twisted, Emma couldn't break herself free of his hold. "That's *exactly* what you're trying to do," she hissed back. Screaming wouldn't have been much help because thus far no one had paid their little tableau any attention. No doubt such interchanges were commonplace in this area and hardly worth notice or intervention.

"No," her assailant murmured in a voice solely for her ears. "I'm trying to protect you."

The statement was so ludicrous, Emma couldn't even respond. Clearly the only person she needed protecting from was *him*.

"A man's been following you," he whispered.

Abandoning her attempts to free her arm, Emma swiveled to look behind them. That *would* explain the chills along the back of her neck. And the footsteps. But she hadn't seen anyone. So far, the only person to accost her was the man pinned to her side.

"Just let me go…please," Emma pleaded, "I'll be fine."

He huffed. He actually *huffed*. "Could you be quiet? I'm trying to think."

Think about where you're going to dispose of my body?

The man might be nicely dressed—much too nicely for this part of town—and Emma might have thought that his expression, when he smiled, was most pleasant. But just because the stranger was handsome didn't mean he wouldn't murder her and dump her body in an alleyway.

So this time, she yanked against his hold.

Hard.

Instead of freeing herself, though, she caused them both to stumble. Emma's shoe caught on the hem of her dress, and there was a suspended moment when she lost her balance. Instinctively, her grip on the gentleman's arm tightened, probably to the point where she was digging her nails into his skin. And when she flailed her free arm at the same time that he leaned forward to offer assistance, Emma's elbow connected with something hard.

And if his muffled "oomph" were any indication, the something hard was probably his face.

That further startled her…to the point that she wobbled even more wildly. Emma would have fallen face-forward if the man hadn't hauled her upward and against his chest.

Her first thought was that his embrace felt unexpectedly nice.

Of course he had to spoil the effect when he opened his mouth.

"Enough," he snapped. "I'm only trying to help you." His annoyance was impossible to miss.

Emma was supremely agitated herself. Both because of his interference and the fact that she couldn't seem to push herself away from him…maybe a little more so about the latter. An interlude with a possibly deranged stranger—albeit a handsome one—wouldn't have been welcome at the best of times, but this was *really* not a good day. Lady Roth was probably watching the clock, ticking off each passing minute with a mean-spirited glee. The viscountess didn't much care for Emma. Which was fair—Emma didn't much care for her, either, or the very spoiled Roth children. But she needed to keep this job. Her parents were almost entirely dependent on her income.

"No one's around now," she said to her self-proclaimed rescuer, casting a look about them. "So while I thank you for your help, I must be on my way."

He opened his mouth, probably to argue, but Emma didn't give him a chance.

"Let. Me. Go," she said forcefully.

And apparently loudly enough to arouse the curiosity of a passing constable.

The short, stocky officer retraced his steps, walking back toward them. Emma could have cried with relief.

"What's the trouble here?" the lawman asked.

I'm being harassed by a bedlamite, Emma wanted to shout. She didn't have a chance to utter the first syllable, however, because the man, who smoothly released her from his hold, was already chatting with the officer.

"How are you, Constable Hilliard?" the stranger asked, tipping back the brim of his hat and making his face more visible.

The law won't care how attractive you are, you're still going to Newgate, she thought when she got a better view of his face.

It was admittedly very attractive. Dark eyes. High cheekbones...a nose that would have been the model of perfection if not for the small, almost unnoticeable bump from where it had likely been broken. And his lips, which were curved in a strained smile, most certainly weren't unpleasant to look at. Her eyes traveled back up his face, locking momentarily with his. Emma wanted to shiver at the depth of them.

In the few minutes that had passed, however, his eye was getting increasingly swollen. For a brief moment, Emma felt a pang of guilt for elbowing him, but had he only let her go, she wouldn't have—accidentally, of course—given him what

would likely become a black eye. And he was clearly crazy...
possibly homicidal. She needed to keep reminding herself of
that before she softened or allowed herself to feel too badly.

When the constable saw the gentleman's face, he floun-
dered for a moment. Then, after several seconds of righting
his uniform, seemingly making sure no crease was mis-
aligned, he executed a smart little bow. "My l— I mean, Mr.
Fairfax, I didn't recognize you at first. How are you doing,
sir?"

"Fine, Hilliard, fine." The man now identified as Mr. Fairfax indicated Emma with his free hand, "I'm just seeing this
lovely lady home safely. There are some ruffians about tonight."

The lawman, who seemed eager to please, bobbed his head
in agreement. "There certainly are,"

"Haven't had any trouble out here tonight, have you?" Mr.
Fairfax asked.

"Not too much," Constable Hilliard answered automati-
cally. But then he looked at Mr. Fairfax closer. "Though it
looks as if you might have met your share of trouble."

Mr. Fairfax's hand went up to touch his swollen and
bruised eye. "Oh, this," he said. "Only a bit of an unexpected
tussle."

"Something you'd like me to take care of for you?" the
constable asked, eager and ready to please the man on
Emma's arm. Apparently he was someone of importance—
or at least of more importance than this neighborhood usually boasted.

And with that thought came the sudden fear that Mr. Fairfax might try to have the constable apprehend her. Emma felt
faint.

But when the moment came that Mr. Fairfax could have
exposed Emma for her unintentional crime, the strange man

waved off the constable's question. "It's of no concern," Mr. Fairfax dismissed.

"Well," Constable Hilliard said, for the first time addressing Emma, "it's a good thing Mr. Fairfax found you. He'll get you wherever you're going safely."

And that would be helpful, she thought, *if he could somehow manage to get me there four hours ago. As it stands, I'm growing later by the minute, and this additional delay is hardly helping.* She smiled tightly at the constable in response.

As if he sensed her frustration, Mr. Fairfax swiftly drew the exchange to a close. "Good night, Constable Hilliard." Then he wasted no time pulling her away and down the sidewalk. "My carriage is not far. I'll take you home," he said to Emma.

Emma let herself be pulled along, while trying to decide exactly what she should do.

It was hardly ideal to accept an escort from a man she had not properly met. If she saw anyone who knew her, the resulting scandal would be sensational. But who were they likely to encounter at this hour? And the constable had seemed entirely convinced that Mr. Fairfax was respectable. The most compelling reason of all to go along with him was that she wouldn't have to walk back to the Roths, costing herself even more precious time in the process.

So Emma allowed him to guide her past the puddles of indefinable liquid on the street, away from the leers and jeers of men congregating in their path. And it was actually rather nice not to feel exposed and in danger.

Mr. Fairfax's carriage appeared in the distance. Within minutes, she was safely ensconced in the luxurious coach and had given Mr. Fairfax the Roths' address, which he conveyed to the driver.

"I appreciate your assistance," Emma said rather grudgingly once the gentleman took a seat across from her.

The man *had* helped her a great deal. Emma had not spotted a single hack during her exchange with Mr. Fairfax and then the constable. Were it not for Mr. Fairfax's offer of his escort, she would be facing the unpleasant prospect of a long walk through some rather unsafe streets.

Not that a carriage ride would save her from being fired.

"Why so pensive?" Mr. Fairfax asked quietly.

"I'm wondering what my employer will say about my tardiness." She didn't know what possessed her to share that; her plan had been to enjoy the ride in stony silence, not wanting to converse with Mr. Fairfax any more than necessary.

"Employer?" he repeated. "You're going to work at this hour? What do you do?"

"I'm a governess."

"Ah," he said.

It was on the tip of Emma's tongue to ask him what *that* meant, but she bit the question back.

Mr. Fairfax stretched out his long legs, and because of the close confines of the carriage, Emma felt even more crowded. She resisted the urge to shy away from him.

"What were you doing in this part of town so late?" he asked.

Emma had no intention of answering that question.

"That's personal." The words came out more snappish than she'd intended.

Mr. Fairfax frowned. "This isn't a safe place for a gently bred lady to be."

"I hardly think that would concern you at all." Emma bristled at his tone.

Mr. Fairfax didn't back down. "You need to think carefully about where you travel, especially at night." Along with the

I-know-better-than-you attitude came a strong note of disapproval.

"Don't trouble yourself, Mr. Fairfax. I think I can manage without your pearls of wisdom—" A phrase she decided on instead of her first choice, which had been "overbearing dictates."

His nostrils flared. "Had I not *troubled* myself this evening, you would have found yourself robbed…or worse," he said ominously.

"So you say," Emma said stubbornly. She didn't want to concede the smallest point to her new adversary. "I never saw anyone behind me anyway."

"I came to your assistance before he had a chance to accost you," Mr. Fairfax argued.

The battle over who could be the most intractable continued until the carriage rumbled up to the Roths' townhome. Emma made a move toward the coach's door, but Mr. Fairfax was faster. Swinging the door open, he jumped down to the street and reached out his hand to help her descend.

"Thank you for your unnecessary assistance," she grumbled, dropping her hold on his hand once both of her feet were on the ground.

"My pleasure." He bit out the words.

When Emma began walking toward the back of the house, Mr. Fairfax followed her.

"What do you think you're doing?" she hissed, reaching around, grabbing his arm and pulling him into the shadows.

"Walking you to the door," he said, as though he were a typical gentleman escorting a young lady home after a leisurely stroll.

Their situation was anything but typical.

"Are you mad? What if someone sees you?"

"Who do you expect to be awake at this time of night?" he asked with a lift of his eyebrow.

Emma didn't bother mentioning that Lady Roth was undoubtedly waiting for her. "You can't very well tell me you expect a band of ruffians or thieves to be hiding behind the bushes, waiting to accost me," Emma said instead.

Mr. Fairfax obviously thought answering her wasn't necessary, because he only held out his arm, indicating she should lead and he would follow. Throwing her hands up in disgust, she resumed her walk to the house and didn't bother to look back to see if he was following.

But of course he was.

When they reached the servants' entrance, Emma motioned for Mr. Fairfax to step back into the shadows. Surprisingly, he complied without comment, and she blew out a heavy breath of relief.

"I suppose I should thank you for the escort," Emma said, hesitating on opening the back door.

"But you're not going to?" Mr. Fairfax asked with a smirk. The shadows obscured most of his expression, including his injured eye. Emma briefly noticed the effect was actually quite dashing.

"Thank you," she replied, working to push the errant observation out of her mind. Her words of gratitude sounded rather grudging, however. Very grudging.

"I'll wait here until you're inside," he told her.

Emma didn't argue. Even with only their brief acquaintance as a guide, she knew it would have been pointless. But she did steal one last look at the handsome man standing in the shadows before she pulled the door shut behind her and stepped into the darkened kitchen.

Back in the carriage, Marcus Fairfax, the Earl of Westin, relaxed with a sigh as the driver turned toward home. His evening had run on longer than he'd expected—and the conclusion of it had been rather more exciting than anticipated, too. He prodded gently at his injured eye and winced at the sting. The fiery little governess had gotten in quite a good blow. He wouldn't be able to see his face in the glass without remembering her for a few days at least.

Not that he was likely to forget her anytime soon—injury or not.

In fact, he couldn't remember the last time a woman had so thoroughly engaged his attention—despite the fact that many had tried to spark his interest over the years. Marcus's title was old, his name was well respected and his fortune was considerable. Not to mention he still had his health, his wits and all of his teeth. Even half so many attributes would be enough to draw the notice of matchmaking mamas and their ambitious daughters. But none had caught and held his eye like the young woman who had seemed so very determined to escape his company.

He was still musing on the fire in her eyes when the carriage pulled up in front of his town house. Before Marcus could open the front door, however, someone pulled it open from the inside. The earl was mystified to find Gibbons standing on the other side. The butler looked remarkably alert, considering the late—or rather, early—hour.

"Gibbons?" Marcus asked, blinking in surprise. The servant actually doing his job during daylight hours was notable. This was flabbergasting.

His butler looked just as surprised to see him. The eye, Marcus supposed.

"Were you waylaid by a band of ruffians, my lord?" the older man asked.

"No, Gibbons." Marcus sighed.

"Attacked by a throng of marriageable young misses?"

Closer to the truth, Marcus reasoned, but still, he shook his head in denial.

"Trip over your feet?"

"Leave it, Gibbons," Marcus ground out. Gibbons was an old family retainer and, as such, had the liberating knowledge that his position was secure. However, for some reasons mystifying even to him, Marcus was too fond of his butler to dismiss him. Although the notion was occasionally tempting.

Gibbons quirked a smile but then sobered suddenly. "Though I'm curious to know who accosted you, we've no time for game-playing, my lord," he said as though the persistent questions were somehow Marcus's fault.

"I couldn't agree with you more," Marcus said, stepping into the house. His eyes—well, the one that wasn't swollen shut, at least—were tired, and his tongue felt thick and unwieldy. He'd been up now for nearly twenty-four hours, and fatigue weighed heavily on him.

"I'm going to bed now, Gibbons," Marcus said, pulling off his greatcoat and passing it to the butler.

"I think you might want to go to the blue salon instead," Gibbons suggested.

"Has my bed been moved there?" Marcus quipped.

"I don't believe you left explicit instructions for us to do so in your absence."

"Then I can visit the blue salon tomorrow. Right now, I'm going to sleep." Thinking was becoming a struggle. If Marcus didn't move quickly, he might end up sleeping in Gibbons's chair because he couldn't make it any farther.

"Shall I tell your estate manager to rest while he awaits your leisure?"

Marcus stopped in his path to the stairs. He turned to face Gibbons, trying to ignore the knot forming in the pit of his stomach. But Gibbons wasn't smiling, smirking or doing anything that suggested he was joking.

"Grimshaw is here?" he asked.

Gibbons nodded. "He arrived twenty minutes ago."

What could his estate manager want? Marcus knew that

whatever had happened, Grimshaw's coming to see him in the middle of the night was an ill omen. Anxiety momentarily banished his fatigue, and the earl nearly sprinted to the salon.

"Grimshaw? What are you doing here?" Marcus asked as he entered the room. Any thought of exchanging pleasantries faded at the sight of his employee's haggard expression.

"My lord," the older man said, rising from the chair. He took a step forward as though to shake Lord Westin's hand but then quickly stepped backward. "I'm sorry to have woken you."

Marcus could have corrected him, but he didn't bother to. "I'm only surprised to find you here so early," he said instead.

Grimshaw nodded. "Forgive me, my lord. I wouldn't have intruded were it not of the utmost importance. But once I received the news, I left immediately for London."

"What news?" Countless possibilities paraded through his mind, each one more dire than the one before.

"You made an investment with Lord Rutherford for some American timber," Grimshaw said slowly.

Marcus nodded. He only vaguely remembered the investment itself—Grimshaw handled those details—but he did recall the estate manager mentioning it to him several months ago. The investment seemed sound, and Marcus had authorized the man to deal with it accordingly.

"What about it?" Marcus prompted when Grimshaw hesitated.

"The ship transporting the goods has been in a storm. We can't say for certain, but I've received some information that the ship and the merchandise..." Grimshaw trailed off, obviously unable—or afraid—to say anything else.

"The ship and the merchandise, what?" Marcus pressed.

"Well...they might have...it's not certain, you understand...really, we won't know anything further until more information surfaces…" Yet Grimshaw still didn't get to the crux of the matter.

"Grimshaw, it's much too early in the morning to be playing guessing games."

"The ship has most likely sunk," the estate manager blurted.

Marcus thought through the ramifications for a few moments before he said anything.

"It's certainly a tragedy if that's the case, Grimshaw. But I'm more concerned about the crew and any other people who might have been aboard the ship. We can only pray that the reports are untrue."

"But the merchandise, my lord?"

Marcus waved the concern away with a negligent slash of his hand. "Undoubtedly, it would be unfortunate. But it's hardly worth traveling across the country before dawn. I appreciate your diligence in keeping me informed, but I don't see that this is a matter of any urgency. Surely nothing can be done until the reports have been confirmed." He made a move toward the door to call Gibbons to ready a room. "Stay here tonight and get some sleep before you return to Westin Park."

"You don't understand, my lord…"

Marcus sighed and paused in his trek. "I'm not pleased to have possibly lost the funds. But that is paltry in light of the other concerns if the ship has indeed sunk. That's why I've never gambled much money in schemes. They all have the potential to fail."

At this, Grimshaw lowered his gaze to the floor.

Marcus noticed the change in his demeanor. "What is it, Grimshaw?"

"You've trusted me for years with your estates and with your investments, have you not, my lord?"

Marcus nodded. Nothing about the shift in conversation inspired confidence in him.

Grimshaw nodded almost reflexively. But he still wouldn't meet Marcus's eyes. "And you've given me the liberty to handle the funding as I saw fit, for the most part."

"Yes?" More a question than an answer.

"I might have funded the investment from the Americas with a larger than usual portion of your ready funds."

The knot of worry in Marcus's gut grew and twisted his insides until they felt like mush. "How much?" he managed.

"In hindsight, more than I should have," Grimshaw hedged.

"What does that mean?"

"Bad news…if the ship has sunk…which of course we don't know for sure…" Grimshaw added hastily.

Marcus didn't want to ask this next question, but he had to. "If it *has* sunk, what does that mean?"

The time it took his estate manager to answer was grossly exaggerated by the fear gripping Marcus. "It means you've lost most of your fortune."

Even though Marcus had been bracing himself, the news still hit him hard. He raised a hand to rub his weary eyes and flinched when he pressed on the growing bruise. It was almost laughable—earlier that evening, he had fancied himself a heroic rescuer, sweeping in to save the fair maiden.

But who was going to ride to *his* rescue?

Chapter Two

Across town, Emma Mercer found herself occupied with her own need for rescue. As expected, she'd entered the Roth residence to find herself summarily dismissed from her position. To make matters worse, Lady Roth had not even allowed her a night's rest before setting her on the street, with her belongings already stowed in her valise by a maid. Notably missing among those belongings was any type of letter of reference.

Emma couldn't return to her parents.

Yes, sooner or later, she'd have to tell them she had lost her position, but she couldn't bear to wake them with that dreadful news so soon. Not until she devised a plan to find different employment and provide them with the income on which they depended.

That left her with only one place to go—Olivia's house.

At Olivia's, the butler, an imperturbable man by the name of Mathis, showed her immediately into the drawing room as though there was nothing unusual about a predawn visitor. Olivia joined her there minutes later, still in her nightclothes but with an alert and determined expression. One look—plus whatever information Mathis had given her—was apparently all it took for Olivia to understand exactly what had occurred.

"I never liked you working for that puffed up snob anyway," Olivia, the Marchioness of Huntsford, announced as she entered the room, talking over Emma's attempts to apologize for the early hour. "You are far too good for those terrors she calls children, and besides, she gave you scarcely any time at all to come by and visit me."

"This isn't exactly good news, Olivia." Emma felt compelled to interject. Although her friend's enthusiasm had a grudging smile tugging at the corners of her lips.

"Nonsense, this will be like a holiday, having you here—because, of course, you'll be staying." Olivia continued. "And none of your protests about it being extra trouble, or me being too kind. I'm being entirely selfish in looking forward to having you stay with me. Mathis will have a maid prepare you a room in no time at all, won't you, Mathis?"

"Certainly, my lady," the butler replied with such assurance that one might have supposed he always kept rooms at the ready for newly dismissed governesses.

"There, you see?" Olivia said as she seated herself on a sofa. "Now, while Mathis takes care of that, why don't you sit down here with me and tell me all about it?"

Relief and gratitude poured over Emma in a wave as she all but collapsed onto the seat next to her friend. Soon, the whole story had come out—oversleeping at her parents' house, rushing back to the Roths', the confrontation with Lady Roth ending in her swift but final exit. The only thing Emma left out was her meeting the man—Mr. Fairfax. But surely she could be forgiven for glossing over that. It had, after all, been merely a chance encounter with a gentleman she'd likely never see again.

Olivia listened with her usual amount of patience—which was to say, none whatsoever—interrupting frequently with exclamations of surprise and outrage on her friend's behalf. Emma was used to constantly having to bite her tongue around Lady Roth and the little terrors masquerading as children, and around her parents. Frankness was a sure way to offend the former and hurt the latter. Despite the bleakness of the situation, it was relaxing to finally say exactly what she thought without fear of the consequences. If Olivia were the type to be easily offended, they never would have become friends in the first place.

Granted, a marchioness and a governess were an odd pairing for a friendship. The origins of the friendship had been equally unique. During a walk through the park a few months earlier, David, one of the Roth children, had flung a handful of mud at his sister, Marie—only to have it miss and hit the unsuspecting Marquess of Huntsford as he and his wife were strolling. Emma had been suitably mortified, but the Huntsfords had been cheerful and gracious.

Since then, Olivia had been a stalwart friend. A stalwart friend who was now entirely too eager to find a silver lining in Emma's situation.

"We just need to build the proper strategy," Olivia continued.

"For what?" Emma asked, her dread rising as she wondered how much of the conversation her reminiscing had caused her to miss.

"For finding you a husband."

"Olivia," she said in a warning voice. Considering the evening she'd had, and the early hour, Emma could think of a hundred reasons not to have this conversation. Maybe a thousand reasons.

Her friend paid her no mind, which wasn't surprising at all. "Emma, it's a good plan."

"Your suggestion hardly constitutes a plan," Emma argued. "Besides, who would have me?"

The question was met with a blank stare. "You must be joking, Emma. There are no end of eligible bachelors in Town for the Season. It will be a small matter to make one of them fall in love with you."

"But do you think I'm going to find it that easy to just fall in love with someone myself?" And Emma prepared herself to receive a lecture on how she shouldn't be choosy. Not only was it much too early for the plan, but for lectures, as well.

But Olivia didn't chide. She looked rather crestfallen. "I'm sure there's someone out there who you might find…"

"Never mind, Olivia. I know," Emma said gently because she couldn't stand how her friend looked when she thought her brilliant plan—that wasn't so much of a plan—wasn't going to work. "But I still don't see how I can be expected to compete with the other eligible ladies."

"They'll be foolish to try to compete with *you*," Olivia insisted. "You're beautiful—no, don't shake your head, it's nothing more than the truth—you're kind, generous, practical, good with children and you're from a highly respectable family."

"A highly *impoverished* family, you mean. Uncle is the one with money, and he doesn't speak to Papa."

Olivia waved the problem away. "He's a recluse. He doesn't speak to anyone. No one will expect you to be his closest correspondent. Simply the fact that you are his niece and therefore, eventually, his heir will earn you entrance into many circles."

"But my uncle won't be the one to provide me with a dowry."

"So we'll find you suitors who don't need to gain money from marriage." Olivia reached out to take hold of Emma's hands. "Truly, Emma, a husband is what you need. As a governess, you will always be subject to your employer's whims. You'll never have security, never have stability, never truly be able to help your parents in any lasting way since you'll never be able to guarantee your income from one month to the next."

The last bit was a low blow, but Emma had to admit everything Olivia said was the truth.

"I know this may not be exactly what you'd planned for your life, but can you at least try?" Olivia asked. "If it doesn't work, we'll figure out something else."

Olivia looked so hopeful, Emma could only nod. "I suppose I can try," she said grudgingly.

"Wonderful!" Olivia exclaimed. And her mouth quirked into a smile, and her eyes sharpened. "It really would be the perfect solution. A handsome, wealthy, godly gentleman will fall madly in love with you and all of your problems will disappear."

"But I wouldn't get my hopes up, Olivia…. My agreement to try doesn't mean…"

It was no use; her friend was hugging her as though Emma had fulfilled her most earnest desire.

"I'll put together a list of the most suitable gentlemen, and we'll go from there."

"And how am I to meet these suitable gentlemen?" Emma couldn't help but ask. She covered her mouth to hide a yawn.

"Leave that to me," Olivia insisted. "I have just the man in mind to help."

Two days after the incident in Cheapside, Marcus wasn't in any better mood. There had been no further news on the status of the ship, so he'd spent his time reviewing his accounts, trying to determine just how badly he'd be impacted if the ship was truly lost.

Very badly indeed, as it turned out.

"So you're convinced the ships are lost?" Marcus asked during his morning meeting with Grimshaw and the Fairfax family solicitor, Mr. Wilbanks.

"I'm afraid so, my lord," Grimshaw said with a sigh.

It was clear that this financial struggle concerned Grimshaw just as much as Marcus. Marcus had learned that his estate manager's cousin was one of the timber merchants involved with the investment. That explained why so much had been funneled in a single project—Grimshaw had seen the opportunity to help his cousin and benefit his employer with a potentially highly profitable venture. He'd acted with only honest intentions, but his family loyalties had made him disregard the risk.

The guilt over acting with so little foresight was clearly weighing on him now.

"What can we do *if* the ships are gone?" Marcus asked. He was unwilling to give up hope that everything might, in fact, turn out fine.

However, his solicitor, Mr. Wilbanks, an older gentleman who had served Marcus and his father before him for years, was silent; obviously, he thought the worst.

"The numbers aren't good, my lord," Wilbanks said with the same dejected manner as Grimshaw. "In your grandfather's time," he explained, "the entirety of the family's income came from the rents on your estates. It was your father who made the decision to begin investing in various enterprises with the surpluses from the estate funds—a practice which you have continued, and which has doubled your income."

Marcus already knew the family's financial history, and he wanted to tell Wilbanks to speed up the explanation. But instead of barking at the solicitor, he tried to wait patiently.

Wilbanks took a steadying breath before continuing.

"But all of the monies in the investment accounts were used for this timber project of Lord Rutherford's. If the ships are lost, that portion of your income is gone. It will take years of surpluses from the estates before you would be able to build those accounts up enough to begin investing again."

"How much is going to be left?" Some claimed Marcus was rich as Croesus, which might have been an exaggeration, but the truth of the matter was that his accounts had been quite large. And now they were empty—and would remain so, unless the ship and its merchandise could be recovered.

All was not lost, Marcus supposed. He did still have a vast amount of property at his disposal. Property that earned a fair amount of income—enough so he would hardly have to worry about starving, or lacking a roof over his head.

But all the other uses he made of his money—the charitable donations, the investments into facilities to help the underprivileged, all his plans to use his wealth and position to drive interest in generating labor and housing reforms...it would all have to come to a halt. The very thought was appalling.

Wilbanks fumbled, but Grimshaw seemed to take pity on the solicitor, naming a number that made Marcus wince.

"It's enough to maintain your estates until the next round of rents come in," the estate manager continued, trying to be consoling. "And to cover moderate personal expenses. Not much more than that, though. No lavish living," he finished.

"Mr. Wilbanks," Marcus said, turning toward the solicitor, who looked like he might rather be having his teeth pulled out one by one and without any numbing effect than to be sitting in the room with them. "Is that right?" Marcus didn't care so much about the not living lavishly part...but it would have been nice if there had been something other than eking by on the horizon.

"From what I can tell of the paperwork..." Wilbanks sighed. "Yes. It is, unfortunately, true."

"How long?" Marcus croaked, his throat and mouth parched.

"How long until what precisely, my lord?" Wilbanks asked. He looked twitchy and uncomfortable. Grimshaw didn't look much better.

Marcus scrubbed a hand down his face. "How long until we can recoup?"

The solicitor consulted some papers in front of him. "It is difficult to say. The estates generate sufficient funds to cover most living costs. Unfortunately, most of the income from the recent rents collection went into the investment funds. The estate expenses are, of course, paid first, so there are no outstanding costs there, but the monies in your personal funds will have to last you until the next rent collection date. At that point, the situation should become more stable—and if you are careful with your expenses, then you may still have some surplus to go back into the investment accounts."

After Marcus muddled through the headache-inducing explanations, he decided that at least that was a bit of heartening news.

"I will also see about possibly leasing out some of your secondary estates to bring in some more funds," Wilbanks continued, "but any significant expenditure—" Wilbanks tiptoed carefully around the reform investments Marcus had discussed with him so many times "—will have to wait for…I'd say six or seven years, at the least. If you begin to conserve, make cutbacks, then the funds will, of course, accumulate faster—"

"I don't care about whether or not I'll be able to go purchase a new pair of boots every week," Marcus interrupted.

"Would you be willing to temporarily raise the cost of rent from your tenants?" Wilbanks asked bluntly.

"No," Marcus said before the man even had time to close his mouth on the question.

"Not even to help—"

Marcus slashed his hand through the air. "I said no." He

wasn't going to burden his tenants to fund his own social-reform agenda. "We'll find another way." He didn't know whom he was trying to convince—the two downtrodden men, or himself. "And I won't abandon all hope that the ship is, indeed, safe."

Grimshaw opened his mouth to speak then promptly closed it again. Another time or two of the same routine, and the estate manager finally found his voice. "I wouldn't get my hopes up, my lord. No one has heard from the ship. Nor have any of the rescue ships sent out located any sign of it."

"I'll continue to pray," Marcus said.

The two men stayed for only a few more minutes. Really, there was nothing left to discuss. And when Marcus was left alone in his study, he felt the weight of his predicament bearing down on him.

What was he going to do? The urge was strong to stay in his study and keep searching his finances for answers. Pouring over ledgers and account books wouldn't make a difference in the reality of the situation, however. He trusted Wilbanks and had no reason not to take the older man at his word. If anyone knew the state of the family's coffers, it was the solicitor who'd been serving the Fairfaxes for years.

Marcus was trying to devise an outing that would occupy his mind for a bit when his butler brought in a letter from his sister, Olivia.

Drop whatever you're doing. I urgently need to see you.

Less than half an hour later, his sister's butler, Mathis, barely had time to open the front door of the house before Marcus was pushing his way in. In the time it took him to ride to the Huntsford town house, he'd had ample opportunity to envision what might be wrong. After Wilbanks and Grimshaw's ill tidings, the earl was primed to expect the worst.

Mathis's stoic exterior should have given Marcus some reassurance that things were fine, but the butler's expression never changed. A thief could have a gun trained on him, and the most the older man might do was blink.

And because of his completely unflappable nature, Mathis didn't say a word about seeing the Earl of Westin with an eye that was an impressive display of mottled blues and purple.

A butler who didn't feel the need to offer unsolicited commentary on everything…it was a refreshing change.

"Your sister will meet you in the yellow parlor, my lord," Mathis said.

Without asking the location of the yellow parlor, Marcus headed down the hall. In the months since his sister's marriage, Olivia's new home had become as familiar to him as his own.

Marcus paced the length of the room while he waited for his sister to appear. Just when he was seriously beginning to contemplate going and finding her, the door opened.

"Good morning, Marcus," Olivia said cheerfully.

"What is it? What's wrong?" Marcus asked, taking a few steps toward her.

Olivia's brow furrowed in confusion as she hugged him. "Nothing," she answered.

Marcus still wasn't convinced. "Has something happened?"

"No." She paused. "Why would you think so?"

"Your letter said to come immediately. It sounded…frantic."

"I think you probably read too much into my request," Olivia said with a shrug.

"When your request contains the word *urgently,* I don't really have to read into it much."

"We're not here to discuss your overly active paranoia," his sister returned. "Besides, I'm in no mood to argue with you. I need your help," Olivia said, taking a seat and offering to ring for tea.

After declining the tea service, Marcus relocated to a chair, curious to hear about Olivia's problem...hopefully, it would distract him from his own. Whatever was wrong with his sister was consuming enough that she had yet to ask him about the injury to his eye.

Not that he minded that omission from the conversation, of course. Olivia would be much too amused by the story. Not to mention when Nick—her husband and Marcus's best friend—found out, Marcus would be lucky if he ever lived down the humiliation.

"What do you need my help with?"

He was pleased Olivia had come to him for assistance. Since she'd married, she hadn't seemed to need her older brother anymore. And as someone who had spent his entire adult life caring for his sister, the sudden change after her marriage made Marcus feel a little bereft.

"I've a made a list," Olivia said, digging in the pocket of her skirts and finally producing a folded-up slip of paper.

"A list?" he echoed, taking and unfolding the paper so he could read it.

His sister sat quietly while he scanned down the rather long collection of names.

"What's this?" he asked finally.

"A list."

Marcus barely resisted the urge to roll his eyes. "Yes, I think I have a fairly good understanding of what constitutes a list. But all I see on here are names. Would it be too much to ask what the significance of them would be?"

"Those men," Olivia continued, pointing to the paper, "are eligible bachelors."

Marcus stared at her, waiting for further explanation.

"They're for a friend."

"A friend?" Skepticism oozed in his voice.

Olivia sighed. "It's a complicated matter, Marcus. And I'm

going to need your assistance and discretion. So I'd appreciate it if you would at least *try* not to be difficult."

"I hardly think my trying to make sense of your inadequate explanations should classify as being difficult."

Olivia sighed. "I have a friend who needs a husband."

Marcus's cravat tightened, and his mouth was suddenly so parched he wished he'd accepted the tea. He couldn't dismiss the suspicion that Olivia had more of his involvement in mind than just being a keeper of the list.

Clearing his throat, he scrambled for an easy way to break it to her that he wasn't going to be eligible bachelor number one. "Olivia…you understand I have quite a bit to focus on right now…" he began, "and I'm not in any place to be considering taking a wife—"

Olivia rolled her eyes. "Do you see your name on the list, Marcus?"

"Well…no…but—"

She waved her hand as though to shut him up. "Then stop being dramatic. I certainly wouldn't have put you there."

"And why's that?" Marcus asked before he could consider the advisability of voicing such a question.

This earned him another look. "I doubt my friend would have you," she said breezily.

"I'm considered a fairly decent catch by most of the matchmaking mamas." Marcus couldn't believe himself or the words coming out of his mouth.

"She seems to think a scholarly gentleman will suit her."

"I was at the top of my class at Oxford." Clearly he was out of his mind.

Olivia only stared at him.

"Fine. I'm not on the list…not that I want to be," he added just in case he hadn't been clear on that. "So, since I'm not *worthy* to be there, would you mind telling me what you think I'm going to do with it?"

"You know the gentlemen on that list, right?" she asked.

Marcus nodded.

"How difficult would it be for you to arrange to bring some of them by here to meet my friend while she's staying with me?" Olivia picked at an invisible piece of something on the skirt of her dress as she asked the question.

He wasn't going to refuse her. There was little he *could* refuse his sister. But that didn't mean Marcus planned to give in easily.

"You want me to round up the men and parade them through the house like a Tattersalls auction?" he asked.

Olivia rolled her eyes. "I don't want them all here at the same time, Marcus. It would make much better sense for you to bring them by individually."

He gaped. "There are at least thirty names here."

"I don't want Emma to have to settle," she said as though he were a barbarian for suggesting otherwise.

Emma.

So that was the mysterious friend's name. He liked it, Marcus decided. Not that it mattered what he thought of the name or even the woman herself. Supposedly, they wouldn't suit.

"Suppose I decide to help," he said finally. "*Why* exactly would I be doing it again?"

Olivia sobered. As she leaned forward, Marcus saw the concern lurking behind the humor in her eyes. "Emma really needs a husband, Marcus. I want to help—and I told her that you would be happy to, as well. You *do* want to help, don't you?"

"A damsel in distress?" he muttered.

Olivia nodded, without any trace of irony.

With that, he was sunk—and he could tell Olivia knew it. But before he could say anything, there was a gentle tap at the door.

"Come in," his sister called out, and Marcus could hear the door behind him open.

"Oh, I'm sorry," a woman—Emma?—said. "I didn't realize you had company." Her voice was pleasant, Marcus noted. Low and sweet, and...oddly familiar.

"No, Emma," Olivia said, motioning her forward. "You're fine. Please come sit with us. Marcus and I were just talking about you." The woman crossed around the room to take a seat beside Olivia, giving Marcus his first look at her. It was a struggle not to let his shock show.

Damsel in distress, indeed, he thought to himself, as he stared at the governess from Cheapside.

So this is Emma. He looked down at the list of names in his hand and frowned. He hadn't liked being left off the list even before he knew for whom it was intended.

For some reason, he liked it even less now.

Chapter Three

"Maybe I should leave the two of you to your meeting," Emma said, rising from her seat and preparing to make her escape from the room.

"Not at all," Mr. Fairfax answered before Olivia had a chance to. His smirk widened.

A red-hot blush stole through Emma's cheeks, making her feel like the temperature in the room had risen dramatically. "No, truly," she argued, "I can talk to Olivia later. Right, Olivia?" she asked, looking to her friend for assistance.

Either Olivia was oblivious to Emma's distress, or she found the situation humorous, because the marchioness didn't seem willing for her to go.

"Of course you won't leave. I have to introduce you," her friend said.

"You really don't," Emma muttered. She was sure no one had heard her until she noticed that Mr. Fairfax's smile had widened impossibly further, and his eyes glinted mischievously.

"Marcus, allow me to introduce my friend, Emma Mercer." She smiled at Emma, as though to reassure her that Mr. Fairfax wouldn't bite. "And Emma, this is my brother, Marcus Fairfax, the Earl of Westin."

Her brother?

An earl?

Emma thought she might throw up.

She had punched an earl in the face…albeit accidentally. Was there any way to slink out of the room and pretend she'd never knocked on the door?

Sadly, it appeared too late for that option.

"There was no need for the introductions, Olivia," the man said, drawing Emma's gaze.

Emma hated the fact that he was more handsome than any man had a right to be. And she hated the fact that she'd noticed.

"There isn't?" Olivia asked. Her look of surprise was almost comical. If Emma had been inclined to find anything about the situation remotely humorous, that was.

Mr. Fairfax—the Earl of Westin, she amended—looked to be enjoying himself far too much. He nodded. "Who do you think gave me the black eye?"

Marcus barely contained his laughter. He wasn't sure whose expression amused him most. Olivia looked like she might fall out of her seat…either that or injure her neck because she kept whipping it back and forth between Marcus and Miss Mercer.

As for the other lady… Well, Marcus quickly decided that anger only made Miss Emma look even more appealing. Which was fortuitous, he supposed, because she looked mad enough to blacken his other eye. Purposely this time.

"Who…she…you…?" Olivia couldn't seem to form a complete thought. With each half-uttered word, his sister looked at him and then back at her friend. The gaze leveled at him was slightly accusatory.

Miss Mercer had her hands folded together in her lap, a beatific look on her face as though to suggest she would be the last person capable of doing anyone bodily harm.

Marcus could have made it easy on her. Could have explained to Olivia that the injury was accidental. But he wasn't in the least inclined to do so and ruin the fun of the moment. Heaven knows, he could use some amusement after the fear and uncertainty that had swamped him for the past few days.

Finally, Olivia settled on a reponse. She turned to look at her friend. "You hit Marcus?" Olivia's tone was surprised... not censuring.

The young woman looked like she was about to answer, even though Marcus thought it seemed pretty clear that the only thing she wanted to do was pick up her skirts and run from the room. "Well...we...it's really..."

He was going to be a chivalrous gentleman and rescue her. "Don't look so surprised, Olivia. I recall you having a violent streak of your own."

The comparison was enough to rile the previously tongue-tied Miss Mercer. "I hardly have a violent streak!" she defended. "It was an accident."

Marcus made a "hmming" noise deep in his throat. Mostly just to irritate his sister's friend. He found that he quite liked the high flush on her cheeks and the fire in her gray eyes.

"And even if it *weren't* accidental—which it was," she added as an impassioned aside to Olivia, "you would have deserved it for accosting me."

If Miss Mercer had noticed how wide Olivia's eyes grew with speculation at that statement, she probably would have stopped her passionate defense. As it was, with the two women sitting side by side, Marcus was the only one with the benefit of reading both expressions.

Olivia's was the height of amused curiosity.

Miss Mercer's bordered on horrified.

Smothering a laugh, Marcus interrupted her. "I was rescuing, not accosting. Which you wouldn't have needed had you not been on such an unsavory street at such a late hour."

Miss Mercer's eyes narrowed. And Marcus had the distinct impression that she might now like to punch him in the mouth instead.

"I was perfectly safe." She turned to Olivia as though she was about to try and convince her friend of the truth of that statement.

Marcus could tell by Olivia's expression that his sister was too busy trying to smother her own smirk than trying to tamp down her interest in the saga unfolding before her. "Don't worry about me, Emma," she said, her voice almost choked with laughter. "I'm just listening quietly."

Emma whirled back on him. "And *you* should tell her it was an accident!" she nearly yelled. "It's not as though I would have hit you on purpose."

"You wouldn't have?" he asked, keeping his face as impassive as he could manage.

"That might not be true right now," she nearly growled at him.

Olivia rose suddenly from her seat. "Did someone call for me?" she asked no one in particular, as though the room were populated with at least a hundred people.

"No!" Emma said at the exact moment Marcus said...

"Maybe."

Olivia smiled approvingly at him. With a nod, she brushed out her skirts and began walking toward the door.

"I think I'll just go check," Olivia said. She spared a look for Emma that was probably supposed to be apologetic. But her expression was too speculative to be sincere. "It's a big house. People are always needing something. You just never know." Then the marchioness shrugged.

"No, you never know," Marcus agreed, relaxing back against his seat, enjoying the rapid-fire emotions that flitted across Miss Mercer's face.

While he would never be so ungentlemanly as to accuse

a gently bred woman of doing so, he couldn't help but notice to himself that his sister ran from the room.

Leaving a murderous-looking Miss Mercer in her wake.

"No one was calling her," the lady said unnecessarily.

"No, they weren't," he agreed with a small smile.

"You're an awful person," she said then.

Marcus tensed a little, wondering if he'd taken his teasing too far and now she was truly put out with him. "Why's that?" he drawled slowly.

"For letting your sister think I hit you. She might be upstairs packing my bags for me." While the words had a forced lightness to them, Marcus could hear the genuine fear underneath.

All the humor drained from the situation. And Marcus felt like a cad.

It was impulsive—and probably foolish—but he rose from his seat and crossed the few steps to be at her side. He covered her hands with one of his, stopping her from wringing them together.

"Olivia's doing nothing of the sort. Honestly, if she thought you'd hit me on purpose, she'd probably be out buying you a gift. I can only estimate how many times she's wanted to do the same." Marcus hoped his smile put her at ease.

That brought out what looked to be a genuine smile… although a small one. Marcus felt a flash of elation and pride at having wrested that expression out of her anxiety. And when he noticed that she hadn't tried to pull her hands away from his, he felt something else…something warmer, more indefinable.

"Olivia shut the door behind her," Miss Mercer said then, surprising him with the sudden change in conversation.

But Marcus followed her gaze and laughed. His sister was nothing if not enterprising.

"So why *do* you think she ran out of the room?" Miss Mercer asked after a few seconds.

Marcus grinned. "She was giving us some time alone."

The complete innocence in Miss Mercer's expression was refreshing. "Why?" she asked.

"To see what we would do."

"What we'd do?" she echoed.

Marcus nodded. "She probably thought you might like the chance to punch me again."

Miss Mercer laughed. It was the first time he'd heard her do so, and Marcus decided that she was exceptionally beautiful when she laughed. Her gray eyes twinkled. And as she tossed her head back, some of her shiny black hair slipped out of her fancy arrangement, tumbling to her shoulders. Her full lips quirked in a smile.

"So what did Olivia think you might want to do?" the lady asked. A guileless question.

Why, then, did Marcus want to answer her with a kiss?

Not that he would, of course. No, it was a completely inappropriate urge, and…and a ridiculous idea, besides. His lack of sleep was playing tricks with his head. After years of ducking and dodging every predatory female on the marriage mart, surely he wasn't succumbing to tender feelings just because a pretty woman—this *particular* pretty woman—smiled at him. The very idea was absurd.

Yet, for all that, he was still careful to take a step away from temptation before he answered.

"Olivia likely thought I'd want to talk about the particulars of finding you a husband."

Emma choked.

On air.

"*You* will be helping me find a husband?"

His teasing smile gave way to a sheepish expression. "My

sister has decided that I will, so it seems highly likely. She's accustomed to getting her way. I'd like to lay the blame on her indulgent husband, but I'm afraid her indulgent brother was the first to set the trend in place."

"So you will…that is…you— I don't understand." Mentally, she scolded herself for sounding like such a ninny, but really, how was she supposed to respond? Olivia had truly asked the man she'd assaulted to find her a husband? What if he married her off to a boxing master in revenge?

"I'm here today by Olivia's summons," the earl explained. "When I arrived, she presented me with the following list." He waved a piece of paper in the air. "It's the names of all the gentlemen I'm supposed to coerce into calling on you— by means of physical force, if necessary."

Emma felt her back go rigid. *Coerce* into calling on her? By *physical force?* As if a man would have to be tricked or strong-armed before he'd consider courting her?

"I'm teasing, Miss Mercer," he said, sitting back slightly when he must have felt her stiffen.

"I know that," she snapped.

"Well, I wasn't teasing about Olivia's plan, but I am certain no coercion will be required once the gentlemen of London learn you are here," he amended. "That's truly my role in this arrangement—to arrange introductions."

"I suppose I should be flattered by your optimism," she said briskly. Rising quickly from her seat, Emma was almost surprised that the earl didn't topple over to the floor. She hadn't realized until then how much he'd been leaning against her.

"Were you aware of my sister's plan to have me bring you a husband?" Lord Westin asked.

"No! That is, yes," she stammered, turning her head to hide the blush. "That is, I was aware of the plan, but I didn't know that you were to be a part of it. How could I have? I had no idea that you were her brother until moments ago! She said that she knew the man to help put the plan into action—I assumed she meant her husband. I hadn't the slightest notion that she meant..."

"Me?" Lord Westin also rose to his feet, the motion fluid and graceful.

She decided then that no man should be able to move with the kind of lethal grace he did. It wasn't decent. Nor, Emma continued—since she was already in a making-pronouncements mood—should any man be quite as handsome as the earl.

Handsome men didn't bother her in general. And she'd known quite a few individuals who she would say had been given more than their fair portion of beauty. Olivia's husband, for instance. The Marquess of Huntsford was attractive. In a completely nonthreatening, pleasant way.

Not so with the earl.

It wasn't merely the handsomeness...although there certainly was that. It was the shrewdness, the playfulness and the intensity in his eyes, which all seemed to coexist in some strange commingling.

But Lord Westin was the last man for whom she should let herself feel an attraction. Olivia had recruited him to help her find a husband, which clearly meant that she did not consider *him* to be a good prospect—and who would know better than the man's sister? Besides that, Emma couldn't help but remember the condemnation in his eyes in the carriage on the way to the Roths', when he scolded her for being in Cheapside. What would he think if he knew that her parents lived so nearby? Surely an earl would disdain anyone with such low connections.

Why should that thought bring her pain? What did she care for his good opinion? He was overbearing and teasing and... and he smirked too much.

"Maybe I should go find Olivia. Maybe she needs help with…whatever it is she's doing." Emma at least had the presence of mind to be embarrassed by her pathetic excuse. That didn't, however, stop her from moving toward the door as she spoke.

"I doubt my sister needs your help eavesdropping," he returned. With only a few, long strides, Lord Westin was by her side.

"I'm sorry if my teasing you has upset you," he said seriously.

Deciding to take his proffered olive branch, Emma assured him she was fine—just worried about Olivia.

When Emma had turned her back to him and was preparing to continue her path toward the door, Lord Westin said suddenly, "You never did tell me what you were doing in Cheapside."

"That was intentional," she returned.

There was a little too much fervency in his tone for the question to be only polite curiosity. But she still had no intention of answering.

Olivia's brother was probably a perfectly decent and caring man. Clearly he had been concerned that his joking had upset her. Maybe he wouldn't treat her with disdain if he knew the truth. But Emma still didn't want to tell him.

Nick and Olivia were the only people she'd told all about her family's circumstances. Not that there were many people she *could* have told. Lady Roth had been entirely uninterested in the details of why she'd sought a position, and there was no one else to whom Emma was close. But even telling her friend had made Emma feel exposed and ready to be judged. She never forgot that she was associating with the nobility.

The Mercers were a respectable family, but even when her father was at his wealthiest, he'd never been a member of elevated society. The second son of a landed gentleman, her father was a scholar…a scholar who was unfortunately an abysmal custodian of the money he'd received as his inheritance in lieu of the estate that had passed to his older brother.

And now even that money was nearly gone. Emma didn't want Lord Westin's pity once he discovered how desperate circumstances were for her family. She didn't want to think about how differently the earl might treat her if he knew the truth.

She'd seen similar situations far too many times during her employment with the Roths. If Emma happened to be visible during one of the family's parties, the young men would flirt with her and act as though they valued her presence and conversation above all else.

The moment Lady Roth let it be known—in a voice that was much louder and shriller than necessary, in Emma's opinion—that she was nothing more than the governess, most of the gentlemen would scurry to far corners of the room. The ones who stayed weren't doing so for any noble purposes.

Emma knew how these kinds of things worked. With the exception of her friends Olivia and Nick, nobles didn't waste their time with those outside their social spheres. And wrong though it might be, Emma was enjoying the ease of this moment with Lord Westin too much to spoil it.

So she clamped her lips together. Let the earl think whatever he wanted. Because as far as she was concerned, nothing he came up with could be quite as bad as the truth.

Chapter Four

Emma really shouldn't have climbed up in the tree. It didn't matter that Olivia's rather extensive garden showed no signs of other inhabitants. With a bit of a self-deprecating smile, she thought that if Lady Roth could see her now, the viscountess would feel vindicated in terminating Emma's employment. Who wanted a tree-climbing hoyden watching over her children?

Olivia and Nick were both gone, visiting Nick's aunt, the Duchess of Leith. Emma had been invited but wasn't quite ready to face anyone else in the *ton*. Especially since there was one particular member of high society that she couldn't seem to get out of her head.

Stop thinking about him.

Really. It will do you no good.

You're being a fool.

Ever since the day before, when she'd realized who Mr. Fairfax truly was, Emma had alternated between being irritated that he hadn't immediately told her who he was, and being irritated with herself for caring at all. Climbing the tree had been a desperate attempt to find something to occupy her mind, which had been much too busy with thoughts of the Earl of Westin. She hadn't even attempted climbing trees since she was a child, and in her aggravated state, it had seemed the perfect challenge for the moment. Frankly, even now she was rather impressed that she hadn't broken her neck. But now that she was treed for the time being, she was left with nothing to do but think.

Her first priority had to be finding another job.

She'd agreed to go along with Olivia's plan, but surely the husband hunt her friend envisioned would never succeed. It was ridiculous to think that rich, eligible men would form a line to catch her attention. And besides, any man who *did* fall all over himself to earn the favor of a former governess of no particular distinction could hardly be sensible. How could she depend on a man like that to shelter and protect her and her family? No, she'd have to do as she had always done—rely on only herself.

It had been three days since Lady Roth had dismissed her without a letter of reference. Three days since she should have gone straight home and confessed everything to her parents. Emma hadn't been able to do it yet, though. She hadn't been able to fortify herself enough to see her mother's and father's hearts break.

Waiting, in the hopes of having some good news of a new position to alleviate the bad tidings of her lost job, was perhaps the most asinine plan Emma had ever concocted. But staying with Nick and Olivia made it so easy for her to not go home yet, to keep the problems to herself for a little while longer. To hope that some wonderful new opportunity would come to light soon.

Emma had already written to the different agencies in London, praying that they might have families in need of a governess. And while her personal contacts weren't extensive, Emma had sent missives to anyone she could think of, asking if they, or anyone they knew, needed a governess or even a lady's companion. Too little time had passed for her to receive any replies.

Father, let me find a job, had become a constant prayer. *And let me forget about that irksome earl,* had become a constant follow-up.

And while Emma was an avid believer in the power of prayer, she never felt any kind of confidence afterward that her entreaty would take care of the matter where Lord Westin was concerned.

Her life had spiraled so far out of her control that Emma wasn't certain she'd ever be able to rein it back in. Like a leaf tossed about by the gusting wind, she had little say over what happened to her anymore. And it scared her. Giving up control didn't come easily to her. Surrendering her concerns to God sounded fine in theory, but it was one of Emma's biggest struggles.

"Why am I not surprised?"

Emma started from her position on the branch, shaking the stout limb until she feared she might fall.

"Careful," the voice cautioned her.

She looked down toward the ground, wishing she could disappear farther up into the tree when she saw that it was Lord Westin standing below her.

Where had he come from?

"You're not about to drop out and knock me down, are you?" His mouth curved in a smile, and Emma felt her own lips upturn in response.

Emma said, smirking, "Not unless you provoke me." Which, considering their short, volatile history, was a distinct possibility.

Lord Westin, once assured that she wasn't going to be taking a nasty tumble, stepped back a few feet. He leaned almost negligently against a gatepost opposite her tree. "I'll try to be mindful of that, then."

Emma tried to look as stern as possible—something a bit difficult considering the undoubtedly ludicrous picture she presented. "You would do well to do so."

"So, are you in the tree for any particular reason or are you indulging a long-held desire to be a bird?" The gleam in his eyes teased her.

"I thought it might be a peaceful place to contemplate," she hedged.

For a moment, Emma was afraid he'd mock her, but Lord Westin nodded solemnly. "Understandable."

The two of them stared at each other for a few moments… it couldn't have been too long, just enough time to make Emma look away uncomfortably. She hated the fact that her wit and social graces seemed to fail her when he was around.

"Did you wish to be alone?" she asked finally.

"Not really," he replied.

Emma waited for him to say more, but Lord Westin didn't offer any explanations.

"Are you sure?" she persisted, "Because I could leave if you wish me to."

"Not at all. You were here first." As he shook his head, Emma noticed how delightfully mussed his hair looked.

Emma couldn't think of anything else to say. She decided that whatever the rest of the conversation held, it would be preferable if her part took place on the ground rather than in the air. Emma thought about asking him to help her down, or at least asking him to turn around so she could descend with a shred of her dignity intact. But without knowing how she would possibly phrase either question, Emma stared at the distance from her feet to the ground. And she jumped.

Lord Westin was at her side in an instant, steadying her by wrapping his arm around her waist.

"Are you all right?" he asked, looking her over as though she'd fallen headfirst.

"I'm fine, Lord Westin," Emma said, trying to step back and regain the distance between them.

"Don't do that again." His voice was harsh, commanding. His jaw was set, and his hands were a vise around her.

Her chin raised, and her eyes glinted in defiance. "How do you think I usually get down?"

Grudgingly convinced that besides being perhaps addled in the head, there was nothing wrong with her, Lord Westin released his hold and stepped away.

As soon as he let go of her, she felt the most disconcerting stab of emptiness.

"I stand in amazement that you made it to adulthood," the earl drawled.

Emma could tell he was trying to calm his own panic by the way he was breathing slowly, exhaling audibly. It was oddly pleasant to have someone so concerned about her welfare even if "show concern" for the earl seemed to translate to "be bossy and insufferable."

"You and my parents," she quipped.

His expression sharpened with interest. "Your parents? I haven't heard much about them."

There's a very good reason for that.

For a moment, she couldn't think of a single thing to say. "It's not like you're brimming with stories about yours," she countered. If she'd been thinking more clearly, Emma would certainly never have brought up the undoubtedly painful subject. She knew from previous conversations with Olivia that their mother had committed suicide after her husband's death.

The Earl of Westin's face shuttered, becoming a blank mask.

"I'm sorry," Emma said, her voice earnest. She even took a few steps forward, thinking she might grab his hand…some physical touch to try and imbue her regret into him.

"Don't apologize." His voice was gruff, although not angry.

But she couldn't leave it there. Emma already felt like a brat for firing back at him. So in an effort to offer an olive branch, she said, "I shouldn't have brought up such a painful subject. Olivia has told me about your mother's…" Emma's words trailed off as her brain caught up to what she'd nearly said. In her rush to apologize she'd forgotten that the circumstances of the former Lady Westin's death were a secret.

Society would shun Olivia and Marcus if it were known that their mother had taken her own life. "Th-that is to say," she stammered, "she has told me what a struggle it has been for you both to come to terms with your losses."

He gave her a considering look. "I see that Olivia has told you a great deal, indeed. The two of you must be quite close."

Emma nodded. "I don't know what I would have done without her these past few days."

The considering look sharpened. "And just how many days *have* you been here? Since about the night that we met?"

Emma shrugged. "Lady Roth didn't appreciate my tardiness." She tried to sound unconcerned. Lord Westin didn't need to know how devastating and upending her termination was. Or how confused and adrift she felt over what to do next…join Olivia in a husband hunt or confess to her parents and beg for their forgiveness?

He frowned. "She's not exactly a sympathetic figure, is she?"

"I see you've met her, then…" she joked.

His chuckle was low and warm. "So, what are your plans now? I know my *sister's* plans for you—but you've already shown that you're entirely unwilling to fall in line with others' expectations." He cast a significant glance up at the tree she'd so recently conquered. "Do you agree with her intentions to find you a husband?"

Emma averted her eyes, suddenly embarrassed. "I'm still trying to figure that out," she said quietly.

Despite her attempts to look away, brown eyes bored into hers. The inspection was so steady that Emma had to force herself not to be the first to break the connection. "What do *you* want?" he asked.

Why did she feel like the question was something more than it seemed?

"To be happy."

Her words hung in the air, almost taking on a life of their own. No matter how awkward she felt or how much she might have wished that she hadn't been quite as frank, it was too late to change the moment.

And when Lord Westin whispered, "Me, too," she was fine with that.

When Marcus saw the wistfulness in Miss Mercer's eyes, he couldn't help but be moved. He'd come into the garden with his mind full of all of his own problems. Another round of endless hours spent analyzing his accounts had brought him no good news. But Miss Mercer, in a situation far more pitiable than his, still seemed to cling to hope for the future. He admired her for that.

What would bring her the happiness she sought? Was it a husband, as Olivia seemed to think? She would hardly be the first woman in London to seek happiness in a wealthy match. Yet Marcus didn't really think that she was a single-minded husband-hunter. While he couldn't claim to understand the feminine mind, something about the fiery young woman being so materialistic didn't quite ring true to him.

But could he really deny his help in trying to make Miss Mercer's life better? Since she'd lost her job, maybe finding a spouse was her only hope.

He chose not to examine the way that thought rankled.

Marcus had come to call on Olivia today with the sole purpose of telling her that he couldn't participate in her matchmaking scheme. Getting his affairs in order to enable him
to live on his new and much-reduced income would be an
enormous undertaking. He'd have little time to devote to ar-
ranging routs and luncheons to find Miss Mercer a husband.
But now, in light of her wistfulness, Marcus found himself
reconsidering.

As he stood there looking at her, Marcus resolved that he
wouldn't tell his sister "no" just yet. Admittedly, he wasn't
thrilled with the prospect of what he was going to have to
do, but if it would bring a smile to Miss Mercer's face...well,
that might make the ordeal worth it.

Chapter Five

Emma shifted nervously in her seat in the pew beside Olivia. This was her first week at church since she'd begun working for the Roth family. While Lady Roth was a faithful church attendee, she hadn't wanted to be bothered with having her offspring underfoot during her time with God. So Emma had always been relegated to staying at the house with the children. She'd always tried to find a moment to herself at some point during the day to say her prayers and read some passages from her Bible, but she'd wished for the chance to attend a regular worship service again.

A wish that she was regretting now.

Oh, the church itself was lovely, and she had no reason to believe the service itself would be otherwise, but even though they had arrived only ten minutes earlier, the stares were already starting to grate. The other churchgoers had quickly noticed the unfamiliar face in the Huntsford pew and were abuzz with rumors and speculation.

Emma's seatmate was just as bad—though Olivia's speculation was of a rather different sort. "That's Mr. Beckett," she said, nodding discreetly at a stout gentleman of perhaps four and twenty making his way down the aisle. "Pleasant man, good family, income of, I'd say, four thousand a year. Very fond of cats. You like cats, don't you?"

"I… No, actually, I hate them," Emma replied. Olivia looked momentarily disconcerted.

"Pity," she murmured, before her expression cleared. "Still, there *is* his cousin, Mr. Wainwright—the one in the blue jacket. Handsome, don't you think?"

While she nodded, Emma remained uncomfortable. Mr. Wainwright *was* likely considered handsome, by most women. It was hardly his fault that he did not quite match her idea of a truly handsome man—tall, tanned, dark hair and eyes along with an irritatingly engaging smile…

She was relieved when the minister began welcoming the congregation, signaling that the service was about to begin. But her relief shifted to shocked dismay when the Earl of Westin slid into the empty space to Emma's left. "Sorry I'm late," he muttered to the rest of them.

Both Nick and Olivia whispered back words of greeting. Emma, however, wasn't able to do much more than force herself to continue breathing. Why did Lord Westin's presence seem to take the air out of the room? It was disconcerting. And even more disconcerting was the fact that none of the other gentlemen Olivia had pointed out had affected her nearly so strongly.

As she tried to ignore the fact that the lack of room on the pew meant that Lord Westin was practically pressed against her, Emma shot furtive looks at the other gentlemen in the congregation. Oh, they were all pleasant-looking enough. Some even could be called quite handsome.

Emma slid her gaze to the left. Her attempt at catching a discreet peek at the earl was thwarted when she caught his gaze. A corner of Lord Westin's lips quirked in a smirk, and he raised his eyebrows in a silent question.

Instead of responding to the wordless query as to why

she was casting furtive glances his way, Emma stared at her hands, clasped in her lap. Hopefully, he'd turn his attention back to the minister so he wouldn't notice that her face was an undoubtedly unbecoming shade of crimson.

What was it about the earl that simultaneously bothered and intrigued her? Emma pondered that question seriously for a few minutes, but came to no conclusion. While not having a wealth of expertise on the subject of men, she'd known her share of charmers and rogues. In all fairness to the earl, however, Emma could hardly deem him a rake—but a charmer, most certainly.

That assessment of him made Emma feel a bit better about the fact that she was quite unable to stop thinking about him. After all, it could hardly be her fault when the man was an accomplished flirt. She would simply do her best to avoid him…well, as much as their close connection would allow.

The minister's impassioned plea for the congregation to show Christ's love to others—which was really a yelled statement—roused Emma out of her thoughts. And she immediately felt ashamed for them. Here she was, in God's house, too distracted by the man sitting next to her to focus on anything else.

To add another sin at her feet, Emma had missed most of the sermon while rambling about in her mind. Whatever it was must have been fairly rousing because an elderly woman a few pews away brushed at gathered tears with a square of linen. A quick look to her right showed Olivia staring at the front, obviously as engrossed in the reverend's closing as she'd been in the entire message.

Good job, Emma. Your first time back at church and you don't even pay attention.

Saying a quick, silent prayer of repentance, Emma folded her hands demurely in her lap, ready to listen to the rest even if her mind became so full of other thoughts that it burst.

And as was her luck, Emma was in time to hear the closing thoughts and the calls for the congregation to heed the words—whatever they had been—of the message.

The reverend concluded his closing with a plea for the congregation to remember the Earl of Westin in prayer.

Emma's eyes immediately swung to meet the man's beside her—she couldn't help the reflex. *Was something wrong with Lord Westin? Was he sick? In trouble?*

Naturally she was concerned. Who wouldn't be? It didn't mean that she felt anything other than supreme irritation at his presence. Emma was simply concerned, wondering what could be so dire that the earl sat stiff and unyielding beside her.

And why did he look so panicked?

Marcus tried to shutter the emotions running through him before Miss Mercer noticed something amiss. His hands clenched. Every muscle in his body clenched in anticipation. What did Reverend Beresford know? How *much* did he know, and who had told him? Most important, what was the minister thinking, bringing up his financial difficulties in front of the whole congregation?

It wasn't as though his new "circumstances" wouldn't surface eventually. There were too many wagging tongues in the *ton* to ever believe he'd be able to keep something as intriguing as a shipwreck and lost fortune quiet. Marcus wanted more time before it came out, however. He wanted certainty, not merely grim speculation or even *near* certainty.

But Reverend Beresford seemed oblivious to Marcus's discomfort.

"His lordship might not appreciate me taking the liberty to discuss this with everyone..."

His lordship certainly wouldn't.

"…but prayer is powerful. And I think we should ask God to give him courage…"

And restraint.

"…to accomplish his task."

What?

"Being a voice for society's abused and neglected is never easy. Lord Westin needs our prayers that he remain a tireless champion of God's work."

Marcus could have whooped with relief. But embarrassment quickly followed. The eyes of those in the congregation honed in on him. He'd always tried to avoid any kind of attention for the work he was trying to do in Parliament. Seeking rights for the underprivileged and ignored wasn't platform for him to build a political career. The earl wasn't fighting for any reason other than to right a wrong.

The stares had almost a tangible weight. Though he noticed the person closest to him was studiously avoiding his gaze. Interesting.

Marcus could honestly say he'd never been so glad to have a preacher begin to pray. At least then everyone should have their eyes closed instead of training them on him. When the congregation was dismissed, Marcus didn't stand right away. He wanted to give the curious folks time to make it out the door.

As though the rest of the family sitting on the pew wished to show their solidarity, neither Olivia, Nick nor even Miss Mercer moved. The four of them watched as others strolled along, chatting with their friends and acquaintances.

"Are you all right?" Miss Mercer leaned over to whisper.

The lovely lady couldn't have surprised Marcus more she'd kissed him on the cheek.

Instead of answering, he turned to smile politely at her. "Am I that obvious?" he asked.

"No," Miss Mercer rushed to assure him. "I was just watching closely."

His strained smile shifted into an honest grin. When she realized what she'd said, Miss Mercer's face flushed. "That's not exactly what I meant," she said.

"I'm fine, thank you," Marcus said quietly instead of pressing her on her statement.

"Good," Miss Mercer said on a sigh. Marcus wasn't sure if that was necessarily a statement about his well-being.

"Emma, look," Olivia hissed, gesturing in a manner that Marcus supposed his sister considered subtle. "There's Baron Chivers—and he's looking right at you."

Marcus had heard of the baron. Actually, the man was supposed to be a decent sort—if a bit young still. And Chivers's mother was actually one of the most giving, generous women Marcus had ever met. Baroness Chivers ran a charity for downtrodden ladies.

Marcus looked casually over in the direction his sister had indicated. Though he hadn't met the baron before, it wasn't difficult to identify him. In fact, it would have been nearly impossible to miss him. He had his mother's hair, his father's bearing and an absolutely besotted expression on his face as he stared unabashedly at Miss Mercer. The speed with which Chivers took an interest in Miss Mercer bothered him…although Marcus wasn't precisely sure why.

Well, he had an idea of *why,* but it was better not to think about ridiculously foolish things. It would be absurd to be jealous. Even before the recent stress to his finances, marriage had not been in his plans for several more years, at least. And now, of all times, the burden and expense of a society wife was the last thing he could handle. Besides, he was all wrong for a woman like Emma Mercer—even his sister,

Olivia, had said so, and every ounce of reason and practicality he possessed told him that was for the best.

So why did it feel wrong to think of Miss Mercer becoming the wife of any man in London except him?

Chapter Six

Three days later, it had become widely known that there was an incredibly beautiful, unmarried lady staying with the Marquess and Marchioness of Huntsford. As a result, Marcus found himself having to fight a sea of callers to get in the front door of his sister's house.

Not that he was vying to add his name into the sea of potential suitors, of course. He'd simply wanted to get away from his home and the pile of letters on his desk reminding him of the work he could no longer do, the assistance he could no longer offer. Some time spent with Em—that is, with *Olivia* would be the perfect distraction.

"Unusual burst of activity, isn't there, Mathis?" he asked the butler once he was shown inside.

"Thanks to Miss Mercer, my lord," the old man said with a surprising grin.

That stopped Marcus in his tracks. He'd never seen Mathis smile. Ever.

It was almost enough to make him remain in the foyer and interrogate the servant as to what had truly happened, but the door was opening once again to let in two more ladies, a mother and daughter. Marcus knew them by sight, although not by name. The younger of the two looked like she'd just swallowed an entire lemon. The mother, on the other hand, looked like she'd be glad to wipe the sour expression off her daughter's face so long as no one was around to see her do it.

"I suppose my sister is..." he began asking Mathis.

Only to be interrupted with, "In the yellow parlor, my lord."

"Of course," he muttered, hurrying to beat the newest arrivals in there.

But Nick caught him in the hallway before he could make it to the parlor.

"Marcus?" Nick asked in surprise. "I didn't know you were coming by today."

Why did Marcus feel guilty to be caught by his friend? It wasn't as though he was doing anything wrong. He was paying a call on his sister...and on the woman he'd promised to help find matrimonial happiness.

When Marcus didn't say anything, Nick steered him toward the stairs. "You don't want to go anywhere near that part of the house. Trust me on that," he said.

"Is that so?" Marcus asked, hoping that he didn't sound overly interested.

Because he wasn't...overly interested, that was.

"I can't count how many people have been in and out in the last day or two. I think I'm going to have to send Mathis away to one of my country estates to recuperate for a while," Nick said with a laugh.

"That bad?" Marcus asked. His voice was a little more dispassionate than he might have preferred it to be. Because there was an incredibly fine line between sounding too interested and not sounding interested enough. Either way was suspicious. And with someone like Nick, a former spy who thrived on the subtle clues a person unwittingly gave away, Marcus wanted to be certain not to draw any undue attention.

"It's almost humorous," Nick said. "I think I understand better how you felt being responsible for Olivia all those years."

Marcus thought back to having to fend off Olivia's more ardent suitors and found that the thought of Miss Mercer receiving similar attention bothered him just as much.

But only in a different sort of way.

"Any offers for her hand?" Marcus asked, only joking in an effort to keep the conversation going while Marcus tried to figure out how much information he could pry for without Nick reporting to Olivia that he was interested.

"One yesterday," Nick said without laughing.

"You jest," Marcus said, so surprised that he almost stumbled on the steps. "Miss Mercer hasn't even been out to any events in society yet. How would a gentleman know enough about her in only a few days of afternoon calls to want to marry her?"

Nick shrugged. "She's very beautiful. The man came calling with his mother yesterday. Apparently, the young buck decided from meeting her that the two of them would suit very well."

Marcus waited for some punch line...like that the gentleman had been the infamous Viscount Danfield, an errant suitor of Olivia's who had loved his mother more than he loved good sense.

Nick didn't immediately confirm or deny, however.

"It was Danfield, wasn't it?" Marcus said, trying to prompt him to finish the joke.

Nick shook his head. "No. Baron Chivers."

A proposal from the baron already? He certainly acted quickly. Too quickly.

Wasn't there some fable or cautionary tale about a man who made up his mind too fast and how he was likely to quickly change it again? If there wasn't one like that, then there should be.

"So was Chivers heartbroken when you sent him away?" Marcus asked as they finally crossed into Nick's study. He was striding perilously close to sounding overly concerned. Yet he didn't seem capable of stopping himself.

Nick looked at him, the expression inscrutable. "I didn't send him away."

It was beyond belief. "You're going to let someone court Emma after only speaking to her once?" the earl asked, outrage and indignation lacing his words. All thoughts of discretion were forgotten in the haze of his incredulity.

Nick held out his hands in surrender. "Emma needs a husband…a fact which my wife reminds me of daily…hourly even. What kind of person would I be to turn away someone as kind as Chivers?"

"He's an infant," Marcus countered, immediately incensed by the suggestion that the baron might be a suitable match for Emma.

Nick gave him an odd look. "He's only a few years younger than we are," he said, his expression suggesting that Marcus was acting crazy.

"A few years can make a large difference," Marcus defended.

Nick didn't dispute that, but he also didn't back down. "Emma can decide for herself if they suit," he said, much too nonchalantly for Marcus's liking.

The earl could feel himself getting angry. How would Emma, who had never been a part of society's marriage mart, know anything about what would be best for her? That was why she needed Nick and Olivia to intercede for her. But obviously, his sister wasn't going to be any help. Marcus had looked at the names on that list…and he hadn't been overly impressed with any of them. Olivia seemed quite prepared to

throw Emma at any gentleman who stood still long enough…
except for her own brother, of course.

And now his best friend was also turning out to be a traitor. Stopping Chivers should have been the first thing Nick
did. It would have sent a message to the other suitors—that
any attempts to secure Miss Mercer's affections were going
to be taken seriously and handled with the utmost care and
discernment.

Instead, Nick had essentially declared open season for any
jackanapes who wanted to try and woo a beautiful woman.

"I actually think Emma will probably get along quite well
with Chivers," the marquess said as though he couldn't bear
to leave the subject alone.

Marcus couldn't sit down like Nick invited him to do. He
was suddenly filled with so much restless energy he thought
unless he could pace back and forth the length of the whole
house he'd have a fit.

"Yes, you've made that clear," Marcus snapped.

Nick didn't acknowledge the abrupt change in tone or the
way Marcus looked like he might want to bloody Nick's nose.

Nick shrugged, the gesture at once careless and calculated.
"Actually, I believe Chivers is downstairs, without his mother
this time. You may want to go see for yourself how they get
along since you won't take my word for it."

Marcus was halfway across the room by the time Nick finished his thought. And Marcus was on the other side of the
door by the end of it. And as such, and since he didn't turn
around, he couldn't tell that his friend was trying…rather
unsuccessfully, actually, to muffle his laughter.

Emma didn't want to be rude to the guests, but wasn't
there somewhere else everybody would rather be? She understood that, at the moment, she was a curiosity, a stranger everyone wanted to inspect for themselves. But she was weary

of the constant deluge of people with their endless questions....

Are you related to Mr. Albert Mercer, that wealthy recluse from Cornwall? "Yes, he's my uncle."

How long do you plan to remain in Town? "Until I'm needed back home."

What musical instruments are you accomplished in? "None. At all."

Question...

After question...

After question...

And Emma wanted to scream.

That would defeat the purpose of being nice to the eligible young men who came calling, however. Olivia sat in one corner of the room, doing her best to keep the most gossipy of the women away from her...a service for which Emma was inexpressibly grateful. That left only a few of the younger women, who had obviously come to see whether Emma was going to be any serious competition.

The rest were gentlemen, varying in ages and stations in life. There was a viscount, a baron and, if she remembered the introductions correctly, there was also an earl in the mix. It was unusual for such loftily titled men to come calling upon a nobody.

She supposed she could credit the interest in her uncle's rather bizarre behavior. But for all his elusive and reclusive ways, the size and scope of his assets had always been sufficient to ensure that Mr. Albert Mercer was well respected in society and would, no doubt, have been well received if he could be bothered to venture to Town. No one knew, of course, that Emma's father and uncle hadn't spoken since her grandfather passed away. Her uncle, the oldest son, had inherited the Cornwall estate, and Emma's father had been given a healthy stipend of money.

It was nearly all gone now, of course. And while Emma most likely would one day serve as her uncle's heir, simply due to his apathy in marrying and having children of his own, she knew that she could hardly expect any support from him for as long as he was alive.

Emma shook her head, trying to clear out thoughts of matters that were better left in the past and instead focus on what *she* was going to do to remedy her family's situation.

Baron Chivers, who sat on her left, seemed like an amiable gentleman. He wasn't much older than she was. Maybe five years at the most, unlike the gentleman who had to be well into his sixties being entertained by Olivia—again on the other side of the room.

The baron had sandy-colored hair, a face that was more rounded than chiseled and eyes that seemed kind. And while Emma couldn't in good conscience call him handsome—had Lord Westin forever ruined that term for her?—he was certainly appealing enough.

The young man was also extremely nervous. Which was odd considering that he had come by yesterday and they had spent an hour conversing about ancient Greek literature. Growing up the daughter of a scholar, she'd been weaned on Greek and Latin.

They had spoken about Homer and Euripides and then ended the conversation with Socrates. The baron had seemed to appreciate that she knew just as much—if not more—about the subjects as he did. So she couldn't account for the fact that today he seemed barely able to look her in the eye.

"Miss Mercer," Chivers said finally, "I was wondering if…"

Before he could get to what he had been wondering about, a newcomer to the room loudly interrupted the conversation. "Good morning, Miss Mercer. It's wonderful to see you again!"

Emma was astonished when she looked up into the overly enthusiastic face of Lord Westin. A frown pulled at the corners of her lips. What was the daft man doing?

Whatever Baron Chivers had been going to say was lost at the effusive greetings of the Earl of Westin.

"Oh, Chivers, I didn't know you were going to be here," Lord Westin said after a few moments, as though he hadn't noticed him sitting there before.

Olivia must have also noticed her brother's entrance—because really, who would have been able to *miss* the earl coming into the room? In one fluid motion, the marchioness gained her feet and crossed over to stand beside her brother. After embracing him, Olivia hissed something in his ear. Emma wasn't sure exactly what was said, but whatever it was, the earl apparently found it humorous, because he grinned at her.

And apparently ignored her, because in the next moment Marcus was walking back toward Emma and Baron Chivers. Within seconds, he'd ingratiated himself in the midst of their conversation.

"How's your mother, Chivers?" Marcus asked.

Emma and the baron both stared at the Earl of Westin. Baron Chivers looked at a loss for how to answer, and Emma couldn't help but wonder what kind of insanity had gripped Olivia's brother. And while she wanted to hear what Chivers had been going to say to her, Emma also couldn't deny the thrill she felt at Marcus's presence.

"She's fine," the baron finally said.

"Wonderful," Marcus said. He looked back and forth between Emma and Chivers. "Did I interrupt something?" he asked finally. His face looked contrite enough, but Emma wasn't sure the expression was sincere.

"No, it's fine," Baron Chivers mumbled. The younger man's complexion was ruddy, as though the only thing more embarrassing than whatever he'd been about to say to Emma was now having to sit through an audience with the earl.

"Wonderful." Marcus beamed.

Emma, feeling sorry for the poor baron, fixed Marcus with a glare. "Wouldn't you rather go talk to Olivia? She appears to want to speak to you."

Actually, Olivia looked as though she wanted to drag Marcus out of the room by his ear.

The earl must have noticed the displeased expression, as well. With a negligent shrug, he reclined back in his seat, obviously intending to stay awhile. "No, I'm sure she'll find time to *speak* to me later."

They were stuck, it would seem. Not that Emma could honestly claim to be overly upset, because despite her best intentions to push Marcus out of her mind, she was still absurdly glad just to be in his company.

Emma offered a conciliatory smile at Baron Chivers, who turned around and looked back at her as if he wished he had said whatever had been on his mind to say minutes earlier.

Emma might have been more curious herself, if not for the handsome, distracting and often annoying presence of the earl.

After the callers disbanded, Emma managed—and sometimes had to force herself to—to avoid the earl for the remainder of the morning and most of the afternoon, but it appeared that he had agreed to stay for dinner—which was to be a more formal event that night than usual, for Nick's aunt, the Duchess of Leith, would be joining them, along with her husband.

In spite of her best intentions, Emma was nervous. Olivia had assured her repeatedly that the duchess, whom Olivia called Aunt Henri, was the kindest, most warm-hearted woman imaginable, but after all those months spent in Lady

Roth's employ, Emma found that hard to believe. Was it really possible for a duchess—the highest possible rank for an English citizen outside of royalty—to lack all the snobbery, the hauteur, the disdain for her social inferiors that Viscountess Roth had shown?

Anxiety over the forthcoming encounter had Emma glad for any errand Olivia could give her—even her friend's request that Emma fetch Marcus from the library. She headed off eagerly and not at all cautiously, which could explain why as soon as she stepped into the library, she immediately collided with a hard body.

Perhaps it was the way her skin seemed to tingle at the impact, or maybe it was the distinctively pleasant way he smelled, but Emma knew she'd found the earl.

His hands gripped her by the shoulders, no doubt to hold her in place so she didn't fall backward. Instinctively, Emma did the same. Her hands clutched the lapels of his coat. Her only aim was to anchor herself so she didn't make herself into any more of a spectacle by landing on her backside. When the threat of falling had passed, however, Emma still didn't release him.

He didn't release her, either.

"What are you doing back here?" he asked. At the same time, Lord Westin pulled her closer as though he expected some kind of assault out in the hallway and was positioned to protect her.

Still, Emma could have dropped her hold, but whether because she didn't think of it or because she wasn't inclined to, her hands stayed entwined in his jacket.

"Olivia sent me to find you. She's expecting the Duke and Duchess of Leith to arrive at any moment," Emma explained.

She thought she heard the earl groan at that announcement.

"You don't like the duchess?" Emma asked, her anxiety deepening.

Lord Westin smiled. "No, I love her."

"But?" she prompted, feeling as though he wanted to say more.

"Aunt Henri considers me her nephew. And she's quite… determined at times."

It didn't take long for Emma to catch the unspoken words. "Determined to find herself another niece?" she asked with a smile, imagining a regal duchess pestering Lord Westin about finding a bride.

He nodded. "She has no children of her own, and now that she has Nick married, she's taken on my matrimonial bliss as her next project."

"Are you expecting her to bring a throng of eligible women with her tonight?"

"I hope not," he said with a grimace.

Emma couldn't help but smile at the thought of a string of women chasing Marcus through the streets on the duchess's commands. She ignored the small burn of jealousy. What was it to her if the earl had scores of women across London pining for him? She, herself, had had quite a number of suitors just that afternoon…and she hadn't been any better pleased with them than the earl appeared at the thought of the other women.

"And what of your sister?" Emma asked. "Does she set young misses on the trail, as well?"

Lord Westin shook his head. "Not yet. But never fear. If Olivia took it into her head to do so, I doubt she would send you."

Emma didn't say anything but cocked her head to the side in silent question.

He understood and answered what she hadn't voiced. "I've been warned we wouldn't suit."

His words should have embarrassed her. And in truth, there was a part of Emma that was mortified at the thought of

Olivia and her brother discussing her. But there was another part of her that wondered how the conversation began…and perhaps more importantly, what the earl had thought when Olivia made her pronouncement.

"Miss Mercer," Lord Westin said, her name the softest of whispers. Perhaps he'd been meaning to draw her back to reality…perhaps to say something else, but Emma couldn't guess because he stopped short.

"Yes?" she prompted, looking up at him.

The moment their eyes met surprised both of them. Whatever the Earl of Westin had been going to say was lost as he sucked in a breath. And Emma might have questioned him again, but she was too busy staring.

Emma was much more aware of the earl than she wanted to be. She felt disconnected from her surroundings, shaken by the man's closeness. And it was with immense satisfaction that she noticed Lord Westin appeared distracted, as well. Nor could he seem to recall what it was he'd been going to say. His hands still rested on her shoulders, and Emma's face was still tipped up to his.

Is he going to kiss me?

The question sprang to Emma's mind, startling her with the ridiculousness of it. She didn't even particularly care for the earl, did she? And even if she didn't *dis*like him, Emma hadn't known him long enough to have an opinion. Certainly she hadn't known him long enough to be thinking of kissing him.

Stiffening, Emma prepared to distance herself…physically and emotionally.

Lord Westin must have felt the shift, for his hands loosened and his eyes lost the sharp razor's-edge intensity. Now they crinkled a bit at the corners—more teasing than serious. "Miss Mercer," he repeated, still in a whisper but not quite as intimately as he had uttered the words only moments before.

"Yes?" she asked again, hoping she sounded nonchalant and not at all like she might want to know what it would feel like if he *were* planning on kissing her.

"You're wrinkling my coat," he said with a smile.

Looking down at her hands, Emma saw she'd fisted them in the garment. She unwound her painfully stiff fingers, realizing with a flush of embarrassment how that probably made her look.

"Sorry," she mumbled. Then, trying to undo the damage to his undoubtedly expensive jacket, Emma smoothed her hands down the front of his coat, hoping to divest it of the worst of the wrinkles.

Lord Westin watched her meager attempts to restore his wardrobe with something a little like shock. Belatedly, Emma realized that in her attempt to be a good Samaritan, she was essentially caressing him.

However, before she could step away, or even stop herself, she heard the sound of someone at the door. When she looked over, she saw a woman who could only be the Duchess of Leith watching her and the earl with a beaming smile.

"They've found each other," the duchess happily—and loudly—proclaimed.

Chapter Seven

Miss Mercer looked like she very much wanted to either die or sink through the floor. Marcus was just as stunned by his reaction to her, and by the very timely appearance of the duchess, but he managed to contain his surprise. He was used to Henri's machinations, having frequently seen the woman in action ever since Henri had decreed at Nick and Olivia's wedding that she'd find Marcus a bride within the year.

Apparently, Aunt Henri had been serious about making an attempt.

A shame she hadn't collaborated with Olivia on the choice of victim.

"Aunt Henri," Marcus said, taking Miss Mercer's hands and lowering them from his coat. No doubt the duchess was salivating, waiting to go tell Olivia what she'd seen. He had to stop that from happening.

The last thing he wanted was his sister taking him to task like an errant schoolboy for disobeying her directive.

"How lovely to see you again."

"And to see you as well, dear," Henri replied, "and in such *lovely* company."

Marcus had no response to make to that, so he simply stayed silent.

"Well," Aunt Henri said briskly, "dinner is ready. So, if you two are through…" Her smile was positively beatific.

"We weren't doing anything!" Miss Mercer felt inclined to utter.

Marcus pulled her hard against his side. Henri had her back to them, and he knew the duchess hadn't heard Emma. Squeezing her hand to tell her to remain quiet, Marcus prayed she'd heed him. Any protestations would only fuel Henri's fire. The best thing they could do would be to act like they hadn't been caught in a near embrace.

By the time they made it to join the others, it was time to go to the dining room. No doubt, since Olivia had charge of the seating arrangements, Marcus would find himself as far from Emma as the small gathering allowed. But as he escorted Miss Mercer to her seat, he was surprised to find his name at the place next to hers. Casting a wary glance at his sister—who pointedly avoided looking at him—Marcus wondered if Aunt Henri had hijacked the settings. In spite of their unexpectedly close proximity, Miss Mercer seemed at first determined to position herself as far from him as she could, short of actually getting up and walking away from the table. It took most of the soup course for her to finally relax into her seat.

Perhaps *relaxed* wasn't the right word to describe her, but Miss Mercer *did* appear to look a little less uncomfortable. Her cheeks, though, hadn't lost the high flush that had gathered there when Henri had discovered them in the hallway. For a brief moment, Marcus thought about reaching over to console her. But even leaning too much in her direction would probably send Henri into a flutter—and Olivia into a dither.

He didn't know why his sister was so adamant about the two of them. But she was…that was one thing she'd yet to back down from. And if he were so inclined, Marcus might have found it offensive that he was good enough to chauffer gentlemen to come meet Emma but he couldn't take any interest in her himself.

Of course, if the goal was to find Miss Mercer the most eligible gentleman in London, then it was true, Marcus was no longer as qualified to fill that role as he had been just a few weeks ago. But Olivia didn't know that yet—*no one* knew that yet—and Marcus planned to keep it that way for at least a little while longer.

He knew his sister would help and support him in any way she could, as would Nick, once they found out about his new financial circumstances, but he couldn't bear to tell her. The death of his father—followed shortly after by his mother's covered-up suicide—had taken Marcus from an inexperienced young man to a nobleman with a title, an estate and a younger sister solely in his care. He'd had to grow up quickly to handle all the new responsibilities. How could he admit that he'd failed so completely? How could he tell the sister who he knew, for all her teasing, loved and admired him that he hadn't protected the family legacy?

And if she didn't think he was good enough for her friend now, how much less worthy would she think he was once she learned the truth?

Despite the awkwardness of their initial introduction, it had been lovely meeting Henri. And it had been equally pleasant—if somewhat confusing—to meet her husband. No one had bothered to warn Emma that Henrietta's husband, the Duke of Leith, was named Henry, as well. On occasion, chaos ruled as a result. Emma had a suspicion the duchess loved when that happened.

But for all the pleasantness of the company, Emma had found herself constantly distracted during dinner. Maybe it was because having the earl right there made it all too easy to compare him to the other men who had come to call that day. It was disheartening for her to realize that he outshone them all, easily.

So dinner had been rife with tension…and now that she was huddled in her bed, Emma found she couldn't dismiss the litany of concerns long enough to rest.

Stop thinking about the earl. There's nothing to be had for it. Whatever you're feeling—stop it. She was being presumptuous in even considering him as a possible suitor. Of course, a person as powerful as the earl would likely find it offensive to have his name connected to that of a lowly governess…no matter how close she was to the rest of his family.

And unfortunately, thinking of *his* family only brought her thoughts back to her own.

No matter how long she tried to put off considering what she was going to say to her parents, it had been over a week without seeing them, and she couldn't procrastinate any longer. But telling them that the money wasn't going to be coming for a while was going to be impossibly difficult. She couldn't bear to imagine looking at her mother's face and seeing disappointment clearly written there.

Still, sitting in the Mayfair mansion and pretending as though her parents were going to be receiving the monthly stipend was nothing short of ridiculous. Emma had to make her confession, and the quicker done, the better. The question still remained, though, of what exactly she would tell them. She knew how dependent they were on her income—how could she reassure them when they realized that there would be no more money anytime soon?

Even if everything went according to Olivia's plan, Emma knew that the chances of her finding a husband in enough time to help her family were slim. Weddings took time and preparation, and even if Emma were betrothed tomorrow, it would be a while before she would have funds available to help her parents. And despite her friend's grand plans, Emma still found it difficult to believe a wedding would take place at all. So she'd sent out inquiries across the country, looking for families who were in need of a governess.

But even if she were successful in finding another position, there would not be any income coming in time to help her out of the predicament she was in, either. Her prayers were composed of requests that her mother and father would be understanding, and that between the three of them, they'd be able to devise a plan or implement a budget.

And keep her father from any more of his get-wealthy-overnight schemes.

So after a bit of mental persuasion, Emma talked herself out of the house early the next morning. Giving up on the notion of getting adequate sleep, she supposed it was better to be done with the deed. But she had to be fairly stealthy to avoid the ever-watchful eyes of Mathis. The butler might go to Olivia and tattle that Emma was leaving the house…or he might not. Emma didn't know well enough to judge. But she wasn't going to take any unnecessary chances. It wasn't precisely that Emma didn't want Olivia to know what she was doing… Well, it *was* precisely that.

The marchioness wouldn't allow Emma to go alone. She'd insist on traveling alongside her, especially if she thought she'd get to meet Emma's elusive parents. As awful as it sounded, and as bad of a daughter as it made her, Emma couldn't countenance anyone, even her only friend, seeing how far her family had fallen. It would embarrass her and her mother to suddenly be entertaining nobility in her parents' humble and shabby abode.

But Mathis had stepped away from his post by the door while Emma was sneaking in the shadows. And she took that as her opportunity to escape through the door and out onto the street. In only a few minutes, Emma found a passing hack, paying him several coins to take her into Cheapside.

If the burly driver thought it was unusual to see a young woman from Mayfair asking to go there, his face didn't show it. Emma jostled and banged about in the coach—much different from the elegant and well-sprung carriage the Marquess had—as it rumbled across the cobblestones.

Finally, just when Emma was beginning to fear the violent bouncing might shake her teeth loose, the hack rolled to a stop. She pulled back the dingy curtain blocking the window, and the familiar sites around her home drove Emma further into despondency.

Hopping out of the hack while still trying to retain a sense of decorum, Emma pushed a few more coins into the driver's hands.

"These are payment for you to wait on me. I shouldn't be terribly long," she said with what she hoped was an encouraging smile.

The gentleman stared at her skeptically.

"Thank you so much for your kindness," she said brightly… and she flinched only slightly at the sudden sound of yelling and what must have been a chamber pot shattering against a wall. The sound blessedly didn't come from her parents' street…but was still from close enough to be clearly audible.

Loitering wasn't the wisest course of action, so Emma flashed the man another smile and another assurance that her business wouldn't take but a blink of time.

Her parents were home and looked surprised—and of course ecstatic—to see her, which, while she wouldn't have thought it possible, made Emma feel even worse.

"That's a lovely dress you're wearing Emma, dear" were the first words out of her mother's mouth when the prodigal daughter walked in the door.

The appreciative comment had Emma wishing she'd made Olivia tell her where she'd hidden her old dresses. After the first delivery from the modiste, Emma's plain—some might even say drab—governess dresses had "disappeared." So she'd had no choice but to wear the beautiful green sprigged muslin her friend had bought her. It was finer, even with its simplicity, than anything her parents had seen her in for the past several years.

Murmuring a thank-you to her mother, Emma prayed there'd be no more discourse on her wardrobe and the sudden improvement of it.

Her mother didn't ask anything else, merely making a comment that it was nice to "see the Roths taking care of you."

Emma could have sunk through the floor.

"How are you and Papa?" she asked, noticing that her father had disappeared into his study. That wasn't particularly odd, but Emma would have thought he would have wanted to visit with her for a bit.

Perhaps it was all for the best; if the hack driver *was* waiting, Emma could just break the news gently to her mother. She'd always been the more practical between her parents. Mother would find a way to let Father down easily.

You're the biggest coward in the whole of England, Emma Mercer....

That might be true, she reasoned, but it was much harder now that she was actually here in front of her mother, who was looking at her with expectant eyes.

"How have you been?" Emma asked.

Her mother blushed, tittered and cast a look down the hall to where Mr. Mercer's study was. "I promised your father I would let him be the one to tell you. He should be back in a moment, darling. Horace!" she yelled back to her father.

Strange.

There was a jumble of commotion from the other side of the house and a muffled returned answer—none of which Emma could decipher.

"Before Father gets in here," Emma began quickly, "there's something I would like to talk to you about. Something serious."

Her mother waved off the request with a negligent hand. "No serious discussions today, Emma. We hardly get to see you enough as it is. You don't think I'm going to let you ruin your father's big moment with one of your 'talks,' do you?"

It took every ounce of willpower she had, but Emma resisted rolling her eyes. "I really have to insist—"

Her mother flashed her a stern look. "No, dear, *I* really must insist. I won't have anything upsetting anyone on our happy day."

Fine. Emma slouched back against the chair, waiting for her father to come out and put an end to whatever foolish moratorium had been placed against reality and reasonable conversation.

Mr. Mercer finally bounded out of the narrow hallway, waving a piece of paper like a white flag of surrender in front of his face.

"Emma, dear, you're going to be exceedingly proud!" he announced as he nearly skipped into the room.

"I'm sure I will be, Papa," she said on the tiniest, almost unnoticeable sigh. "Why don't you tell what it is and end the suspense for me?"

Her father and mother exchanged glances, looking like both of them might just burst into joyous celebration at any moment. They practically thrummed with enthusiasm.

"Will *someone* tell me?" Emma nearly snapped. "Before I leave, I have something to discuss with you, something important."

"Should we tell her, love?" Mr. Mercer asked his wife, the excitement clear on his face.

In spite of herself, Emma felt her interest pique.

Her mother nodded, blinking back sudden tears.

"You get to come home," her father said, tearing up a bit himself.

Emma gaped.

"I told you she'd be speechless, Horace," her mother crowed, clapping her hands together.

"What do you mean, I 'get to come home'?" Emma asked slowly.

Her father blew out an exasperated breath, as though he hadn't anticipated questions or anything but her dancing around the room with them. "You can leave your position. You don't have to work anymore."

For a moment, an indefinable blink of time, Emma's heart soared. Could it really be? But the rational—serious—part of her nature snapped the reins on her enthusiasm.

"How is that possible?" she asked. Emma, of course, neglected to mention that she *wasn't* working at the moment. Besides, that seemed to pale in comparison to their announcement.

"Your father's gotten a windfall," her mother sang out.

"A windfall?"

At this, Mr. Mercer looked a bit sheepish; the change in his demeanor immediately made Emma sit a bit straighter. She had a sinking feeling where the conversation was heading, but she didn't want to be hasty. Better to let him tell her than for her to make assumptions about how this windfall came about.

"A man at church was telling me about a speculation…" her father began, clearing his throat every few words.

"Stop there." Emma put a hand up to rub her temples. "I can guess the rest."

Her father waved the paper he'd been holding. "But it worked this time. We have enough money to last at least three months. Your mother's been tidying up your room so you'll have space to bring your things from the Roths'."

Emma, for the life of her, couldn't think of a single thing to say.

"Would you like your father to go with you to turn in your notice and help pack your things?" her mother asked while her daughter was still trying to articulate her thoughts.

"No. No, no, no," Emma added hastily before her father could drag her out the door in his excitement. "We need to talk about this."

"There's nothing to talk about, Emma, dear. We have the money," her father insisted.

"But you admitted yourself it's only enough for a few months. What do we do after that?" she asked.

Both parents paused, as though they hadn't anticipated that question.

Her father was the first to break the awkward silence. "The chap I went in with says he has several more guarantees. It's really only a matter of backing his ventures with more money."

Frustration made Emma want to rip her hair out strand by strand. "Father, don't you understand? Money's the one thing we don't have enough of. And we certainly don't have enough to throw away on foolish speculations—which are nothing better than swindling schemes, if you ask me."

Her father wore a hurt expression; her mother, however, appeared to be losing patience with her only child.

"I hardly think you can call them swindling schemes when the money made off an honest venture is going to be the way you get to come home," Mrs. Mercer said, her voice and expression full of reproach.

"I can't come home when there is only three months' worth of funds. And did you factor in the additional cost of feeding me? Or coal to heat my room?" She could bundle up in blankets, so that really wasn't a necessity, but Emma just wanted her parents to understand that…yet again…they were being foolish by not thinking through all of the variables.

And apparently, they *hadn't* considered that, because they were stunned into silence.

"It's no matter," her father said finally. "We might not be able to keep you in the Mayfair comfort you're used to, but we've enough to get by."

"What about when the three months are over?" Emma persisted. "Once we're out of money again, do you really think it would be so easy for me to walk out and find another position after leaving my last one?"

Funny how she was talking about staying at the Roths' as though it were an issue, or even a possibility. But this wasn't the time to tell them about her termination. They would only use that as a sign from the Lord that she needed to come home. And in three months, they would be in the same position they had been…perhaps one that was worse if her father continued insisting on funding the speculations of some nameless stranger.

No, she'd be better served to continue as she had been this last little bit…to keep searching for positions, and praying that God would open up whatever door He wanted her to walk through.

Her father was perilously close to tears, although he valiantly fought to hide it. Her mother didn't suffer from any such compunction about decorum. It was just family present, after all, and she was crying as though her grief would flood the room.

"Mama," Emma said, rising from her seat and moving to lay a comforting hand on her mother's shoulder. "It's not that I don't want us all to be together."

She looked at her father for help, but one glance at him proved he was going to be of no use. He was trying to hide his sniffling in a handkerchief.

Could they possibly make her feel any worse? Emma was trying to be responsible! Was that a punishable offense?

"I *do* want to be home," Emma insisted again to her mother, but she cast her father a glance so he'd know she was talking to him, as well. "But I don't want the time to come for me to need work and for there to be none." If she weren't at that place already, she added silently.

Now stoic, her father nodded. "Emma's right, my love."

In response, her mother sniffed and dabbed at her eyes with a tattered handkerchief. The display was heart-wrenching.

But something in her father's frame snapped and straightened. "I *will* make these investments pay out, Emma. This is just the beginning. In three more months, we'll have enough money to move somewhere in the country and live comfortably for the rest of our lives."

Her mother rallied a bit, nodding her head to agree with her husband. "Yes, you'll see, Emma. This isn't like the other times. Your father knows what he's doing now. And soon, we'll be together again."

Emma nodded. But why was it that when that knell rang out in the room, it felt like a sentence instead of a promise?

Chapter Eight

"Could you explain once more how I found myself obligated to come this evening?" Marcus asked, grumbling as he pulled on his cravat.

While standing in his sister's foyer with Nick, Marcus didn't really expect an answer, especially considering that he knew *exactly* how he had gotten himself mixed up in all of this.

He was incapable of telling his sister "no." Especially when it had to do with the lovely Miss Mercer and ensuring that she had the best possible experience at her very first social event. The steady stream of callers had clearly demonstrated that society was interested in her charms, but the ball was where gentlemen would truly make their intentions known. Marcus was fully aware of the importance of the event in the on-going quest to find Miss Mercer a husband— a quest that aggravated him every time he thought of it.

Marcus forgot his irritation when he saw Olivia's friend descend the staircase. Olivia had already made her way to stand beside her husband, leaving Miss Mercer to make a grand, and no doubt nervous, entrance.

The sight of her was a punch in the gut.

Oh, he'd known she was lovely. He could tell it even that

first meeting in Cheapside, when the moonlight had illuminated only parts of her features and the darkness of the night had obscured the rest. She'd been breathtaking then, and her beauty had dazzled him again and again on their encounters ever since.

With whatever changes Olivia had convinced Miss Mercer to let her make for the ball, however, she moved out of the realm of just being beautiful. She was something else entirely that Marcus wasn't even sure the most accomplished poet had devised a rhyme for yet.

"You look beautiful, Emma," Nick said, moving forward with an extended hand and a gallant bow. Olivia was clapping soundlessly in the background, as though to say, *See, I told you you were ravishing.*

Marcus wished he'd been the one to step forward first… and then he caught himself, shaking his head at the foolish notion of being jealous of his best friend. His best friend, who was happily married to his sister.

The woman looked every inch the dignified, innocent English miss as Nick handed her the rest of the way down the staircase.

Her dress was cream-colored, making a stark and impacting contrast between the pale porcelain of her skin and the dark sheen of her hair. While he knew that some would say the ensemble was too simple, it was perfect for her. Marcus shook his head before he could spend any more time analyzing the woman's fashion.

Olivia jabbed him in the back. "Say something nice," she hissed.

Marcus shot his sister a withering stare. He'd been *working* on it. Could he truly be held responsible that the sight of Miss Mercer stole any flattering words out of his mind?

He certainly wasn't going to admit that to his sister, though.

Because such an admission would undoubtedly be followed again by the lecture about how he wasn't suitable for her friend.

Once had been more than enough for that.

Hoping that the motion looked much more elegant and graceful than it felt, Marcus stepped forward, taking Emma's hand from the marquess. Bowing over it, Lord Westin kissed the back of her gloved hand.

"You look lovely," he said, still feeling the words were inadequate.

From the corner of his eye, he saw Olivia nodding her approval in the background. "See, Emma," his sister chimed in, "I told you, you were being foolish. You look gorgeous. Everyone will love you. There's no need to worry."

Marcus could feel the faintest tremor in the hand he was still holding, and his heart twisted. He, while never an avid or particularly eager partygoer, had at least never been *afraid* of society. The realization that Miss Mercer was terrified made him wish he could stay by her side all evening.

Marcus led Miss Mercer out to the carriage, and he tried not to let it bother him that she had nothing to say to him. He wasn't sure what conversation he was expecting, but anything would have been preferable to the sensation that Miss Mercer was trying to ignore him.

Why do you care? a niggling little voice wondered. *You're not getting involved in this. You're helping Olivia help Miss Mercer. That is all.*

Right. This was a job. A mission. Nothing more.

So why was he having trouble believing his own rhetoric?

Emma hated being nervous.

She considered it such a weakness that she'd always made every effort to face challenges head-on and without the smallest smattering of anxiety. Her mother—the Lord love her—

was a nervous woman…although who wouldn't be after living with Emma's father? And while both of her parents were good, God-fearing people, ones who had raised her the best way they knew how, one of the greatest things they'd done for her was to lead by example. Mostly that meant she'd learned how to live because of the way her parents acted.

In some cases, it meant she learned how *not* to live.

But Emma couldn't help the nerves this time. Her hands shook as she gripped the banister and walked down the stairs.

Olivia had neglected to mention her brother was going to be downstairs, as well. Which was probably for the best because that might have been just the piece of information to have Emma turning the bolt in her bedroom door and refusing to come out.

It wasn't that she didn't like the Earl of Westin…but the more time she spent with him, the more deeply she was affected by his presence. That was bad enough on an ordinary occasion. It was far worse when she needed, above all, to appear at her best.

There wasn't any time to turn and run back upstairs, however, before Emma found herself being herded into the waiting Huntsford coach. Even if she'd chanced it, Lord Westin's grip on her arm had her firmly anchored to his side.

Olivia kept up an incessant string of conversation for the whole ride. Emma heard maybe two or three sentences of it.

What did she think she was doing? There was absolutely no way she was going to be able to present herself in society and convince everyone she truly belonged there.

And just when she felt like her heart might run away with her, to beat so fast that she'd never be able to slow it, Emma felt a gentle pressure on her hand.

She'd had her hands tucked on the seat at her sides, with the volume of her skirts hiding them from view—she certainly didn't want anyone to see them shaking and trembling—and at the touch, she flinched, looking downward.

Lord Westin's gloved hand covered her own.

And he squeezed it reassuringly.

It was the smallest…and most touching gesture.

He didn't let go of her hand. And Emma didn't try to remove hers. The weight of it was comfortable and reassuring. And she could use a little bit of comfort and reassurance right now.

Emma felt slightly ridiculous.

It wasn't the dress she had on. No, the shimmering gown was without question the most luxurious and beautiful garment she'd ever worn. It wasn't her hair. Abigail, her maid, had managed to pin the black tresses into something both she and Olivia deemed to be the height of fashion. It wasn't anything about Emma personally that made her feel conspicuous and attention-grabbing, when her greatest wish was to recede and disappear in the crowd.

No, it was the veritable posse surrounding her.

Almack's was the first test.

In order for this crazy scheme of Olivia's to have a chance of succeeding, Emma needed to make her entrée into society. And what better place to do that than the most discriminating establishment in the whole of London?

There was nothing hallowed about the halls of Almack's. Nothing from the outside that would indicate that many a young woman's dreams for a successful Season had met a grim end inside the four walls. In fact, Emma thought the building rather unremarkable, if not a little shabby—not that she'd ever voice that thought aloud. But she knew better than to underestimate the patronesses—a group of women who prided themselves on their discriminating tastes and social influence. One look askance from a patroness, and

Emma might as well slink back to her family and beg their forgiveness.

Olivia had told her to stop being so dramatic, that everything would be fine, but Emma had seen her friend chew on her lip when Olivia thought no one was looking. Tonight meant a lot. If Emma made a poor showing, a wealthy uncle and influential and titled friends wouldn't be able to salvage a dowryless and socially ostracized nobody.

So while Emma had determined not to do anything that might embarrass herself or her friends, Olivia had been strategizing.

"No one would dare deny you tonight," Olivia had promised in a whisper on the coach ride over.

And it seemed as though her friend had good reason to be optimistic. Emma and her posse did look rather intimidating. After presenting Emma's voucher, Henrietta and Olivia had bustled her off to a settee in clear view of the rest of the assembly. Instead of trying to parade her through the crowds of people, Henri and Olivia had decided to make the gentlemen come to Emma.

Which was nice in theory, but in reality Emma felt like an exhibit at the museum.

To be fair, however, Emma didn't think that all of the curious looks were because she was an unknown in the presence of such esteemed nobility, but rather because the gentlemen in her company had their own idea of how to ensure Emma's social acceptance.

And apparently, their plan was to glare everyone into submission.

Each of the three gentlemen—Nick, Lord Westin, even the duke—stood behind the settee, with their arms crossed and mouths set into grim lines of challenge.

Emma suspected she wouldn't be doing much dancing that evening. Undoubtedly, any potential partners would be too terrified of the gentlemen to approach her. Aunt Henri must have had the same vision as Emma, because she turned around and snapped at her husband, "Henry, stop glowering. You're not a watchdog."

The duke, who Emma was coming to believe liked to bluster for the fun of it, softened his expression a minuscule amount. Aunt Henri, however, had already decided that she wasn't going to win the ensuing argument.

"Idiots," she muttered as she turned around.

It would have been a gross exaggeration to say that everything in the ballroom had suspended itself when they'd arrived and that now everyone stood staring back at the group of six renegades across the dance floor. The scene before Emma wasn't nearly so dramatic, but it certainly at moments felt that bad.

At least she'd be getting up to dance soon, with or without being approached by the young men in attendance. Her dance card already bore three names. She was set to stand up with the duke, the marquess and the earl.

The men had strategized that they would lead off with the most prominent member of their group. Emma was beginning to feel like an integral and necessary component of a military campaign.

Again, her friends claimed necessity. There was only one opportunity to win the good favor of the *ton,* and while everyone agreed that they didn't care for society's good opinion, it was a necessary condition in this instance.

An hour later, Emma had to concede the plan had worked.

After receiving the all-important nod from Lady Jersey, one of the patronesses, Emma had found herself beset by gentlemen wanting to dance with her, wanting to fetch her a glass of lemonade, wanting to see whether "her eyes were as blue as they'd appeared from across the room."

Emma hadn't the heart to tell the last gentleman that perhaps he needed spectacles, since her eyes had never been anything but gray.

Olivia and Henri had congratulated her and then each other. It appeared they both just barely reined in the instinct to engage in a group embrace to celebrate their victory.

And it was because the evening had, thus far, been such a resounding success that neither lady had complained when Emma had begged to have a moment to get some air.

She hadn't made it out the crush, however, before the Viscountess Danfield, one of the ladies Henri had said to avoid, stopped her.

"How are you enjoying your evening?" the woman asked. Her tone was polite, but Emma could feel the assessing gaze sizing her up while she waited for an answer.

"Very well, my lady," Emma said with what she hoped was an acceptably respectful curtsy.

"You seem to have made some advantageous friends," the woman continued, moving her gaze to where Olivia and Henri had ceased their conversation and were watching Emma with concerned expressions.

Their concern made Emma nervous.

"Yes," Emma agreed. "Olivia is my dearest friend."

Emma didn't know where the conversation was headed. And she never found out because she noticed that someone was approaching in her periphery. Emma's heart sank as she realized it was Lady Roth.

"Ah, Emma," Lady Roth said as she drew beside Lady Danfield.

Was it her imagination, or did the two other women have matching sly smiles?

"Lady Roth," Emma said, bobbing into another curtsy. While it would no doubt be bad form to turn and run in the other direction, she suspected that would be the only way to salvage the upcoming conversation.

And while it probably made her a coward to admit it, Emma cast a look backward to see if Henri and Olivia had noticed the arrival of her former employer. But a throng of people obscured her view, so she figured it was unlikely they'd noticed.

She'd be receiving no help from that quarter.

"Imagine how very shocked I am to find you here," Lady Roth said. Her voice barely concealed her distaste. Turning to the other woman, the Viscountess Roth arched an eyebrow. "I was under the impression that Almack's had standards."

Emma fought the urge to wince at the pointed jab. Meanwhile, Lady Danfield was attempting to assure her friend that while occasional oversights might be made, the proud Almack's tradition of discrimination would be upheld in the end. Then both women turned their focus to the interloper.

Straightening her back, Emma decided that she was in no way going to cower before these two women. Lady Roth was quite possibly the most unpleasant individual Emma had ever had the misfortune to meet, much less work for. And Viscountess Danfield was not winging her way into Emma's good graces, either.

"I couldn't agree with you more, my dear Eugenia," Lady Danfield said to Lady Roth as though Emma weren't standing inches away from them. "I know the Huntsfords enjoy charity work, but I'm surprised to find their social duty extends this far." She peered down her nose as though she were regarding an offensive puddle.

"I—" Emma began.

"Miss Mercer, I believe it's time for our dance," Lord Westin said, sliding in between Emma and the two other women as though he hadn't the slightest awareness that they were standing there.

She couldn't have been happier to see him. Not that she needed to be rescued, of course. But, well…it was nice not to have to face the scrutiny, disapproval and hostility of these women by herself.

"Of course, my lord," Emma said. With a bright, somewhat relieved smile, she accepted his arm, wrapping her hand around his.

Emma's two adversaries gaped at her, which was rather foolish. Hadn't they seen her enter with the earl? Why would they be so shocked to discover he'd requested a dance?

It took her a moment to realize they were appalled at Lord Westin's lack of manners. When he'd approached, he hadn't extended a greeting to either one of the other ladies.

Emma had to smother a smile at his audacity.

Lord Westin beamed at her as they began to walk away. Emma pointedly didn't beg the women's pardon. Nor did she bid them farewell. They seemed to be beyond exchanging empty pleasantries.

In a surprising rally, Lady Roth called out at their backs, "Lord Westin? I need to speak with you for a moment." It wasn't really a request.

The earl halted in midstep, causing Emma to jolt to a stop. They had quite a few spectators watching them, probably mostly due to the Viscountess Roth's shrill call. In pausing, Lord Westin made it clear that he had heard the command.

Then, without any further acknowledgment that the lady had spoken, Lord Westin walked onward.

Emma felt herself flush at the realization that the Earl of Westin had just *cut* her former employer and Viscountess Danfield.

For her.

Chapter Nine

Marcus heard the dual gasps of feminine outrage behind him, but he didn't slow his pace. His primary objective was getting Emma away from the two vipers masquerading as upright matrons of society.

He wasn't sure how long she'd been talking to the women, or what had been said prior to him sidling closer to eavesdrop. Nor did he much care. As far as he was concerned, he'd heard more than enough to convict the two of flagrant disrespect. And before he could stop to think of the potential scene he might cause, Marcus had cut the two women, even though he knew that their outrage would in no way match his.

"What are you doing?" Miss Mercer whispered, leaning close enough to his ear to waft the scent of roses about him. Surprisingly, she didn't sound put out with him or embarrassed, merely curious.

Turning to favor her with what he hoped was a charming smile, he answered, "Dancing with you."

Miss Mercer's eyes widened, but she didn't press him on the issue. Marcus wondered when she'd notice that they'd drawn the attention of the entire assembly. Perhaps he'd erred in his very public support of her. Not that he was worried for himself. While there were certainly consequences to his action, such as Lord Roth and Lord Danfield—imbecile that he was—trying to stymie every bill he backed in parliament, Marcus was more concerned that Emma would buckle under the increased attention.

One look at her face when they'd arrived that evening had been all Marcus needed to tell him that she was terrified of rubbing elbows with the same people who had employed her and generally looked down upon her. He only prayed that she wouldn't be upset by his defense of her right to be among them.

Marcus knew the exact moment Miss Mercer noticed the additional scrutiny. The hand on his arm tightened, and her step faltered. If not for the fact that he pulled her tighter against his side, the lovely young woman might have fallen.

"Don't be nervous," he whispered.

"Couldn't they all look somewhere else?" she murmured back. At least she didn't look quite as pale as she had only seconds before.

He smiled, more to calm her nerves than to put on a show for their audience. "They'll find something else to stare at before long."

Miss Mercer tightened her fingers on his arm, nearly gouging his skin.

"What if you're wrong?" she asked.

He smiled then, a slow, self-assured smile. "I'm never wrong. It's one of my greatest attributes."

"Let's hope so," she muttered.

The musicians were oblivious to the tableau unfolding in the middle of the ballroom, else they would have held their instruments rather than lifting them to begin the next set. Marcus led a slow-moving Miss Mercer to stand in line to begin their dance together.

Marcus decided then that if the *ton* wanted a spectacle,

he'd be happy to comply. Let them see how fond the nobility—at least one member of it—was of the former governess.

He bowed deeply—more deeply than he'd ever bowed to anyone, save the King—over her hand and raised it to his lips.

"You look radiant this evening, Miss Mercer," he said. His voice was loud enough that the people in the immediate vicinity would have no doubts over anything he said to her, and those who were farther out on the edges of the ballroom would hear from someone else before the next fifteen minutes had passed.

"Thank you for the compliment," she said, a smile playing at the edges of her lips.

"I could pay you many more, but I'm afraid that would take up most of the evening."

When she realized that they were nearly the only couple ready for the set, Miss Mercer's confidence flagged again. Marcus half feared that she would run off, leaving him standing alone in the middle of the room.

"Dance with me," he said quietly.

Instead of answering, Miss Mercer cast another anxious glance at the assemblage.

"They don't scare me," he told her, still with his voice pitched low. "And they shouldn't scare you, either." He extended his arm toward her. "Come, let's show them together that we couldn't care less what they think."

The musicians seemed to suspend and slow, as though wondering if they should waste their musical talents on one mismatched pair of dancers. But before Miss Mercer could utter a refusal, someone lined up beside her. Marcus turned to grin at his sister. And if Olivia's smile were a little tighter and strained than normal, he doubted anyone else would be able to tell the difference.

Nick took his spot beside Marcus.

Then, on Emma's left, the Duchess of Leith appeared,

nodding reassuringly to the young woman when their eyes met. The duke took the vacant spot on Marcus's other side. Slowly, other couples began to line up with them.

Marcus was grateful for the sign of acceptance, even if it seemed to be moving rather slowly. It was as though the others still hesitated to join the dancing, even with three other couples on the floor. Or, worse yet, as though they feared that by dancing alongside Emma, they were forfeiting the right to talk about her later.

When he was dancing with Miss Mercer, however, Marcus forgot all about his shocking cut of two of society's most lauded matrons. He didn't think about the fact that he and the others were on a mission to prove Emma's right to cavort with the *ton.* The only thing occupying this mind was the fact that he rather enjoyed his close proximity to the woman in question.

An enjoyment which must have shown on his face, because it was certainly remarked upon later.

In less than ten minutes, they—the ones who made all-important, grand and sweeping pronouncements—declared that Lord Westin had, by giving the *cut direct* to the viscount-esses, made Miss Emma Mercer one of Society's *nonpareils.*

Within the hour after arriving at the ball, Emma was finally beginning to enjoy herself. Several gentlemen had been flatteringly eager to fill her dance card, and not one person had taken a look at her and told her to leave immediately because she clearly didn't belong. Probably they were afraid of incurring the Earl of Westin's wrath. Which was fine with Emma. As a general rule, she liked to stand up for herself, but Marcus had done a much better job of effectively quashing any further unpleasantness.

When Emma retreated to the wall of the assembly hall, hoping for a respite for her poor feet—which unfortunately had been the recipient of many crushing blows throughout the evening—she found herself cornered by Aunt Henri.

"You've made quite an impression this evening, dear," the duchess said with a proud, motherly smile.

"I hope it hasn't been for the wrong reasons," Emma said, still wondering what the ramifications of Marcus's attention might be.

"Nonsense. I've never seen two ladies more in need of a proper set-down," Henri assured her. "Besides, if their intent was to shame you into anonymity, they've failed horribly. I think every unattached male has been eyeing you tonight."

Well, that was a rather disconcerting thought. Emma, however, tried her best to look pleased with that bit of information.

"And since you now will undoubtedly have no end of eligible suitors, perhaps we should turn a discriminating eye to which gentleman will capture *your* heart."

"I'm not sure—" she began, certainly not about to confess that a certain earl might already be doing an admirable job of earning her affections.

Aunt Henri patted her on the arm, completely misunderstanding Emma's reluctance. "I know it can be a bit overwhelming. I remember my first Season. So many beaus." She smiled at the remembrance. "But no ever held my heart like Henry."

Emma was about to remark on how sweet that was when the duchess barreled along, not stopping too long in her mission. "But proper planning can only speed the cause of love along. So…"

"Emma, look," Olivia interrupted a few minutes later as she bustled up to them, saving Emma from Henri's question about what color waistcoats she preferred for a man. "Baron Chivers is approaching."

So he was. Emma straightened her posture and pasted a

smile on her face that was mostly sincere as she prepared to greet him.

Sadly, she didn't get a chance. The Earl of Westin got to Chivers first.

Marcus saw Chivers approaching Emma from across the assembly room.

When he might have stalked off to find Nick and Henry, who were avoiding the Almack's melee with an admirable skill and gusto, Marcus found that he didn't want to stray too far from Emma. Didn't want to give anyone the impression that he wasn't standing at the ready to protect her again if she were threatened.

But he had to admit that his further assistance didn't seem necessary. The viscountesses had left the assembly early, and no one else had uttered so much as a disparaging syllable in his presence. So perhaps he was safe to go find a place to hide from the simpering ladies who tried to throw themselves in his path.

That was one thing he hadn't taken into consideration when he'd agreed to escort Emma around the various *ton* events. His entrance had been noted, and within moments, Marcus had patrons coming to parade their eligible, extremely accomplished, exceedingly biddable daughters in front of him. He'd danced with several of the ladies, had listened to inane recordings of the latest *on dits*…all the while, he'd been hard-pressed to pull his attention off Emma.

Regardless of where she was in the room, Marcus could innately find her. And while she might be safe for the moment from the viperous tongues of some of "proper society," he had to be honest and admit that he didn't want to disappear from the crush.

He wasn't going to deny himself the pleasure of watching her.

And since he was being such a diligent observer, Marcus immediately saw the way Emma straightened and smiled when she realized Baron Chivers was approaching.

That was a situation that had to be remedied right away. For Emma's own good, of course. Because, as in that fable about indecisive men which Marcus may have possibly made up, men like the baron could not possibly make any woman lastingly happy—they lacked the steadiness of resolve. And Emma deserved to be happy.

"Chivers!" Marcus called out as though the man were standing on the other side of the building.

The younger man turned to look at him in surprise. "Lord Westin?" he asked.

"I've been meaning to talk to you," he said even as he wondered what it was he was doing.

Apparently, his sister wondered as well because she glowered at him from her position near the wall. Ignoring Olivia's outraged expression, Marcus crossed over to have a chat with the determined Baron Chivers.

As they walked together, Marcus could tell the other man was nervous. Good. Marcus didn't know exactly what he was going to say yet, but he had a feeling that whatever it ended up being would be more effective if the other man was terrified.

"You wanted to talk to me?" Chivers asked, his voice wavering.

Marcus tried to offer a friendly smile. "Yes. I like you, Chivers."

The baron eyed him suspiciously. "You do?"

Marcus nodded as he continued in their path across the room, away from Emma. Without wanting to distract Chivers, the earl shot a look over his shoulder to make sure that his sister wasn't barreling toward them in an effort to tackle him to the ground. Oh, she was glaring at him, all right, but thus far, Olivia didn't show any signs of coming after him. Perhaps she was surrendering to her sense of decorum.

"Are you having a pleasant time tonight?" Marcus asked.

Baron Chivers didn't even hide the backward glance—presumably at Emma. "I'm enjoying myself very much."

Marcus gritted his teeth and tried to suppress his irritation at the way Chivers's face brightened upon seeing the object of his affection.

"She's quite beautiful, isn't she?" Marcus said, following the man's look.

Chivers slanted him a look. "Yes, extraordinarily so."

The baron was still eyeing Marcus with a mix of wariness and speculation. It seemed as though the man was trying to decide whether he was about to be threatened away from Emma.

He was, of course.

But Marcus didn't want it to seem as though he was trying to claim Emma for himself. That wasn't the point of the discussion. Marcus had his own problems to contend with without adding in any additional concerns. He just didn't think that Chivers would be a good fit for Emma.

"I think deciding to settle down at your age is commendable," Marcus said.

Several beats of silence. "Thank you?" Chivers made it sound like a question more than a response.

Well, it was clear that Baron Chivers wasn't going to be doing anything to help speed the conversation along. And Marcus wanted to work quickly before Olivia came and tried to drag him away by his ear.

"I mean, so many young men see marriage as the death of all their freedoms. It's a refreshing change to find someone willing to sacrifice all his hobbies and pastimes for the sake of becoming a father to bouncing, raucous offspring." Marcus couldn't venture a look at the other man's face, because he didn't want anything in his expression to make the baron suspicious.

Apparently, one didn't need to see Chivers's face to be privy to the turmoil suddenly rolling through him. "Death? Sacrifice?" and then in the most horrified whisper of all, "Offspring?"

Marcus nodded happily. "To all three. But just because a husband can't spend any more time at White's or Gentleman Jackson's doesn't mean that all of your friends will abandon you. In fact, perhaps you'll be able to tempt them into visiting by offering your new French cook's legendary scones with a prettily arranged tea service."

The baron stopped walking, causing Marcus to have to backtrack a couple of steps to return to him.

"My new cook?"

"Just an example. Your wife probably won't disband *all* your servants. Maybe if you're extraordinarily lucky, she'll be too busy rearranging your house, ordering new pink drapes for the bedroom and getting rid of the dining set that's been in your family since the Battle of Hastings to notice what you're doing, and you'll be able to sneak a few of your favorite ones into permanent employment."

A garbled "My dining set?" was the baron's only response to that, as though the man really did own such a historic piece…though as far as Marcus knew, the set was only a figment of his imagination.

"But all of those trials will pale in comparison to the joy you feel when you set up your nursery," Marcus continued on, feeling fairly assured now of his victory.

"I'm not thinking of children right now." The younger man's face had a decidedly green cast to it.

Marcus waved off the objection. "Who ever is? Other than the women, of course…" He forced a hearty chuckle. "And once that happens, naturally, your days will be spent with the little rapscallions sitting on your back while you gallop about the hall like a pony. Or maybe you'll stick your foot in your best boots only to find honey inside and on your stocking—just a little joke from the children, harmless of course. Adventures! Which would probably be quite an immeasurable amount of fun if you care for that sort of thing."

Marcus knew the precise moment the enemy thought of hoisting a white flag of surrender. Chivers visibly paled and his step slowed.

"Oh," Marcus pressed, as though remembering something long forgotten, "you were wanting to talk to Miss Mercer. We should probably walk back…wouldn't want to keep a prospective mother to your children waiting, right?"

"I'm not so sure," Baron Chivers said, his throat sounding clogged, like he might be choking.

Marcus gave him a friendly whack on the back. "Buck up, man! Miss Mercer is probably an excellent candidate for the future Baroness Chivers…I can't honestly say, though, since I've never been *married* to her."

Without a word of farewell, the other man started walking at a fast clip in the opposite direction from Emma.

"Aren't you going to come back with me?" Marcus called after him, trying to smother a victorious smile.

Baron Chivers kept right on walking. "I need to get back to my mother," he tossed over his shoulder. "She might start to miss me."

"It was nice talking with you," Marcus said to the man's back.

Chapter Ten

After Emma's evening at Almack's, and now, three days later, her first literary event—which was really the hostess's fancy way of saying she would be conducting dramatic reenactments of Shakespeare's greatest monologues *all* evening long—Emma could say with surety that she hadn't been missing very much by staying out of society. Of course, it was entertaining to see the women in the their finery…some of which would make Henri's concoctions look tame. And Baroness Ludly's dramatic readings were…well, dramatic. But Emma was less than overwhelmed by some of the gentlemen she'd met. Many of them had proven to be decidedly heavy on their feet—the ones she'd danced with at Almack's—and others light on conversational topics of interest.

Pretending to find them all charming and fascinating was more of a strain than she had expected. And while she'd certainly tried to envision each man's husband potential, Emma had to be honest and admit she hadn't yet met one she could possibly endure for a lifetime…except possibly Lord Westin, who clearly wasn't an option. Tired, overheated and rather disgusted with poor, innocent Shakespeare, she needed a few minutes away from it all.

So when Lady Ludly began her interpretation on Hamlet's lament for "poor Yorick," Emma made her excuses to Olivia. When her friend offered to accompany her, Emma assured her that she simply needed a moment alone. She made her way to the ladies' retiring room. Blessedly, she was the room's only occupant. And as soon as the door swung shut behind her, she was at the oversize mirror.

Outwardly, she didn't *look* on the verge of coming apart. That was a small blessing.

Get a grip on yourself, she chided.

Moving quickly to a pitcher of water and several cloths stacked neatly on one of the tables, Emma dampened a cloth, pressing it to her forehead. The water was cold, startlingly so, and after a few applications, Emma felt a bit more in control.

She heaved a sigh of relief.

You can do this. Flirt. Flatter. Find a husband. How hard could it be?

Unfortunately, it wasn't just the strain of being charming that Emma had to deal with, but Olivia's brother, as well. Not as a potential groom, of course, but as an obstacle to any of the men who might wish to fill that position. Every gentleman she talked to, every partner she danced with, every possible suitor who handed her a glass of punch had to face down the inscrutable—yet clearly menacing—glare from Lord Westin.

It was making her daft.

Why couldn't he leave her alone…find some other unsuspecting victim to irritate? Emma had witnessed firsthand the number of young ladies who had enthusiastically flocked toward him once his presence in the house was announced. So she couldn't understand why he'd eschew their company in favor of spending his time aggravating her.

It hardly mattered, Emma supposed. Regardless of the dark looks she shot his way, Lord Westin seemed determined to stay latched to her side.

And in truth, it wasn't the fact that he took an inordinate amount of pleasure in frightening any gentleman who approached her that bothered Emma. No, that was actually mildly humorous. What was disturbing was that being in such close proximity to him caused Emma to be too distracted to properly converse with the men brave enough to weather the earl's foreboding presence.

Several minutes of peace in the retiring room, however, and Emma was fairly confident she could face the Earl of Westin without melting into a puddle, or flinging herself at him. She pulled open the door and stepped out into the hall.

Moments later, Emma wasn't sure how she had lost her way from the ladies' room to the drawing room, but she had. As she passed through a darkened hallway, it was fairly clear she had no sense of where she was going and might be doomed to wander aimlessly for hours. The sounds of the crowd were far off in the distance, but the voices were too muffled to be able to tell from which direction they were coming.

"Great job, Emma," she muttered.

"Who's there?" a male voice demanded.

Her heart pounded frantically in her chest. Emma forced herself to breathe slowly. This was actually the best thing that could have happened. She would just ask the gentleman how to get back to the rest of Ludly's captive audience.

"Sir?" she called out hesitantly. The hall was awfully, oppressively dark, and she was only able to see a vague outline of where the man was standing. "I need your help."

A tall gentleman stepped forward. A slant of moonlight coming in through one of the windows illuminated his face. Despite his intimidating height, he looked kindly enough, with an affable face and a warm smile. Very nonthreatening. But despite his pleasant appearance, he lacked even the smallest amount of Lord Westin's heart-stopping handsomeness.

Could she keep the earl out of her mind for five minutes? Obviously not.

"I'm always happy to be of service to a beautiful lady," the man said. The words of chivalry were endearing, and Emma found herself relaxing. Clearly she hadn't stumbled upon a deranged killer in the shadows.

"I've lost my way back to the drawing room," she explained, feeling stupid. Offering him a self-deprecating smile, Emma invited him to laugh at her inability to accomplish such a simple task correctly.

Instead, the man swept a bow. "Mr. George Barnwell at your service, my lady."

Emma nodded and quickly introduced herself.

Had Olivia begun worrying about her yet? Emma wanted to find her way back as quickly as possible. "I would appreciate if you could point out which direction I should walk in, Mr. Barnwell."

Mr. Barnwell, however, was apparently too much the gentleman not to see the task accomplished to his satisfaction. Stepping forward, he had ahold of her hand before she could guess his intention.

"There's no need to escort me, sir. I don't wish to be an imposition." What she really didn't want was for anyone—Lord Westin, especially—to see her returning from a mysterious disappearance with a gentleman on her arm.

"It's no imposition at all, my dear." He patted her hand with a brotherly affection.

Mr. Barnwell began walking her through the hallway. The man kept up a running commentary on who was in attendance, what everyone was wearing. Mr. Barnwell might be harmless, but he was also quite the dandy.

"I haven't seen you much in Town this Season," Mr. Barnwell said suddenly.

Emma was certainly not about to discuss what had kept

her from the amusements of the *ton* with a stranger. So she said nothing at all.

They were drawing closer to the noises of the drawing room and the carrying voice of the baroness. Emma breathed a sigh of relief.

"Thank you so much for your assistance, Mr. Barnwell," she said when they were in a small alcove set off from the crowd. "I'm quite sure I can make it the rest of the way on my own." And she smiled brightly so he wouldn't think anything of her abandoning him.

"It was my distinct pleasure, my dear," he said.

"I hope you pass a pleasant evening," she said, feeling genial and generous. It was a singularly wonderful feeling to spend a few moments with a gentleman and not come away twisted in knots and unable to think.

Mr. Barnwell had a cup of something that looked like the weak lemonade they'd been serving all evening, and Emma thought the darkness of the hall had been the reason she hadn't noticed it earlier. What followed next was a clumsy attempt to bow to her. But since he was still anchored to her side by their entwined arms, he used his cup-holding arm to flail upward and outward. Such a flourish might have looked charming and graceful if it weren't so unwieldy.

Since his cup wasn't empty, however, the courtly bow resulted in a large splash of drink on Emma's dress. The lemonade dripped from her neck down the front of her gown, turning the light green fabric dark wherever the trails of liquid went.

"Oh, dear," he muttered, clearly horrified by what he'd done.

The gentleman seemed so upset, Emma's natural instinct was to rush to reassure him. "It will be fine, Mr. Barnwell." Which wasn't a very easy thing to say with the lemonade making her feel both chilled and sticky.

"Please allow me," he said quickly, fumbling in his pocket for something.

"Really, it's fine," Emma insisted, sighing inwardly at the thought of having to return to the retiring room. Perhaps this time she'd be able to find her way back by herself.

Mr. Barnwell waved off her protests with his retrieved white handkerchief. The square of linen flapped in the air like a flag of surrender. "No, no. It will just take a moment to set this to rights."

Emma froze with surprise as he began to clumsily mop at the dripping liquid at her neck and lower.

Which was exactly how Lord Westin found them.

Marcus didn't have to use much imagination to figure out what was going on in front of him. Both Emma and the gentleman—he used the term in the loosest possible way—turned to look at him. Marcus had yet to say anything.

In truth, he didn't plan on talking very much. He knew Nick was somewhere behind him; they'd come looking for Emma when Olivia grew worried for her. All Marcus could hope for at the moment was that his friend hadn't seen Emma in the compromising position.

It was, of course, too late to block out of his own mind the picture of another man touching Emma.

Marcus shrugged out of his evening coat. Then with dedicated, deliberate motions, he tossed his jacket onto a nearby chair. Afterward, he deftly flicked open the cuffs of his white cambric shirt, rolling the sleeves up to his elbows.

It'd be a shame to get any more blood than necessary on his evening shirt. His valet would have a fit.

"Lord Westin? What are you doing?" Emma asked worriedly, taking several steps away from the other man.

"Stand on the other side of the room, Miss Mercer," he said without halting his attempts to ready himself for battle.

"No." She didn't stamp her foot, but with her belligerent tone, she might as well have.

Marcus shrugged. "Fine, then go back to the drawing room."

He spared her enough of a glance to see that she had her hands propped on her hips. Her lovely mouth was set in a mutinous line, and her shoulders were rigid. "I absolutely will not," she said.

"Emma," he said with all the warning he could muster into his voice. But Marcus didn't lose focus on the other man, who was beginning to look a little bewildered and maybe even angry.

"How dare you talk to the lady with such disrespect?" the man demanded.

That was exactly the kind of thing the man shouldn't have said considering that Marcus was *this close* to pummeling him into the ground for manhandling Emma. And no, he hadn't yet stopped to consider whether Emma had been a willing participant.

They'd discuss that later, Marcus decided.

"Miss Mercer, step back."

She must have heard in his voice exactly what he'd wanted her to hear, because she took several steps backward.

The other man was too foolish to keep his mouth shut. He turned to Emma. "You don't have to listen to this…this… barbarian."

Marcus paused in his advance forward. Regardless of the fact that the man had clearly been taking grave advantage of Emma, could Marcus really punch him in the face? That *would* be rather barbaric, he supposed.

"You shouldn't have interrupted us, anyway," the stranger continued. "I was nearly finished." Then he looked pointedly at Emma's…

At her...

Well, somewhere he certainly *shouldn't* have been looking.

And Marcus decided, yes. Yes, he could punch him.

Somewhere in the distance, Emma groaned.

"Perhaps you could handle this like gentlemen," Emma suggested to the room at large once she was done huffing under her breath.

"How about we just handle this like men?" Marcus countered.

The man took several steps toward Marcus, and the earl tensed, wondering what he was going to do.

"How dare you impugn this lady's honor by making such a spectacle," said the stranger...not making even the smallest modicum of sense. And before Marcus could decide for certain what he was going to do, the man decided to go on the offensive.

He swung right at Marcus' head.

Marcus ducked, sliding out from in front of him.

In spite of the fact that he'd moved, however, Marcus still heard the man's fist connect with something. That was followed by a muffled grunt of pain. For a horrified moment, Marcus thought the idiot had punched Emma.

Marcus was crouched and didn't wait for any confirmation on who had been the man's victim; he vaulted forward and tackled him to the ground.

"Did he *hit* me?" Nick's voice came from somewhere above Marcus.

The earl wrestled his opponent into stillness then looked upward. Nick had a smear of bright red on his white gloves and was busy pressing his fingers to the corner of his mouth, where blood beaded from a cut.

"This is a joke, right?" the marquess continued.

Marcus pointed at the man, who was starting to resent his confinement and was bucking at Marcus's hold. "Can I get a little help here?" he asked Nick.

"What have you done to Mr. Barnwell, Marcus?" Emma cried, rushing forward to press her tiny hand to the man's forehead, as though checking to see if the altercation had resulted in a fever.

"What have *I* done?" Marcus snapped. "Were you not watching what was happening here?" Well, at least now he had a name to put with the villainy…Barnwell.

"I was watching," Nick supplied obligingly as he helped restrain Mr. Barnwell.

Emma stamped her foot in disgust. Had she not been wearing dainty slippers, the effect might have been more commanding. "Let. Him. Go," she demanded.

"Thank you, my gracious lady," Mr. Barnwell said from his position on the ground.

Marcus thought about hitting him just to shut him up.

Nick just laughed.

"I would like to punch both of you," the delicate *gracious* lady ground out through her tightly clenched teeth.

Nick dabbed at his cut again. "I've already been hit this evening," he said ruefully. "Marcus hasn't, though." The marquess supplied the alternative with a smile.

"I can remedy that," Emma threatened.

Marcus decided they'd prattled enough about laying him low. "If the two of you could refrain for a few minutes, I could figure out what to do with this man."

"If you hadn't knocked the poor Mr. Barnwell to the floor, there'd be nothing to figure out," Emma decided to point out.

"If what I've heard about the man can be trusted, your Mr. Barnwell is anything but poor," Nick supplied.

"Thanks for the helpful commentary," Marcus snapped.

And then he turned his attention to Emma to see her reaction to that bit of information.

It was then that he noticed the front of her dress was drenched by…something. Looking quickly around, he spotted an empty cup on the floor…along with a dampened handkerchief still clenched in Barnwell's hand. And Marcus's stomach sank. Reluctantly, he eased up on the knee he had pressed into Barnwell's back.

"Mr. Barnwell was only trying to help me," she said to Marcus.

"Strange way to be helpful," he said, but now thinking he finally understood what had transpired.

Obviously, Mr. Barnwell had spilled his drink on Emma. And Marcus grudgingly admitted that what he witnessed could have been part of the attempt to clean up the mess.

Odd, but he still wasn't inclined to let the man up. Not with where his hands had been cleaning.

As for Emma…he couldn't very well let her go back to the gathering looking like that. It would be enough to keep the gossips busy for the next fortnight.

"Emma," Marcus said, forgetting once again to call her Miss Mercer, and not correcting himself at the omission.

"What?" Her tone didn't exactly suggest that she was going to be amenable to his request.

"Would you please go wait outside for me?"

She crossed her arms over the damp fabric of her chest. "I certainly will not."

"You certainly will too," Marcus argued back.

"You don't have to go anywhere you don't wish to, Miss Mercer," Mr. Barnwell counseled from the floor.

"Be quiet," Marcus told him. Then he nodded his head at Nick. "Where's Olivia?"

Nick strode over to the doors and cracked one open to take a look inside. "She's keeping my aunt entertained."

Marcus could only breathe a sigh of relief about that. He had absolutely no desire to hear Henri's observations on the scene before them. "Well, then, will you accompany Emma outside until I can get there? It's best she not be left alone."

Nick nodded curtly, moving to usher Emma out of the room.

"I'm not a child," she said to the room in general.

"Then don't pout like one," Marcus fired back. In one fluid motion, he gained his feet. "Don't move," he told Barnwell, "we're going to have a chat."

The earl crossed to the chair where he'd thrown his coat. Picking it up, he draped the garment around Emma's shoulders.

"It's cold out there," he said simply. Perhaps his own hands lingered on the lapels she was clutching, but he wasn't going to deny himself the small moment to be close to her.

Foolish though it may be.

Emma blushed at his attentions. Her hands moved up the lapels, sliding against his own. Marcus wasn't sure why he thought so, but the action seemed almost involuntary.

"Careful," he warned her, his face a picture of mock seriousness. "You might wrinkle it." He was thinking about the last time she'd clung to him.

And from the fire flashing in her eyes, Marcus could tell she remembered, too.

Ridiculously pleased by that, he smiled back innocently.

"Can this little flirtation wait until later?" Nick asked, looking at Mr. Barnwell, Emma and then to the drawing room not far from them.

"It's not a flirtation," Emma snapped.

"It can wait," Marcus said at the same time.

Nick laughed, and Emma glared at him. Marcus smirked at the venomous expression from his proper lady.

His proper lady?

Marcus shook his head as Nick ushered Emma toward the back of the house, where there was another set of doors to the gardens.

She wasn't *his* anything. He couldn't marry her, not with his current disastrous finances. And she couldn't marry *him,* not when her friend and sponsor seemed determined to throw her at every eligible man in London who *wasn't* him.

"Get out of here," Marcus said with a sigh, turning back to Mr. Barnwell.

"What?" the man asked, rising up on his elbows.

"I said leave." Marcus knew he had no right to decide who could attend to Emma. Mr. Barnwell had not compromised Emma's honor. And while pummeling Barnwell into the ground because he'd touched her would be undoubtedly satisfying, it would also be rather unfair.

"Do you want me to change my mind?" Marcus asked when Mr. Barnwell didn't move.

The man shook his head vehemently. Clearly, he thought the earl was deranged.

And perhaps he was.

"Do you need assistance to your carriage?" Marcus asked, a little more kindly this time.

Mr. Barnwell still shook his head with the same conviction as if Marcus had asked if he'd like to have his nose broken.

"Fine," Marcus said with a shrug. Although, he did lean over and help Mr. Barnwell gain his feet. The ungainly man was really no worse for the experience. "I wouldn't mention this to anyone if I were you."

For the first time, Mr. Barnwell stared him levelly in the eye. They were of similar stature, so Marcus was denied the satisfaction of being able to tower over the man. "I wouldn't do so even without your implied threat," Barnwell said courageously.

Marcus's only answer was a nod.

But the gentleman seemed to have mustered even more courage during his rest on the floor. "And you may also thank Miss Mercer for her kindness," he said. "And pass on that I intend to pay a call to show my…appreciation."

Marcus wasn't going to pass on anything of the sort. Instead of replying, he merely watched the man lumber away. With one problem solved, Marcus wondered what he was going to do with the woman waiting for him outside.

Chapter Eleven

By the time Nick had her safely escorted outside, Emma was so mad she wanted to throw something.

The marquess, blessedly, was silent during their walk. Whether it was to give her enough quiet to nurse her anger, or whether it was because his cracked lip hurt when he tried to talk, she didn't know or much care.

A wind blew through the garden, picking up tendrils of her hair and whipping them across her face. Instinctively, she pulled Lord Westin's coat tighter around her to ward off the chill. And maybe when the wind wafted his scent around her, Emma breathed in a little deeper.

Just maybe, of course.

The two of them found the side gate, where they waited on the earl to join them.

"Why don't you send for the carriage to come and take me home?" she asked Lord Huntsford.

His flinch suggested he was surprised to hear her speak. Maybe he knew enough from Olivia that it was often better to leave a furious woman alone.

"You're not returning home by yourself, Emma," he said in a mildly placating voice.

"No, you're certainly not," Lord Westin seconded as he

came to join them. And there was nothing soothing or placating in his tone at all. It was intractable. And if the set of his jaw were any indication, he wasn't going to be in any mood to argue.

Well, that was really going to be unfortunate for him.

Emma crossed her arms over her chest, trying to ignore the fact that she undoubtedly looked ridiculous swallowed up in Marcus's coat. Her hands didn't even poke out through the long sleeves.

"Fine," she said. "I'll wait here while you two go get Olivia and the carriage."

"I'll send for the carriage," the marquess said quickly... and a little too eagerly.

It didn't go unnoticed that Lord Westin didn't volunteer to go fetch his sister.

Emma glared at him.

"I'm not leaving you out here alone," he said, interpreting her pointed look correctly. His raised eyebrows dared her to argue with him.

"Nick," she said, calling out to the man who appeared to be trying to sneak out without being noticed. "Maybe you should tell Olivia to ready herself first. That way she'll have plenty of time to make our apologies to our hostess." If their hostess could manage to curb her dramatics long enough to hear them.

"Actually," the marquess began, "I was thinking Marcus could escort you home."

Emma and Marcus answered at once.

Emma—"Absolutely not."

Marcus—"Splendid idea."

When she heard the earl's contribution, Emma whirled to face him. "Absolutely not," she reiterated.

"It *is* the best plan," Nick said. His apologetic tone did little to soothe her temper.

"He," she countered, jabbing her finger in Marcus's direction, "just attacked a defenseless, innocent man. He's crazy." Emma didn't necessarily believe that…but she certainly didn't want to be stuck in a carriage alone with him at the moment. She was too angry.

"In my defense," Marcus said in cultured tones that only served to make her angrier, "the man appeared to be groping you."

She blushed at his frank explanation. "Well, he wasn't. Which you might have realized if you hadn't been so pigheaded."

Lord Westin didn't have a valid defense.

Emma thought she might have won because the men remained silent. But Nick was the one brave enough to break the bad news to her.

"Emma, imagine how strange it will seem if we all leave in the middle of the festivities…before dinner, even. It will look like we're attempting to hide something. For the sake of your reputation, Olivia and I should remain here, for appearances' sake."

"He's absolutely correct," Marcus said, nodding affirmatively.

It was bad enough to have to deal with Lord Westin, but when he and the Marquess of Huntsford teamed against her… well, defeat was inevitable.

But that certainly didn't mean she was going to be pleasant about it.

"Fine. Whatever you brilliant gentlemen think would be best. It's clear I'm hardly bright enough to walk down the street without getting myself in trouble."

"Clearly, you can't even walk down a hallway without getting yourself in trouble…" the earl said in response to her sarcasm.

She sputtered at the insult. "You know very well that's not what I meant. I was being figurative."

Lord Westin smirked. "Then you should have made sure your words had no literal application."

Brushing aside his argument, Emma continued, "Besides, what happened in the hallway was not my fault."

Marcus raised a skeptical eyebrow. "Why were you alone in the hall in the first place?"

"Am I required to report everything I do to you?" she demanded, only a small breath away from stomping on his foot.

Out of the corner of her eye, Emma noticed the marquess backing away. The man had an expression on his face that was much too sly for her. And with something that looked suspiciously like a wink in Marcus's direction, Lord Huntsford disappeared behind the hedgerow.

"Traitor," she mumbled under her breath.

Lord Westin heard her; she could tell by the way his eyes narrowed. But he obviously thought it best not to press for what she'd said, because he moved forward with his tirade.

"Perhaps you don't understand the significance of being caught *alone* with a gentleman," he said.

"You're the one who *caught* me," she fired back. "So unless you plan on saying something, there's little to be worried about."

"What if it hadn't been me? What if it had been one of London's notorious gossips? Even the barest hint of scandal is enough to have you shunned from society."

Emma said nothing. It was clear that arguing would not stop him, so the best course seemed to be to let him continue his rant unimpeded and hope he finished soon. But all the same, she quietly fumed, resenting the implication that she was a sheltered, naive miss, and he was the stern but wise disciplinarian trying to guide her toward an advantageous future.

Laughable. She had been the primary support of her family for some time now. She knew quite well how to take care of herself—and how to deal with men who couldn't be trusted.

"You don't believe me?" he continued, mistaking her silence for disbelief. "That's how Nick and Olivia ended up betrothed."

He'd no doubt meant to shock her. But Olivia had already shared that story. So it was no surprise to her. She already knew how malicious circumstances, and the villainy of one Baron Finley who had attempted to blackmail Olivia into marrying him, had caused Nick and Olivia to be found in a compromising position by a number of ladies of society. Nick had informed the women that Olivia was his fiancée in order to protect her reputation and while Olivia had confessed that she'd been furious at the time, it had all worked out for the best.

"Well," Emma said briskly, "I don't see either of them complaining about that now."

He raised that insufferable eyebrow of his. "So you wouldn't mind wedding Mr. Barnfield?"

"Barn*well*," she corrected then shrugged. "He seemed amiable enough."

"I've only known him for twenty minutes, and I'd say you'd be lucky if he didn't trip over himself at the altar and knock both of you to the floor."

"You almost sound jealous," she snapped, really just to irritate him further.

With those words, however, the air charged around them. Marcus's spine stiffened. His hands fisted. The muscle trailing his jaw ticked furiously. "Forget about Barnwell," he snapped. "And remember your reputation."

Emma's eyes flashed fire. "Why, Lord Westin, perhaps *you* should return inside, then, as well." Her voice was sweet enough, but a hint of steel ran through it.

He waved off her concern. "We are an entirely different matter."

"Is that right? How do you suppose that's so?"

Opening and closing his mouth a few times, the earl struggled for an answer. "Well...I'm your friend's brother."

"And wasn't Nick Olivia's brother's friend?" she asked sweetly.

Really, could he not see how ridiculous he was being? Not even sticking by his own cautionary tales?

Lord Huntsford's carriage rumbled up then, sparing the earl from having to answer the pointed question. Emma didn't think she imagined his sigh of relief.

The marquess met them at the back gate. "Marcus," Nick said, "Olivia and I will bring your carriage home. That way, if anyone passes you and sees Emma, it won't look suspicious with her in your coach."

The men touted the brilliance of that plan while Emma marched toward the carriage and hoisted herself up. And while it would have been very gratifying to do so, she resisted the urge to slam the door closed before the earl could follow in behind her.

But only just barely.

Marcus gave a few parting instructions to Nick. He wasn't particularly worried about someone noticing Emma's absence and remarking upon it. By this time, it had been nearly an hour since she'd been spotted inside, so if someone was going to be speculating on what she might or might not be doing, Marcus thought it would probably already be filtering around the party.

And Henri would be sure to have heard something.

Marcus didn't know how the woman did it, but she managed to be the gatekeeper of nearly every shred of information that passed through the *ton*. But the fact that Henri had given Nick the clear to send Emma home alleviated any of Marcus's concerns in that area.

Now what he was worried about was the lady waiting for him in the carriage.

For his life, he couldn't understand her.

What did she want from him?

Well, obviously not for him to interrupt any of her meetings with her gentlemen. And in this particular case, Marcus was sorry for the way he'd acted. He had, of course, charged into the situation without having any knowledge of what exactly was going on. But really, what else could he be expected to do, considering the circumstances?

And he'd been close to apologizing before Emma started acting like he was out to ruin her life. Was it so bad that he didn't want her exposed to unscrupulous rakes? Was it such an awful thing that he was worried about her reputation— because clearly she wasn't? There was so much in his life now that was out of his control—his finances, his ability to oversee his estates, the reforms he still hoped to pass through the House of Lords. Was it really so bad that he was being proactive in this one responsibility, to ensure that Emma was well protected from rogues and scoundrels as she sought a husband?

Throwing his hands up in the air and mumbling over the indecipherable nature of females, Marcus followed the young woman into the coach.

He almost laughed when he saw that she'd squeezed as far into the corner as humanly possible. For a brief second, Marcus thought about going and taking the seat right beside her just to further torment her, but his gentlemanly instinct won, and he took the opposite bench.

The ride was going to be tense enough without adding any additional insult to whatever perceived injuries she was nursing.

"Just so you know," Emma said, crossing her arms over her chest, "I think this is ridiculous. I can ride back to the house by myself."

Marcus noticed that she had burrowed into his coat for warmth, and the image gave him a strange sense of satisfaction. Shaking his head as though to distract himself from those thoughts, he tried to focus on what she'd said.

"Of course you think it's ridiculous," he said as reasonably as possible. "You seem to have absolutely no concern for your safety."

"Don't presume to know so much about me, Lord Westin." Emma's voice could have frozen boiling water.

But he wasn't going to back down from the bait. "I think I know quite a bit about you. You genuinely seem to think that you are immune to danger."

"I've been handling myself well enough for years, Lord Westin," she intoned, her voice as cold and imperious as the most severe of matriarchs. "And I've managed to get by just fine without your help. I don't see why the rest of my life has to be spent under your tutelage…regardless of what you *think* you know about me."

And of course, as she said that, Marcus thought back to their first meeting, when he'd come across her in Cheapside in the middle of the night. He'd never gotten a satisfactory answer for her presence there—even though he'd gone so far as to question his sister about it. Emma, of course and unsurprisingly, was close-lipped. And his sister wasn't any better. Olivia only insisted that it wasn't her story to tell, and if Marcus wanted to know the answer, he was going to have to go to the source.

Something he hadn't done yet…but even the reminder of how reckless she'd been to be parading around that part of town by herself made Marcus's hackles rise back up.

"Oh, I beg to disagree," he said. Leaning forward, propping his elbows on his knees, Marcus stared straight through her. "You might have forgotten how we met, but *I* haven't."

"I no more needed your assistance then than I do now," she maintained.

He barked out a laugh. "How long do you think you would have lasted traipsing down the sidewalk like you were taking a Sunday-afternoon stroll?"

Now it was her turn to laugh. "You think you're so brilliant, don't you, Lord Westin? I've made that *stroll* a hundred times," she nearly shouted in his face.

Well, that shut him up.

And he actually didn't process what she'd said right away. After a few seconds of uncomfortable silence, Marcus finally comprehended the words she'd just said.

"A *hundred* times?" Marcus couldn't help it. Yes, he yelled.

Loudly.

Emma, wincing from the sound, shrank back into the seat. Not out of fear, no. That had been his first thought when he shouted at her, but he could still see the fire in her expression. She wasn't afraid of him. More likely, she was regretting what she'd let slip.

As well she should have.

Still, she said nothing.

"A HUNDRED times?" he repeated…a little more forcefully this time.

"That was an exaggeration," she said in a tone no doubt to mollify him.

It didn't work. The only image Marcus had in his head now was Emma frequently making that dangerous trek by herself. It was shocking that nothing disastrous had happened to her before.

"Why don't I believe that you're exaggerating *that* much?" he asked.

Having apparently learned that sometimes silence was the best way to deal with his hostility, Emma let her crossed arms and set jaw do all the explaining for her.

"How often do you go there?" he demanded.

Still no answer.

"*Why* do you go there?" he asked.

Nothing.

Like a steadily rising temperature, Marcus could feel his anger ratcheting up with each extended beat of silence. If she didn't come up with something believable and perfectly innocent soon, Marcus was afraid that he might not be culpable for his actions.

Too soon, because he hadn't been able to get any further answers out of her, the carriage pulled up to the front of the Huntsford town house.

"You're not getting out of this carriage until we talk about this," he ordered.

Emma had apparently already anticipated something like this, because as soon as the wheels stopped rolling, she had ahold of the handle on the door and was pushing it open. And with a motion sprier than anything Marcus had ever seen from a lady in a formal evening gown, Emma jumped down to the sidewalk.

His instinct was to yell after her to stop…but that would have only caused a scene for any neighbors that might be awake and near enough to their windows to look outside.

His reluctance to draw attention was probably exactly what Emma was counting on.

Without missing a step, the demure-looking woman raced up the steps to the house. But Marcus wasn't one to be thwarted so easily. He launched himself from the carriage, following quickly in Emma's footsteps.

He heard her say something to Mathis as soon as the butler

pulled the door open, but the earl was still too far away to hear exactly what was being said.

No sooner had he made it halfway up the steps than the front door slammed shut.

With Emma safely on the other side.

Oh, she wasn't going to best him so easily. It might delay him by a couple of seconds, but as punctual as Mathis was, Marcus would be inside in no time. And then, they *were* going to have this conversation, no matter how distasteful she might find it.

But the door never opened back up.

Strange. Surely Mathis had seen him following Miss Mercer. And he was close enough to them that the butler couldn't have mistaken him for some sinister stranger. So, when it appeared that the butler had taken a page out of Gibbons's book and was declining to do his job, Marcus knocked on the door.

Hard.

Mathis opened it the smallest crack.

"Yes, my lord?" the servant inquired as though nothing unusual were going on.

"I'd like to finish my discussion with Miss Mercer," he said tightly, pretty sure he wasn't going to like anything that was about to transpire.

He was right.

Mathis looked around him with a convincingly bewildered expression. "I believe Miss Mercer attended a function this evening with his lordship and her ladyship."

"Yes. I know she did. I was there." Marcus took special pains to make his words crisp and intelligible. "I have only seconds before brought Miss Mercer home. Now, I would like to finish talking about something with her."

He didn't say, *So let me in,* but it was definitely implied by the way he was trying to get his foot close enough to wedge it in the door should Mathis try to close it on him.

And that was exactly what the butler did. With the graciously muttered, "Forgive me, your lordship, but I am now under orders."

And *slam.*

Before Marcus had a chance to squeeze his foot in all the way.

And before he had the chance to ask under *whose* orders.

As he turned to walk back to the carriage, however, he could hear Emma laughing on the other side of the door.

Chapter Twelve

It had been a week since the memorable meeting of Mr. Barnwell and Emma's spat with the Earl of Westin.

Barnwell had become a frequent visitor during calling hours...and Marcus had become an even more permanent fixture. Everything in Emma wanted to beg the earl to leave her alone. How could she possibly think of courting someone else when he was always nearby?

And today, in particular, Lord Westin had pushed her too far.

Emma waited until Mr. Lovelace disappeared through the front door and walked out to the street before she wheeled around and marched back into the drawing room. Grabbing the doorknob, she slammed the door behind her so forcefully the teacups rattled in their saucers.

Lord Westin, however, didn't so much as flinch at the sound.

Her hands balled into ineffective fists. Emma wanted to stomp around the room, throw a flower vase or box the earl's ears.

But while indulging her violent flash of temper might have been momentarily gratifying, Emma had to struggle to maintain some decorum. So she settled for marching several steps toward him.

"What. Were. You. Doing?" she snapped—each word punctuated by another ominous step closer.

"I was *trying* to take a nap," Lord Westin said with a completely unaffected drawl. "But you're not making it terribly easy for me, are you?"

"You know what I'm talking about, Marcus. What were you trying to do to Mr. Lovelace?"

His eyes were wide with feigned innocence.

Emma wasn't fooled.

"The gentleman had done nothing to you," she continued.

The earl raised a brow. "Did I suggest he did?"

"You poured tea on him!" she yelled.

Marcus didn't offer a defense, which was wise—as there really was none that would have been believable.

She shook her head at the memory. Mr. Lovelace *really* loved his clothes. Almost unnaturally so. "The poor man was nearly in tears over his ruined waistcoat."

"It will wash," Marcus said, still appearing completely unmoved and unconcerned.

"And if it doesn't?"

The man shrugged. "It was an ugly waistcoat anyway."

Well…he had her there.

"That's not the point," Emma argued. "You can't run around ruining every article of clothing you find ugly."

"You're right. Most of your suitors would be down to their underclothes if I did so," he muttered, low enough that he might not have meant for her to hear.

"Again," she ground out, "that is *not* the point."

To the casual observer, Marcus's reclined position would have indicated he was relaxed…but Emma could see the tension in the stiff lines of his frame at her persistent questioning. His irritation didn't stop her.

No, this time he'd pushed her too far.

It was bad enough that for some inexplicable reason Marcus had to be present every time a gentleman caller came. It was as though he lounged in the corner solely to gather material to laugh about later. And that was to say nothing about his habit of interfering with any gentleman who approached her at social functions.

"So what *is* the point, then?" Marcus asked, drawing her back into the conversation.

"Why are you doing this?" she asked, defeated and slouching into a chair.

Lord Westin, as if drawing strength from her surrender, sat forward, looking more alert than he had for the past hour. "Doing what, exactly?"

This earned him a slanted look and a frown. "You know exactly what you've been doing. Mr. Lovelace—"

"People accidentally spill things all the time," Marcus interrupted.

"You're not *people*." Exasperation made the statement come out harsh.

And of course Marcus took advantage of that, slumping a little and pretending hurt. "Well. That's insulting."

Emma brushed off his remark. "I've never seen you do anything clumsy. And you just *so happened* to spill the tea right after he'd mentioned that he'd just purchased that waistcoat."

"I've always had impeccable timing," he said with a shrug.

The look Emma hurled at him suggested it would be wiser if he just stopped talking.

Clearly, now that Marcus realized he hadn't even the remotest believable defense...and perhaps because of her dark look, he remained quiet.

Which suited Emma just fine, as her arguments were only

mounting and gaining speed, and she didn't want anything
to distract her from yelling at him.

"What about Lord Whipshaw?" she asked, thinking of
the gentleman who had come to call yesterday, but had also
stormed out of the house less than an hour after his arrival.

"What?" Marcus asked, his face a blank mask that was
perhaps meant to look innocent. Emma knew better.

Frustration heated her face.

"You tricked Lord Whipshaw into making a fool of himself," Emma accused.

"I hardly think he needed my help with that particular en-
deavor."

"Marcus," she warned, feeling oddly like a mother chiding an errant child.

"Fine," the Earl of Westin said, throwing his hands up in
surrender. "But I hardly see how having a scholarly conversation could classify as tricking anyone."

He wasn't entirely wrong. It wasn't as though Lord Westin
had *forced* the other man to confess that he thought America
was somewhere north of India. As soon as that utterance had
passed Lord Whipshaw's lips, however, Emma had struck
him from her mental list of eligible suitors. There was no
excuse for laziness when it came to broadening one's intel-
ligence. And really—it hadn't been that long since England
had been at war with the colonies, so he should have known
better.

Emma would concede that point. "Fine. But what about
Mr. Kirkland?" Another gentleman caller, of course.

"What about him?" Marcus linked his hands behind his
head, kicking back even farther in his seat.

"He stormed off in a huff several days ago. I'm sure you
can remember that far back," she snapped.

"I do. And as per my recollections, it wasn't from anything
I said."

Emma's blush deepened at the memory. Mr. Kirkland had left in a billowing haze of disgust. Mostly because she'd said she didn't understand the unhealthy attachment some men had for their hunting dogs…which might not have been so horrible if she hadn't followed that with the observation that most men of that ilk she'd met were singularly unexceptional and perhaps even terribly awkward with actual people.

Mr. Kirkland had turned out to be, of course, one of *those* men.

Which was something Marcus had undoubtedly known when he'd brought the topic up. And something she reminded him of now.

"Why have you been doing all this, Marcus?" she asked him. Hating the way her voice sounded a mixture of beseeching and defeated. But his behavior had been so odd that she wasn't going to let him go without answering the question.

Emma had thought they were friends of a sort.

It was a marvelous relief to talk to a man who didn't seem surprised when she expressed opinions outside matters of fashion or housekeeping. She enjoyed their conversations, and he fascinated her with tales of his travels, and sharpened her mind with debates over books they had both read and music they had enjoyed. He'd told her all about the reforms he hoped to implement, and she'd been moved by his determination to help those less fortunate. The earl was truly a remarkable man.

Except, of course, for when he was an unmitigated *pest*.

As pleasant as he was when they spoke alone, or with only Nick and Olivia in attendance, he became another man entirely when faced with one of her suitors. From the displays of the week, it would seem that his first priority was making her look foolish…or trying to deter any interested man from darkening her door.

And he was remarkably proficient in his mission.

Marcus gained his feet…maybe to storm out of the room after all the accusations she was hurling at him. But the earl didn't make a move toward the door. He stepped toward her instead.

"Have I done such a bad thing, Emma?" Marcus asked. His voice was low and smooth, a subtle caress.

Ignoring the feelings it stirred within her, and believing the question was a trap, Emma didn't say anything.

It didn't stop Marcus from continuing, "Do you really want those kinds of men—men obsessed with rivaling Beau Brummell for style, men who don't know enough about anything to realize the country they live on is an island or men who will show their pets more devotion and attention than they do you?"

Put that way…no.

"But you knew all of these little character—" Emma struggled for the right word to say "—quirks about these men already. So if you had such strong feelings, why did you bring them by? Why make the introductions?" It wasn't a sarcastic question or an accusation; Emma waited to hear the answer.

"Perhaps I felt you might suit in spite of it," Marcus mumbled. His eyes averted, it was clear he wasn't going to give any more of an explanation than that.

"Then why sabotage it before I could decide for myself?"

Her soft-spoken question ignited a fire in his eyes. "Why do you keep pressing me, Emma?" Marcus asked, advancing on her.

Her mouth went dry at the intensity in his expression… the heat in his words.

"Do you want me to say I envy them their time with you?" he continued. "That I'd pour tea on a thousand waistcoats if I thought it would get everyone to go away?" Marcus laughed, the sound mirthless and maybe a little broken. "And knowing that they're here because I paved the way only infuriates me more."

Emma sat, stunned into silence.

Marcus wasn't through, however.

"Or," he continued, "would you rather I confess that when another man smiles at you, and you smile back, it's a knife twisting in my gut?" he rasped. "And that I would gladly help the man look a fool just so you would save your smiles."

"Why should I save them?" Emma asked because most of what he was saying didn't make sense. She rose, thinking that if she were standing, he couldn't loom and it wouldn't look like she was cowering.

Marcus was so close to her that she could feel the heat, the trembling, the emotion rolling off him. "Those men don't deserve your smiles—don't deserve *you*," he said almost desperately.

She'd never heard him talk this way. It scared her. And thrilled her.

Striving to keep her voice light, Emma said, "It doesn't have to be that way." But even as she said it, she didn't know exactly what she meant by that.

Marcus, apparently, did…and he disagreed. With a dark look and a muttered "Yes. It does," he stormed out of the room himself.

Emma stared at the door, wondering if Marcus might reappear on this side, laughing and beckoning her to join in with his joke. The echoing of a slamming door, however, dispelled that possibility.

Her heart hammered in her chest, and Emma backed up a few steps before sitting down on the settee behind her. She didn't know what to think. Her relationship with Marcus was, for the most part, comfortable. Of course there were the occasional moments when perhaps he looked at her with an intensity that overwhelmed her and seemed to surprise even himself, and possibly Emma had forced her thoughts to turn from wondering what it might feel like to be loved and cherished by a man like Marcus...possibly even more than once.

But this afternoon was the closest he'd come to shattering the tenuous truce of friendship between them.

What were his motives?

Could it be that he...

No, Emma couldn't let herself think that. Surely his reaction today had been borne of a frustration for having to help play matchmaker for her. After all, he'd been faithful in visiting every day, wading through the callers and offering his opinions on who would make a good match.

It just seemed as though he didn't think *any* of the men would make a good match for Emma.

Was that because he wanted her?

The possibility, while thrilling, terrified her. What would she say if he declared himself? What *could* she say?

Never, while dreaming up the idea for finding a husband, did Emma think she would have to contend with matters of the heart. It would be an arrangement for convenience— something she would make sure her prospective groom understood. And in return for the security a husband would provide, Emma would be a dutiful wife.

It was all so simple outlined that way.

But there would be nothing simple and certainly nothing convenient about entangling herself with Marcus. And that was more of a shame than Emma could bear to contemplate.

"I'm an idiot," Marcus muttered as he pushed open the front door to his home.

"You certainly *can* be, my lord" was Gibbons's answer as he stepped forward to take Marcus's greatcoat, hat and gloves. Marcus didn't bother to ask why the butler hadn't been alert enough to open the door for him. He'd long ago stopped expecting the older man to do anything remotely butlery.

"I was having a private conversation," the earl said instead.

The old servant bowed in fake submission. "In the future, I will refrain from commenting so you might field both ends of the conversation yourself."

"Not in the mood today, Gibbons."

The butler sighed. And Marcus steeled himself to fend off more of Gibbons's rapier wit because the man wasn't any better at following orders than he was at opening the front door in a timely fashion.

His long-time employee surprised him, however. "What troubles you, my lord?" Gibbons asked without an ounce of insincerity.

Marcus motioned for Gibbons to follow him to the nearest sitting room and closed the door behind them.

"A woman," he found himself saying before he considered the advisability of the confession.

Gibbons lounged in the seat as though he'd reclined there every day.

For all Marcus knew, he very well might.

"I see," the butler returned. "They can be the worst kind of trouble. But also the best." The sage advice was accompanied by a small smile.

Marcus's lips quirked in spite of how miserable he felt. "What have you been hiding?"

"We all have secrets, my lord." Gibbons grinned but quickly sobered, as though he could tell it was not the time for levity.

Marcus found himself under Gibbons's scrutiny. And, like that, he was stripped of title, rank, position, and was a small boy ready to be lectured by an elder. It was a singularly uncomfortable feeling.

"Perhaps you should propose to Miss Mercer yourself, then," Gibbons finally said.

Marcus's answering laugh was dry, brittle. Apparently, everyone knew at least one of his secrets.

The Earl of Westin surprised himself with how strongly he was tempted to follow Gibbons's advice. Marriage had been the furthest thing from his mind for so long, even before his recent financial disaster. And now, with his income so drastically reduced, and the evidence of his poor ability to provide for the estates and tenants under his protection, could he really be contemplating offering himself—shoddy specimen that he was—to Emma?

"And what would I say?" he asked. "Hello, Emma. I have lost a vast fortune, one which I may never be able to rebuild, but if you'd be content tying yourself to an inept and struggling man, then you might as well marry me."

"I think I would employ a bit more finesse and romance than that, my lord," Gibbons said.

"It was just an example," he muttered.

"It was a bad one," Gibbons reiterated.

"I know that," Marcus snapped. "But isn't that basically what she'd be getting?"

And didn't Emma deserve better than that?

Marcus might have lived the past few weeks with a shadow of uncertainty hovering over him, but one thing he *was* sure of was that he wanted Emma to have the best of everything. Never had he met a woman who managed to both confound and entice him. She was bright and funny…and certainly not afraid of standing against him. He admired that about her, even when it frustrated him.

He loved her.

The realization didn't knock him to the floor. Rather, it was more of a quiet acceptance of something he'd been thinking from the earliest moments of meeting her. Marcus had always known that he didn't want a simpering young miss, concerned only with getting her hands on the Countess of Westin's coronet. No, he needed someone exactly like Emma.

She was practical and determined. Perhaps they would be fine financially, since Emma didn't strike him as a woman who would sulk if she didn't have the newest fashions from Paris. In fact, if he remembered her mutterings well enough, Marcus was fairly sure keeping abreast of fashion was positively painful for her. It wasn't unrealistic to think the two of them could be happy and content. Was it?

And while his finances might be in something rather like shambles, he would love her. Not a day would pass that she wouldn't know she was cherished and loved, that she had his complete and utter devotion.

But with his current circumstances, was that enough? Did he deserve a woman like Emma?

But Marcus didn't voice that question, mostly because Gibbons was probably frank enough to tell him the truth. Then Marcus would lose any courage he might have to consider the idea.

The butler shrugged. "And what if that's exactly what your Miss Mercer wants?"

"She's not 'my' anything," Marcus said. But his mind was reeling from the question and the possibilities it presented.

"And for that, you have no one to blame but yourself, I'm afraid."

Could Gibbons be right? Could it be as simple as asking Emma for her hand? Would she say yes? Marcus was relatively certain that she at least cared for him, and while caring wasn't necessarily love, maybe she could see the potential for the emotion to grow. Besides, she seemed convinced that she needed a husband.

And he needed her.

Marcus straightened. Determination pounded through his

veins. He was going to do it. Going to ask for her hand before whatever flare of temporary insanity left him and he had time to consider how rash and inadvisable it might be.

He was halfway to the door before Gibbons's voice stopped him. "I wish you success, young Master Marcus," he said with a ghost of a smile. The term of endearment was reminiscent of days when Marcus had been nothing but a boy romping through the house, carefree and following whatever whim suited him.

Marcus hadn't been that boy for a long time.

"I didn't say what I was doing," the earl countered, feeling a bit more sporting now that his mind was made up—now that he was foolish enough to think his proclamations of love might actually work.

The butler inclined his head. "No, you didn't. But I know everything." Then, stretching his long legs forward and leaning his head on the back of the chair, he closed his eyes. "Now, I believe I shall take a nap."

It was the middle of the day, and surely Gibbons had things of importance to see to, but Marcus only smiled.

"Sleep well. And thank you," he said.

And then, Marcus marched through the hall and back out the front door before sanity and reality came crashing back down on him.

Chapter Thirteen

Emma was still trying to digest Lord Westin's earlier words when a servant told her the man occupying her thoughts was waiting for her downstairs. Her hands trembled as she reached for the door handle. But before walking into the hall, she checked herself in the mirror. The reflection staring back at her was wan. A touch too pale. A touch too nervous-looking.

She stopped her hands before they could rise to pinch her cheeks or push back the tumble of black hair that was falling around her shoulders. They would all only be temporary fixes anyway.

Lord Westin was waiting for her in the yellow parlor.

"You wished to see me, my lord?" she asked as she walked into the room. Her heart beat harder, and her hands trembled.

He turned quickly, obviously surprised at her entrance even though he was supposed to be waiting on her.

"Emma," Marcus said, his voice rough.

They faced each other. Both unsure and wary. Emma had thought she would have time to prepare before seeing him again. She'd wanted to understand what his words had meant…what *he* had meant, before having to look in his face again.

Marcus broke the silence first. "I'm sorry for what I said to you," he said simply.

Why didn't she feel any better hearing that he regretted his tirade? It should have put her at ease…lessened her anxiety.

But it only made her sad. If he truly were sorry, were his words, his jealousy, the insinuation of his feelings meaningless?

Before she could tell him he was forgiven, Marcus continued on, "I won't lie to you and tell you I didn't mean what I said, but I *was* wrong to have said it aloud."

Emma hated herself for the thrill and anticipation she felt at that confession.

"I don't understand what you're trying to do here." Excitement warred with her confusion.

Marcus pushed his hand through his hair, mussing the strands. And when he looked back at her, Emma's heart lurched. Never had she seen the earl look so…vulnerable. Conflicted.

"I'm not an impulsive person," he said.

Emma had discerned that much, but it seemed as though he was waiting for some recognition of his statement, so she nodded.

"So I don't normally do things without thinking about them thoroughly first."

Another nod. Slower this time.

"But you…" he said, halting after the word. "You…upend me." And Marcus shrugged helplessly.

How was she supposed to take that statement? It didn't *sound* particularly flattering. Should she apologize for doing so? For goodness' sake, she didn't even know what Lord Westin meant, so how could she possibly apologize?

"We might not have known each other long…" Marcus continued, "but…" Then he stopped.

Emma couldn't say anything to either encourage or discourage him. It was as though all breath and words had been stolen from her.

"I'm not very good at this sort of thing." Marcus halted and then laughed at his own statement. "Actually, I wouldn't know because it's not as though I've attempted this before…"

The prolonged wait was killing her. "Marcus," she began, "I—I…"

Rising to his feet, he moved closer to her. Now she had to look up to see his eyes, to see the emotions barely concealed there.

The fear in them surprised her.

"What is it, Emma?"

Too busy thinking to respond to his question, Emma tried to decipher what she thought she saw in his expression. Might he love her? He seemed genuine. And his words earlier— well, once spoken, they were knives that had seared straight through her.

Marcus took her silence for confusion. "I haven't done a good job explaining," he said.

"Explaining what?" she breathed to buy time. The question was only a thin whisper of sound. He was very close to her now. And Emma was very sure she had stayed still.

"Explaining this," he said just as soundlessly. His hands traced along her arms, settling on her shoulders. The weight, the feel of them was comfortable and right.

His hands turned her, pulling Emma until she was in the circle of his arms. Her body was malleable. Relaxed. Yet even in his arms, part of her mind screamed at her to run… to put as much distance between the two of them as she could manage.

For once, however, Emma shushed the fear and doubt. Sinking into his embrace, she tremulously held her breath and waited for whatever he might say.

* * *

Marcus couldn't suppress his smile when he felt Emma relax in his arms. This wasn't something he'd intended when he'd crossed the room. He didn't know *what* he'd intended. But the call to hold her had been too strong to resist.

It was strange how completely this woman had managed to turn everything in his life upside down.

Never would he have imagined proposing.

And certainly never would he have imagined being excited, eager and terrified by the thought of it.

A little sigh escaped her lips, and Marcus felt his own heart contract with the sound. Whatever reservations he might have felt earlier, this proved that it was right...*this* is what he should be doing. Her response made it clear that she shared his affection. Confidence edged away his fear. He would, of course, explain to her his true financial situation—she deserved to know before she heard his proposal—but once that was out of the way, he would pledge his heart to her, beg her to become his wife. And she would say yes, he was sure of that now, and the conviction filled him with relief.

When Emma looked up at him through eyes that had grown heavy-lidded, eyes that betrayed a bit of her own nerves, Marcus couldn't stop himself from saying, "Don't look at me like that," but the command was whispered and lacked any real heat.

She caught her lower lip between her teeth and worried it for a second before asking, "Why not?"

Marcus should have said something flippant, something to defuse the strange pulling intensity between them. He *should* have. He didn't.

"Because when you look at me like that, I want to kiss you," the earl said softly, watching her eyes for any change, any revulsion to his words.

There was none.

Relief overwhelmed him.

His Emma surprised him further when she said in such a soft voice that he could barely hear, "All right."

There was a suspended moment of time, where Marcus weighed the wisdom of what his heart wanted him to do. And when his mind didn't step in soon enough to stop him, Marcus lowered his head, touching his lips to hers.

But he hadn't been prepared for the shock that rolled through him at the simple contact. Forcing himself not to tremble, not to let her know that *he* was at *her* mercy, Marcus tightened his arms around her. Emma melted against him.

Moments passed…he wasn't sure how many of them. All Marcus knew was that he didn't want to step away. His hands twined upward, threading through the strands of her hair.

This was right.

And any hesitancy he had about asking Emma to be his wife was chased away by the eagerness in her returning his embrace and the feeling of completion he felt with her in his arms.

Unfortunately, they couldn't stay that way forever. Finally, Marcus raised his head, looking down at her beautiful face. Taking in her slowly blinking eyes and her mussed hair, he felt a powerful urge to kiss her again.

He contained the impulse.

The moment called for some type of ceremony, so Marcus dropped down to the floor, still holding one of her hands and resting his weight on one knee.

The uncomprehending look in Emma's eyes transformed into something much like panic.

He decided to ignore that and focused on the question that was all but burning his tongue. Explanations and discussions could wait—right now, he needed to hear her promise to be his bride.

"Emma, I don't have any pretty words, although I wish I did. All I can ask is that you spend the rest of your life by my side. As my wife."

Long seconds passed with her silence.

"I'll care for you, Emma," Marcus assured her, hoping to spur her to respond. "And I'll do everything in my power to see that no sorrow ever touches you."

Again, she fretted her lip with her teeth. It was as though he could read every line of indecision on her face. Marcus had been so certain moments before that she would say yes… but now doubt started to intrude.

"I don't know what to say," Emma finally answered.

Marcus searched her face. Refusal was in her eyes…how could he have missed it? But so, too, was acceptance, and it was the flash, the recognition of that that gave Marcus a resurgence of hope, spurred him onward.

"Say yes, Emma," he all but pleaded. Rising to his feet, Marcus looked her steadily in the eyes, as though the power of his gaze alone would be enough to sway her.

Emma drew in a breath…maybe even to say "Yes," but then she stopped herself.

Her inner turmoil was clear.

A thought occurred to him. "I haven't asked your father for permission," he said, having just thought of the oversight, and now wondering if that was why she was reluctant to accept his proposal.

At that, Emma stiffened. And Marcus watched as the smallest signs of softening in her expression hardened into a grim determination. He couldn't understand the rapid change in her demeanor. And he was powerless to soften her again.

After several shuddering breaths, Emma closed her eyes, tipping her head back, much as she had before he'd just kissed her. But there was no nervous anticipation coloring her features. There was anguish, or something very much like it.

Marcus knew her answer before she even opened her mouth to speak it.

Instead, it seemed Emma couldn't even summon up the words she needed. All she could do was shake her head in an unarguable—albeit sad—"No."

"I see," Marcus said tightly. His feet, of their own accord, took him several steps away from her. And some inner part of his mind, which he could neither predict nor control, hardened all the places, the emotions that he had only moments earlier laid exposed and vulnerable before her.

Her rejection strengthened his weaknesses.

Emma—Miss Mercer, he corrected himself—saw the change in him as easily as he'd seen the one in her.

"Marcus, you don't understand…"

He raised an imperious brow, all the while hating his necessary regression. "On the contrary, I think I understand perfectly." His tone was cool, cultured, giving no hint to the profound loss he felt might tear him apart from the inside out.

Anger. Sorrow. Confusion. They all warred for precedence. Anger won. It was easier, and he didn't have to admit to any deeper feelings that way.

The earl could feel his muscles tightening in reaction. He wasn't mad at Emma…but at himself, for believing he might deserve happiness, that he might deserve Emma.

And angry most of all at himself for being hopeful.

"I'll see myself out," he said with a curt nod.

Before he could turn on his heel, Emma found her voice. "Don't leave this way…angry," she clarified.

Marcus didn't bother to look at her as he asked, "How would you prefer me to leave, then?" His voice was an emotionless monotone.

He could almost see and feel her helpless shrug. "I don't know," Emma finally said.

He nodded sharply. "I suppose angry it is, then."

And his long, striding steps echoed his words. If Marcus was a gentleman, he'd explain the source of his anger, would exonerate her from any guilt. But he didn't, not because he wanted her to suffer—how could he even want that considering how much he loved her?—but because he couldn't trust his voice to speak the words.

But Marcus couldn't stop himself, once he reached the door, from turning to look back at her.

Emma's face was pale. Her gray eyes stark against the pallor of her skin. Only her lips provided any color. Was it his imagination, or were they trembling?

In an obvious attempt to avoid his scrutiny, Emma began fussing with her hair, trying to push the unruly black tresses back into their pins. His gut tightened, remembering how her chignon had ended up in shambles in the first place.

Her eyes watched him with a barely concealed wariness. And she seemed poised to bear whatever scathing commentary he might unleash.

But he couldn't do it. As much as a cutting remark would sever any hope for resurrecting this conversation, something Marcus probably needed to prevent himself from acting a fool in the future, the words wouldn't come.

His second choice was to exit in silence. He didn't think his throat, which had painfully constricted, could manage to push out any words anyway.

Marcus surprised himself, however. When he should have been cold or quiet, his words were tender. "Stop fretting, Emma," he whispered as she started jabbing pins into her hair—clearly frustrated with everything. In several strides, he was back at her side.

"What?" she breathed, her hands stilling.

Caressing her cheek with the backs of his fingers was a bad idea. Marcus did it anyway. "Don't worry," he said. "You look beautiful."

Chapter Fourteen

"Emma, is something wrong?" Olivia asked as soon as Emma walked out of the parlor. Marcus had left minutes earlier, and there was no way to ask Olivia if she'd conversed with her brother without further piquing her friend's interest.

"I am well enough," Emma said quickly. Even if the siblings *had* run into one another, it seemed doubtful that the earl would have shared what had happened in the parlor moments before. Because if he had, Olivia would likely have begun the conversation by asking her if she'd lost hold of her senses.

And Emma wasn't entirely certain she hadn't.

But the untimely reminder that Marcus knew nothing of her parents had quashed any intentions she had of agreeing to his proposal. The rational part of her argued that she'd done the only thing she possibly *could* have in the situation. Any confessions about her parents or their circumstances would have ended the conversation anyway, logic argued. What man would want to tie himself to a family that was notorious for its inability to stay solvent?

And Emma had to be honest with herself and admit that she didn't want to see if Marcus's opinion would change once he realized that irresponsibility with the finances was why she had to resort to being a governess in the first place.

Those were the practical reasons for telling Marcus "no."

For once, however, Emma hadn't wanted to be practical. In fact, she was fairly sick of being reasonable and rational. Her heart had wanted nothing more than to cling tightly to him, to allow him to whisper endearments and promises.

Realizing that she hadn't said anything else to Olivia, Emma cleared her throat, rasping out a fairly unbelievable, "I'll be fine."

"You look pale, Emma," Olivia continued, undeterred by the denial.

She resisted the urge to cover that evidence by pinching color into her cheeks. "It's been an overwhelming day."

The front door creaked open before either of them could say another word. When Emma turned, she was staring into Marcus's eyes. She turned away before she could stop herself.

"Marcus!" Olivia exclaimed. "I didn't know you were coming by."

Lord Westin cast a look at Mathis. "I forgot my gloves," he said quietly. While it had been only minutes earlier that Emma had seen him, his face appeared changed. More haggard, less assured, perhaps. Whatever the change, it was hard to define. All she could say was that Marcus looked *different*.

And he was making a valiant attempt at not looking at her at all. Emma might as well have been a statue for all the notice he paid her. Not that she could blame him, she supposed.

"When did you leave your gloves here?" Olivia's eyes narrowed slightly. "You haven't been by since yesterday."

Emma fidgeted with the chain of her necklace, silently trying to will Lord Westin to secrecy.

"I was by earlier," he said vaguely.

Olivia vacillated between appeasement and an even more ravenous curiosity. "Whatever for?"

Marcus didn't so much as flick a glance at Emma when he said, "Business matters."

Those two words twisted the knife in Emma's gut. Well, there was no use in feeling any sorrow or guilt over what she'd done. All she could do now was deal with the aftermath as gracefully as possible. Everyone in the foyer—Emma would include Mathis in that number—knew Lady Huntsford was dying to press the issue, and Emma was afraid she might actually do so, so she rushed Olivia down the hall.

"You must look at my gown for this evening."

Olivia nodded and bid a farewell to her brother. "Don't forget what you promised me," she called over her shoulder.

Emma had no clue what she was talking about, but apparently Lord Westin did, because after a flash of a scowl, he nodded and left.

Olivia, who had no idea that Emma truly didn't care about the gown that she'd chosen for that evening, pushed along beside her. But that didn't stop the marchioness from keeping up her steady stream of commentary, when the only thing Emma wanted was to brood over what had happened with Marcus in silence.

"Didn't you think Marcus was acting oddly?" Olivia asked as they climbed the stairs toward Emma's room.

Emma's step faltered, and she grabbed on to the ornate banister for support. "Why would you ask me that? I can hardly claim to have any understanding of the earl and his moods."

She didn't like the suddenly speculative gleam in her friend's eye. "Perhaps not," Olivia said slowly, "but I should think that his behavior was different enough for *anyone* to notice."

Emma couldn't keep protesting without confirming whatever suspicions seemed to be taking root in Olivia's mind. So Emma resumed her trek up the stairs, shrugging her shoulder. "I can't say why he would be acting oddly, as you called it. Maybe there is something unsettling about his business." That would, perhaps, be the largest understatement Emma had ever uttered.

"You may be right. I would have thought that, maybe, he might have said something to you about it," her friend continued.

Emma's heart slammed in her chest. "To *me?* Wh-why would you think that?"

Olivia's manner was too unaffected, too unconcerned for Emma's comfort. "You two seem to talk a great deal."

"I wouldn't so much say 'a great deal.' We have sporadic conversations."

"You're not telling me something," Olivia said. Her tone indicated she would brook no objections.

So Emma didn't offer any.

"What is it?" the marchioness pressed.

"It's nothing, Olivia. Everything is fine." And Emma prayed that sounded believable.

Olivia's eyebrows rose. "Did my brother offend you?"

"No, no, not at all," Emma said quickly. The last thing she wanted was Olivia accusing Marcus of mistreating her.

Her friend scrutinized her.

"When was the last time he kissed you?" Olivia asked after several minutes of silence.

Emma almost choked. "What?"

"Marcus…when did he last kiss you?"

"How did you know?" Emma whispered, horrified that Marcus might have told his sister about it.

So she wasn't sure whether to be relieved or even more mortified when Olivia said, "I just guessed."

Emma groaned, but Olivia's manner had become brisk

and efficient. "Don't worry, Emma. I'll take care of Marcus for you."

That was *exactly* what she was afraid of.

"Marcus Crawford Fairfax," Olivia demanded as she stormed into Marcus's breakfast room the next morning.

"Good morning, Olivia." He didn't bother to glance up from the paper he was reading. He had a suspicion that he knew exactly why she was barreling into his house so early in the day, and if he was correct, her appearance didn't bode well for him. Quashing a stab of pain caused by thinking of his failed proposal, Marcus tried to keep his expression blank.

"Don't 'good morning' me," she snapped.

Marcus folded the top of the paper down so he could look at his clearly put-out sister. "Would you rather I bid you a bad morning, then?" The banter came easily. And it was much preferable to having any kind of deep or meaningful conversation. Everything was still too raw. He wasn't sure he'd be able to sit through that.

"I'm not here to discuss the pleasantness of the morning, and well you know it." She maneuvered herself toward the table, and a footman pulled out the chair before Marcus could even rise to do it himself.

"What are you here to discuss, then?" he asked, hoping his voice sounded disinterested. The whole time his heart hammered in his chest.

"You kissed Emma," she accused.

That hadn't been what he was expecting. In truth, Marcus wasn't completely certain what manner of tirade he was expecting from his sister. He supposed he was expecting to hear much of the same. That he was to leave Emma alone. That his rejection was justified because hadn't he been warned away from her from the very beginning?

"She told you?" he managed to get out in spite of his surprise.

Olivia narrowed her eyes. "So you don't deny it?"

"Emma told you that?" he persisted, ignoring his sister's simmering indignation while he grappled with what would be a suitable response to the accusation.

"You've given me all the confirmation I need," Olivia said, managing to be both angry and smug at the same time.

Marcus sat back in his chair. "I don't really think this is the kind of thing I need to be discussing with you, Olivia."

"Stuff it, Marcus," she said. "I'm a married woman now. I think it's entirely appropriate for us to talk about you taking advantage of my friend, one who's also under my protection."

"Actually, she'd be under Nick's protection," he said, more just to buy himself some time to think about how he should steer the conversation.

"It's not at all proper to run around kissing a woman, Marcus," she said with a beleaguered sigh.

He quirked a brow. "Do you mean to tell me Nick never kissed you before you married?" he asked.

Olivia blushed bright red. "That would be entirely different."

"How's that?" Marcus asked, buttering a piece of toast with a knife. He hoped his sister didn't notice how he'd almost pulverized the bread by gripping it too tightly.

"Nick is not my brother."

"Well, I should hope not. That would have made things ridiculously different."

Olivia frowned at him. "This is not precisely the time to be making jokes," she said. "This is serious."

Lifting his eyes to meet hers, Marcus let her see a little of the pain he'd suppressed. Let her see just how seriously he took the matter.

Olivia recoiled at what she saw in his face. "You're being

incredibly contrary today," she said, forcing a lightness into her voice. "I come by simply to ask a question—"

"You weren't simply asking a question," he interrupted her. "You were prying."

If her glare were any indication, his sister took offense to that. "I wouldn't have to pry if you would simply do your brotherly duty and keep me informed."

He said nothing.

"She is my *friend,* Marcus!"

Something in him broke at the reminder. Marcus wasn't going to sit idly by and pretend that he was fine any longer. He certainly wasn't going to listen to his well-intentioned sister trying to warn him away as though he'd been dallying with Emma's affections.

"The friend I'm not good enough for, isn't that it?" he asked, his voice deceptively quiet. What he really wanted to do was yell, rail at someone, anything that might help alleviate the tension building inside of him.

Olivia blinked at him. "I never said you weren't good enough for her, Marcus."

"You didn't have to say it, Olivia. What else could you mean by making every effort to let me know that while I could be useful in bringing stuffed-shirted dandies by, I couldn't be considered a contender myself?"

Perhaps it was the passion in his voice, or the cracking force of his words, but Olivia looked like she couldn't decide whether to come and hug him, or run from the room. Marcus would have preferred the latter merely because he felt the overwhelming urge to wallow in his grief alone.

Was it his imagination, or did his sister suddenly look guilty? "Marcus...I..."

"What is it, Olivia?" he prodded, his voice tired, sad, even to his own ears.

"I'm sorry," she said simply.

The tone of their conversation had shifted, and Marcus struggled to keep up. "Sorry for what, exactly?"

"I figured that if I pushed you toward Emma, you'd ignore her just because you thought I was trying to meddle." Olivia ventured a sad sort of smile. "I *was* trying to meddle, of course, but only because I know how seriously you take your work. Seriously enough that finding a wife wouldn't be a priority."

Marcus might be oblivious sometimes, but he wasn't stupid. "So you thought by roping me into helping you find Emma a husband that I'd fall in love with her myself?"

"Yes?" Even his sister didn't sound too sure of her scheme now.

Marcus couldn't think of what to say. Should he confess to her that he'd asked Emma to marry him and had been refused? That would probably only upset his little sister. Or make her more determined to rectify whatever problems there were between them.

And he most definitely couldn't take either of those at the moment.

Olivia knew she had probably interfered too much already, and she seemed nearly desperate to make amends. "She's a good woman, Marcus. And you're a good man. It wouldn't give me any greater joy to be able to call Emma my sister in truth."

Marcus supposed it was too bad that Emma didn't feel the same.

"I love you both." She assessed him with a level stare. "And I hate to see either of you hurting."

Marcus wanted to ask if Emma seemed hurt, but there wasn't a way to phrase the question that wouldn't sound needy. And he wasn't ready for Olivia to see the depth of his own pain.

"Let's just leave it for now, Olivia," he said, not unkindly.

She nodded. Then, however, almost as if she couldn't help herself, Olivia pushed back from the table, ran to his side and threw her arms around him.

"Whatever it is that's making you both so miserable will work itself out," she mumbled into his shoulder.

He nodded because the silent seeming agreement would mollify her. And because he didn't want to dash her optimism. There had been enough dashed hopes already.

Chapter Fifteen

Unfortunately, life went on. Went on without Emma having even a moment to pause and reflect on how miserable she was. That didn't stop her from feeling miserable, of course, but when she might have wished for some solitude to sort out her feelings, Olivia had informed her that they didn't have time to waste. After all, she still needed a husband.

And since Marcus…

Well, it was better to banish those thoughts before they even had time to take hold in her mind.

"This looks ridiculous," Emma complained as her maid tied the mask around her face. She wouldn't come right out and say that the young girl was relishing her job…perhaps with too much vigor, but Emma winced as the ribbons of the mask were secured to her head with a yank.

"Sorry, my lady," Abigail said with a cockney accent Emma found delightfully charming. Apparently, the Marchioness of Huntsford had made it a practice to attempt to reintegrate the young women of workhouses into respectable positions as maids or perhaps seamstresses.

"What did you say, Emma?" Olivia asked, the smile on her face evident in her voice.

"You do realize that I look ridiculous, don't you?" Emma returned.

"It's a masquerade ball, Emma. You'd look ridiculous if you wore a regular evening gown." Olivia, who was unsurprisingly resplendent in her costume, looked on Emma much like a doting mother would.

"Besides, ridiculous is the last thing you look," Olivia continued.

"I think you look lovely, my lady," Abigail said.

Emma smiled at the girl and then, with the same motion, turned to scowl at Olivia. "I look like a peacock."

"That's what you're supposed to be," Olivia said with the same long-suffering tone she'd been using all day. The path to even getting the gown over her head had not been an easy one. It wasn't that Emma wasn't grateful for all the trouble Olivia had gone through to pick out the costume. And she supposed that many people would look at the shimmering blues and greens of the gown and declare it a visual feast. No matter where the wearer went in the room, there would doubtless be eyes drawn right to it.

And Emma supposed *that* was the problem.

This was her first masquerade, and the last thing she wanted was to stand out so uncompromisingly. Her vision had been to rather drift into the background, emerging only if Olivia twisted her arm and made her dance with someone. She knew that she was supposed to be drawing eyes—and suitors—at every opportunity, but ever since refusing Marcus's proposal, it had grown harder and harder to motivate herself to look for a husband.

And that was a dangerous position to find herself in, since between the suitors that Marcus had frightened away and the ones who had left in a huff after finding out about her nonexistent dowry, the selection was growing scarce.

But her friend, who possessed a surprising and somewhat

frightening amount of tenacity, had obviously thought ahead on how to circumvent these difficulties.

Olivia had to beg Emma to come down the stairs. And even though the marquess was nothing but flattering—he didn't even grimace at the profusion of aquatic colors, no doubt accustomed to the far more garish arrangements his aunt put together even for ordinary occasions—she was still nervous. Although she was properly and modestly clothed, Emma felt exposed for the whole world to inspect. Such was the life in the *ton,* she supposed.

An hour later, she was actually grateful that Olivia's choice of costume had been so discreet…comparatively, of course. Ladies ran about in shepherdess costumes, Roman togas and—her personal favorite—even as a fruit bowl. Emma cringed as the woman dressed in fruit bobbed and moved. If a piece of the costume didn't fall off the dress and roll across the floor by the end of the evening, it would be nothing short of astonishing.

She stood along the perimeter of the ballroom, grateful that the costume provided her with the anonymity to simply hide. Tonight, Emma preferred to watch. The gentlemen were nearly indistinguishable from each other. Of course, there were those who had dressed to match their lady-loves. A humble shepherd, a gentleman in his own toga, but fortunately, no accompaniment to the bowl of fruit.

Most had simply worn their evening attire with nothing more than a black half mask as a nod to the occasion.

She wondered what Marcus might be wearing.

And then wished she hadn't even thought his name.

Because the thought was a summoning for the man himself.

"Hello, Emma," the Earl of Westin's voice whispered in her ear. His warm breath puffed on the sensitive skin, sending a chill skittering through her.

Turning to face him, she was disturbed to find the sight of him made her heart pound harder and more erratically.

"You're not supposed to know who I am," she said, a touch too breathlessly.

Of course she knew who *he* was. Even if his voice had not given it away, the sight of him would have. No half mask could hide the stark handsomeness of his features. Or the muscular, broad shoulders that were perfectly accentuated by the cut of his black formal coat. With his towering stature, Lord Westin didn't have much of a chance at anonymity.

That was what she preferred to believe, anyway. It was infinitely better than believing that she were so attuned to him she would know him no matter what he appeared as.

Apparently, Marcus didn't have any reservations making similar statements. "I would know you anywhere," he whispered.

Predictably, she blushed. Why did he have to say these kinds of things to her?

Emma turned slightly, giving him more of her back and hoping he would just go somewhere else…anywhere else. Everything was still too raw, and Emma knew for a certainty that she wouldn't be able to pretend nothing had happened between them.

Ever contrary, however, instead of leaving, Lord Westin asked her for a dance.

Before she could advise herself, and him, about the foolishness of such an idea, he snatched her dance card, penciling his name into a blank slot—conveniently for the next set.

Which is how, only moments later, she found herself facing him in the crowded ballroom. And while her costume was likely enough to keep anyone from knowing with any surety who she was, Emma still felt exposed and awkwardly on display.

She was more aware than she wanted to admit of the heat

emanating from her dance partner. Much as she wanted to ignore her feelings for the earl, it was becoming increasingly difficult with him so near, and with him staring so intently at her. Her feelings were ridiculous in light of the heartache that lay between them. But the simmering attraction, now, was much more of a nuisance than an excitement.

Regardless of all that had happened, however, how could she really blame herself for her attraction to him?

Lord Westin was, as always, handsomeness personified. His elegant attire, stark in black and white, only emphasized the rugged plains of his face, the cut of his jaw and the shape of his brow—both masculine and appealing. She let her gaze wander, lingering on the features that weren't obscured by his mask.

Too late, she realized he'd caught her staring at his lips. The corners of his mouth quirked in response.

"Something interesting?" he asked her in a low tone.

Emma wrenched her eyes away. Shame and embarrassment heated her face. Blessedly, her mask hid most of the evidence. And she hoped the couples on either side of them hadn't heard the exchange.

Lord Westin was too much of a gentleman to remark further on her frank appraisal of him.

Or so she thought.

"You don't have to turn your face from me." The statement was a gentle reproach, even sounding a little sad.

"I'd rather not look, my lord," she said before she could realize how her words sounded. *Because then I might break and say something I shouldn't.*

But she could tell he'd hardened almost immediately at the perceived insult.

His grin was too sharp. Too…something. "Ah, fair lady, you wound me." And his words held a hint of bite.

"Stop it," she hissed.

Even with his mask firmly in place, she could tell he'd raised an eyebrow at her. "How else do you expect me to react when you slight me so grievously?" His words were light, but she suspected the emotion behind them was real enough.

"That wasn't my intent," she said, feeling like she should make amends.

Marcus noticed the shift in her manner. He narrowed his eyes, searching for something in her expression. Although uncomfortable with his frank, unapologetic inspection, Emma forced herself to remain still.

"Something interesting?" She'd meant the question to be a taunt, a mocking of his earlier one...but it sounded too earnest for that.

"Yes," Marcus answered without hesitation.

Well, that admission was unexpected, and it rattled her. "Stop looking at me," she commanded.

"Where would you prefer I turn my attention, then?" he asked. "The punch bowl? The terrace doors?" He furrowed his brow in contemplation. "Although if I did that, people might speculate that I'm going to spirit you outside."

"I don't much care where else you look, my lord," she snapped, "as long as it isn't at me."

This created even more mock concern in him. "What will people think if I do not so much as brave a look at you while we are dancing? Either it will be said that you repulse me so much I cannot even glance at you, or that I am an abysmally inattentive dancing partner."

"You shouldn't care so much what everyone thinks, Lord Westin," she snapped back.

At his victorious grin, Emma realized she had fallen into a trap. He didn't have to say the words "Neither should you." She read them in his expression.

Rather than giving Marcus any additional satisfaction by

trying to explain that her legitimate concerns were vastly different from his histrionics, she ignored him.

The musicians drew the strains of the dance to an end. Emma wasted no time dropping his hand.

"I've offended you again, haven't I?" he asked her quietly...almost like the thought of it bothered him.

"It's nothing a bit of fresh air won't cure," she said. Before he had a chance to offer his escort, Emma was striding toward the terrace doors. Once she made it outside unhindered, she breathed a sigh of relief.

The air held an uncharacteristic crispness given the time of year. A chill seized her, and she shivered.

"You shouldn't be out here," Marcus's voice came from directly behind her.

Emma turned to look at him. "Because I might find myself scandalized by an unscrupulous rake hiding in the shadows just waiting for some silly chit to venture out alone?" Her sarcasm was meant to ward off his.

He was grinning, but there was no amusement in the expression. "Because you might catch a chill."

Taking a step forward, as though he meant to wrap her in his arms to ward off the cold, the earl advanced on her. Emma stiffened, but she didn't retreat. Lord Westin stopped no more than a breath away from her. One look upward, and she could read every flicker of indecision in him. His hands even clenched and unclenched restlessly as though he'd love nothing more than to pull her to him.

The earl sighed, the sound seeming much louder than it really was.

Emma had had enough. Her heart beat frantically, and her thoughts raced. Was he going to kiss her again? Did he even want to? Why had he followed her outside? Why had he insisted on a dance? Why couldn't he just leave her in peace?

Tears sprung to her eyes. And the only reason she didn't

brush them away was because she didn't want to draw attention to the fact that she was about to cry. And admittedly, brushing them away might have been difficult considering her mask and plumage.

The earl saw the gathering moisture anyway. Any hints his demeanor had held of the teasing, rakish gentleman disappeared.

"What is it, Emma?" he asked. With annoying gentleness, he lifted the mask away. His hands moved to cup her face, and with a featherlight touch, he brushed away her tears with the calloused pads of his thumbs.

Looking up at his wavy and watery appearance, she asked quietly, "Why are you doing this to me?"

He didn't bother to ask what she meant. He knew.

She could tell that from the way he flinched from her question as though she'd struck him. His hands dropped back to his sides. "I don't know."

They stared at one another, each looking for something in the other, with perhaps neither of them knowing for sure what it was.

Impulsively, Lord Westin took her hand. Bringing it to his lips, he flipped it over, pressing a kiss to her palm. "This is the end," he said cryptically.

He left to return inside, leaving her to decipher his statement.

The problem was, Emma was fairly sure she knew exactly what he meant.

This time, she didn't try to hold back her tears.

Chapter Sixteen

Emma was happy to be back in her church. It had been several days since the incident at the masquerade with Marcus. Blessedly, Olivia had not noticed their interlude on the balcony—or if she had, she'd refrained from saying anything. But she had been watching Emma with a certain measuring look in her eye that Emma didn't know how to interpret. Dearly as she loved her friend, it had been something of a relief to get away from her for a day. And Emma was looking forward to spending time with her parents.

The minister preached from the book of Esther about trusting in God even when circumstances were beyond one's control and consequences of failure were dire, and Emma sat a little straighter in the pew.

Wasn't that exactly her problem?

She'd fallen into the trap of fear. She was afraid of telling her parents she'd lost her position because she worried that *they* would worry or would be disappointed in her. Afraid of abandoning this ridiculous hunt for a husband because she'd convinced herself it was the only option she had left when all of her applications for a governess's post went unanswered. Afraid of being honest with herself. Afraid of Lord Westin because…

Because…

Well, she couldn't bear to think of her life without him in it…even if only as a friend.

Yet, instead of turning her concerns and fears over to God, she'd clutched them to her chest—afraid to let go even the tiniest bit.

Reverend Jacobs continued to preach, but Emma was too wrapped up in her own thoughts to hear much else of what he said. But she figured the Lord would understand since she was trying to work out things in her own mind.

What exactly am I supposed to be doing here, Lord?

There was no thunderclap of divine answer coming out of the sky. Nor was there a fiery handwriting on the wall. Instead, there was a rather quiet prompting that insisted she already knew the answer to her question.

But she had no idea how to begin.

After the service, Emma told her parents it would take her only a moment, and she headed toward the front of the church to search out Reverend Jacobs. While knowing that she wouldn't have an opportunity to bare all of her problems— there were of course other parishioners around—she was hoping for a brief word of wisdom.

"Reverend Jacobs?" she asked, as she approached.

He turned to face her, his elderly face lighting in a smile. "Miss Mercer, it's wonderful to see you again. It's been a while, has it not?"

"Yes, sir. I've been attending a church closer to Mayfair… it was more convenient with where I've been staying."

"I'm not chiding you, dear. It doesn't matter to me where you go as long as the message is godly and the people inviting."

"Would you mind if I speak with you for a moment?" she asked.

"Of course." He motioned for her to follow him toward a

secluded nook in the corner of the church, one that would at least afford them a modicum of privacy.

"What's troubling you, Miss Mercer?" the kindly minister asked as soon as they were both seated on a ledge that jutted out from the wall.

"There's a man…" she began, feeling stupid for starting with Marcus.

The man's smile turned knowing. "Yes?"

"Well, I don't know what to do." What she needed to do was to excuse herself as gracefully as she could under the circumstances and go back to her parents rather than continue to make an idiot of herself.

But Reverend Jacobs must have had a bit too much of the matchmaker in him, because he was poised, ready with a barrage of questions.

"What exactly is the problem?" he asked.

"There are too many to go into."

"Is he an unbeliever?"

Emma tossed her head in denial. "No, Mar—the gentleman is a devoted, godly man."

"Do your parents disapprove?"

She thought for a moment and then answered honestly. "No, I think my parents will love him."

"Well, does the gentleman in question not reciprocate your feelings?"

"He's asked me to marry him."

This caused the older man a moment of pause. "Forgive me if I'm not understanding, but *what* exactly is wrong, then?"

Here was where she was going to sound ridiculous. "I told him no."

The look the minister gave her was only slightly less shocked than what she anticipated. "You refused him?"

Emma nodded, feeling miserable. And like even more of an idiot.

"You say he's a good man, and it's obvious that you care for him, or else you and I wouldn't be having this conversation. So, why did you refuse him?"

She'd asked herself that exact question. And she hadn't liked the answer she'd come to. But she was going to share it anyway. When Reverend Jacobs asked it of her, she could hardly refuse. "I was…am afraid."

He leaned back against the wall, contemplating her confession thoughtfully. "It's hardly surprising," he said after several moments.

"What is?"

"That you should be concerned. But just so we're clear and I make sure I understand you, what are you afraid of the most?"

Tears stung her eyes when she thought about it. Making painful confessions to herself was one thing, but giving the thoughts a voice was entirely another.

"I'm…I'm afraid of loving like my parents love."

The minister looked startled. "But my dear, your parents have a wonderful marriage, full of love. Why would you be afraid of that?"

"Because they allow their love to blind them to their circumstances!" Emma retorted, her mixed emotions giving over to frustration. "Mama loves Papa, so she goes along with every scheme, supports him in every ridiculous speculation, when she should tell him he's being a fool for throwing money away. And Papa…he loves Mama so much that he seizes on every false claim, every scheming trickster who promises him easy riches. Love has *beggared* them because it keeps them from showing any sense." She had to take a breath after her speech.

"Now, Emma, don't be saying things like that," but his tone was not harsh, merely chiding.

"When I was a child, whenever we got a bit of security,

something would happen, and we'd be destitute again. When I grew old enough, I was the one who had to become independent and find a way to support my family. And I'm...I'm proud of my independence. If I allow myself to marry this man that I...that I love, what will be the price?"

Reverend Jacobs folded his hands together on his lap and sighed. "My dear Emma, love *will* change you—love changes all of us. It's God's gift to us. That's what makes love such a blessing. It does not make us less than who we were, it makes us more." He reached over and patted her hand.

"That's not to say that love will solve all your problems—we both know that it won't. But a true and sincere love could never alter anyone for the worse. It isn't love that causes bad things to happen. Love is what helps us through them and gives us the strength to persevere. Your father is a good man," the preacher said. "He loves you and your mother very much. Now, is he misguided on some things? Yes. But aren't we all?"

Emma nodded.

"Everyone has flaws. Everyone makes mistakes."

"I know that, Reverend," she said rather dully.

"Well, do you want to know what *I* think?"

"What would that be?" she asked, smiling in spite of herself because he seemed so enthusiastic.

"I think that you need to remember that not every man is your father. And I think you need to go and get this gentleman. He sounds like a prince."

"Almost," she said, laughing. *He's an earl.*

After a pleasant luncheon with her parents, who didn't seem to notice their daughter's distraction, Emma walked out into the streets feeling lighter of heart than she had that morning. The reverend had been correct. Marriage to Marcus wouldn't make her less than who she was, it would make her more, because only as his wife could she achieve the one goal she'd always cherished.

To be happy.

She didn't just want a husband.

She wanted Marcus. Marcus, who took his responsibilities so seriously and who would *never* be as incautious as her father. Marcus, who encouraged her to speak her mind, and even argue with him, as her mother had never done with her father. Marcus, who determinedly protected her from every danger—even if the potential for harm only existed in his mind.

And it had been her own foolishness that had taken away her chance to be happy.

Not watching where she was going, Emma had wandered off the sidewalk in an effort to avoid a mass of people coming from the opposite direction. Completely lost in her internal struggles, she missed the sound of a carriage barreling down the road.

Nor did she hear the shouts from onlookers…or the yelled warning of the coachman, who was pulling hard on the reins but without any real effect. Oblivious to all of the commotion, Emma took another aimless step to the left…for no reason other than her mind was too busy to be guarding her feet that closely.

"Lady! *Move!*"

Finally, a warning pierced Emma's haze. She looked toward the man who had yelled at her, not realizing that it would cost her precious seconds in getting out of the way of the carriage. By this time, the stupor had worn thin enough that Emma could actually absorb the chaos of her surroundings. In less than a second, she took in the gathered crowds, the gasps and shouts…and, most important, the coach that seemed unable to stop.

I'm going to be run over, she thought.

Shock paralyzed her. When she might have been able to jump backward and just barely miss being hit, Emma couldn't seem to find the energy to so much as take a breath.

A pair of hands gripped her around the waist, hauling her backward and up against a hard form, out of danger.

The carriage careened past without incident.

As unlikely as it was, Emma knew exactly who was holding her…who had saved her.

Marcus.

She knew it before he sighed out her name and buried his cheek against the top of her head. His hands didn't release her. If anything, Lord Westin clasped her tighter to him. Emma fought her embarrassment—facing the street, she could tell that people were still watching her with unabashed interest. But she also warred with her emotions. Being in his embrace was perfect.

"Emma," he sighed her name. The word sounded relieved, shocked and ragged. "What were you doing? You could have been…" He trailed off, unable to detail what the outcome of her battle with the carriage would have been. But clearly he thought it, because a shudder racked through his powerful frame.

"Thank you," she managed. Her words came out hoarse, husky, as though she'd been screaming in the middle of the road and had lost her voice.

"Emma…" he began again. Then, as if Marcus realized that his tone conveyed his emotions so much better than words could, he just held her closer in silence.

This was wrong.

So why then did her heart thrill at his presence? She wanted to tell him that she'd changed her mind, entreat him to propose again—though perhaps not on one knee this time, as the streets were rather filthy and would ruin his fine trousers. But how could she bring such a subject up? She couldn't—it

was as simple as that. Having refused him, she had no right
to assume he had any interest in reopening his suit. Awkwardness swamped her, and she straightened away from him,
brushing down the front of her skirts, ridding the fabric from
the dust the carriage had kicked up on her. "I appreciate your
assistance," she said a little more formally.

His nod was curt. "You're welcome." Marcus shook his
head. The gesture meant something, but Emma couldn't
decide what.

"What were you thinking?" he demanded once his surprise
ebbed into anger. Taking ahold of her arm, Marcus pulled
them off the street and into a less public alleyway.

"I'm sorry to have upset you, Marcus." Unintentionally,
his name came out quietly…almost like a caress.

A lot had passed between them, and it wrenched Emma's
heart the way his eyes shut at her simply speaking his name.
Certain her refusal had dampened whatever affections he'd
had for her, she was surprised to see the flash of pain cross
his expression.

And as though he were hardening his heart to her, his
mask of temper and disapproval fell firmly back into place.

"What. Are. You. Doing. Here?" Each word was punctuated by his taking a step closer to her. Emma fought the instinct to retreat. But they were on a busy street, so there was
hardly room for that maneuver.

"I don't want to tell you," she whispered.

"Why not?" he asked, his voice dropping lower to match
hers. Marcus cupped her cheek in his palm.

Emma's body betrayed her. When she should have turned
away, she turned into his touch. Reveling in the rasp of his
skin against her face, she sighed in satisfaction.

It seemed to undo him, as well. The expression he wore
looked agonized, as if he couldn't bear to touch her, but just
as much, couldn't bear *not* to.

"Ah, Emma." He sighed, lowering his mouth to hers, almost in defeat. It was just the barest touch of lips before he pulled away. His hand still lingered, though.

While she knew nothing good could come from giving in to her desire to return his embrace, that didn't mean she didn't *want* to. He'd stepped back before she had the chance, however. Emma supposed she should be grateful Marcus had a better sense of their not-so-private surroundings than she did.

"Are you going to tell me, Emma?" he asked, their brief kiss apparently not a deterrent to his getting information.

"I—"

"Are you seeing someone down here?" Marcus interrupted, asking through gritted teeth.

Emma only nodded.

Just as quickly, Marcus's hand was gone, and as though he had literally jumped back, there were suddenly several feet of distance between them, where moments earlier there had been only inches.

"What's his name?" he asked, surprising her with the question.

"Whose name?"

"Your sweetheart's name."

"Sweetheart?" She certainly might have wished for more elegant responses, but Emma was having difficulty following Marcus's jumping thoughts.

He whirled on her, the tenderness of the earlier moment forgotten in his new burst of temper. "Your beau," he clarified, still not making any sense. "The man who feels so much affection for you that he would let you wander around by yourself unescorted."

She was beginning to understand, but before Emma answered and disabused him of his foolishness, she was too busy being thrilled by another thought.

Lord Westin was jealous.

The thought shouldn't have, but it empowered her. She wanted to reach out and wrap her arms around him. To lay her cheek against him, to listen to the pounding of his heart.

But she didn't. Mostly because they were still outside, where anyone might see. Even the alley they were in wasn't foolproof protection.

"I wasn't seeing a beau," she said quietly.

He stopped midpace. "You haven't been seeing a man?" he asked slowly.

"Well, I have…but it's nothing like what you think," Emma rushed to reassure him.

"Well, what is it like, then?"

"I've been seeing my father."

"Your father?" Marcus echoed, feeling almost weak with relief. Because while he had no claims on her—at her choice— he couldn't quite abide the thought of another gentleman being the recipient of her affections. Perhaps someday the thought wouldn't gall him as much, but right now, it was like a twisting knife to his gut.

"Well, and my mother," she added.

"And your mother?" he repeated, wishing he could stop parroting every word, but unable to do so.

She nodded, her expression so guilty it was Marcus's initial reaction to doubt her. Because, really, who would go to such pains to conceal visiting one's family?

Yet, when the irrational jealousy of only moments earlier reared its head, and the urge to press her, to question her further became almost an unstoppable compulsion, Marcus thankfully stopped himself.

Emma had never lied to him.

At times, she'd withheld information, but she had been blunt and unflinching with the truth, as well.

Steadying his breathing, since he didn't want her to know how close to the edge—of what, he wasn't sure—he really was, he turned fully back to her.

"Why the secrecy, then?"

One of her shoulders arched and fell in a delicate shrug. But the careless gesture belied the tension in the rest of her frame. "It was easier."

"Easier than what?" he pressed.

"Than *not* keeping it a secret." Emma's eyes roved over his face. He stood still while she sought *something* out in his expression. He didn't know what she was looking for, but he was going to give her ample time to find it.

Finally, she heaved a sigh, coming to some sort of inner resolution. He could see the momentary flash of resolve cross her face. "I couldn't bear to have you think badly of me."

Did he hear her correctly? "Think badly of you?" he echoed.

Head down, she nodded glumly.

That didn't quite illuminate the situation any more for Marcus. "Why did you think I would change how I felt about you?"

Emma wouldn't meet his eyes. "My parents live in Cheapside. They depend on me to work, to make enough money to maintain the family." The words sounded so anguished, so ashamed that Marcus wanted nothing more than to cross the few steps between them and pull her head down to his shoulder.

"You worked as a governess because your parents couldn't afford to live without the income?" He tried to make sure his voice was gentle and without censure.

Emma nodded. The lovely woman looked more miserable than he had ever seen her.

"But I knew you were a governess, Emma," he said, confused still. "So why would you think my opinion of you would change?"

"Now you know my background. The fact that my parents don't have enough money to keep a roof over their heads. I knew that would change how you looked at me." With that, she turned her back on him as though she couldn't bear for him to look at her.

Several different reactions warred within Marcus, each one fighting for precedence over the other. He could scarcely believe what she'd said. But Emma wouldn't want him to express the compassion within him. Doing so would only pique her shame even more.

Which was probably best, because the emotion that seemed to be winning the war to be heard was hurt.

"What kind of person do you think I am, Emma?" Marcus asked rather sadly.

The unexpected question had her turning back to face him and furrowing her brow. "What?"

He took a step toward her. "Obviously, since you hid this information when it would have been simpler just to be honest, you must have feared something. So I'm asking you, do you have so little faith in me?"

"I know how the *ton* thinks," she said quietly.

Marcus fought the rise of anger. "So you think I'm like every other nobleman you've known?" he asked, his voice hard now.

"I didn't know you at the time," Emma defended.

He wasn't going to accept that excuse. "That might have worked for the first few weeks, Emma. But you've known me long enough by now. You've had every opportunity to tell me."

"I was afraid, Marcus. All right? Afraid." She refused to meet his eyes.

And Marcus refused to press her further.

How surprised would Emma be to know that the truth of her family situation did change his opinion of her? Considering the heavy burden she'd borne for years, and her fierce loyalty to her family—when many women would have been angry at being forced to take employment—Marcus found it made him love her more.

Perhaps he should be thankful she'd refused his proposal, Marcus told himself. He'd known that Emma needed to marry. And while he'd deluded himself into thinking it would be fine to propose to her even though his finances were struggling and might take years to fully recover, Marcus knew now that it wouldn't have been fair to her or her parents if they'd married. Emma deserved a better life than the one he'd be able to offer her and her family at his current level of income.

If he'd met her six, or even three, months earlier, he wouldn't have accepted her refusal. Once he realized that he loved her, Marcus would have never stopped or conceded defeat. He would have wooed and courted her until she agreed.

But now, he had to leave her be.

Even though it was going to nearly kill him to do so.

Chapter Seventeen

"What were you doing in Cheapside?" she asked as they walked—toward where, she wasn't sure—in silence. As peculiar as he might find it that she kept popping up in Cheapside, Marcus had never explained his presence, either.

When long minutes passed and he didn't say anything, Emma thought her question was going to go unanswered. She would deserve that, she supposed. She hadn't precisely been forthcoming with her own confessions, had she?

Finally, however, the earl pushed his hand through his hair and answered. Was it just her, or did he still seem shaken? "I volunteer some time at the workhouse there, giving lessons on how to read and handle basic arithmetic." Then he turned his face from her as though the admission embarrassed him.

"Th-that's wonderful," she said quietly.

He didn't say anything.

"How long have you been working there?" she pressed, curious to know more about the social activist he was.

"Awhile" was his only answer.

"Are you going there now?" she asked.

"I *was*. Now, I'm taking you back home."

While his tone indicated he wouldn't brook any argument on the subject, Emma was much too curious about this part of Marcus's life not to at least ask her next question. "Will you take me with you?"

He paused in midstride. "Absolutely not."

Emma paused as well, turning to him with her arms crossed over her chest. "Why?" Although she knew exactly what his argument would be, that he didn't want her in such a dangerous place. That she was a lady…blah, blah, blah.

"It wouldn't be proper for me to take you there. These people are desperate, destitute…it's not pretty," Marcus said with something very like tenderness in his gaze.

"I'm not a sheltered miss, Marcus. I would like to see what you do."

Seconds passed before he grudgingly nodded his consent. And Emma wasn't certain which of them was more surprised. Marcus muttered to himself that he couldn't believe what he was doing, and he took her arm, pulling her hard against his side.

"Stay right with me," he commanded.

Emma was so glad that he had relented, she likely would have obeyed any high-handed dictate he issued.

She watched as the farther they went, the streets fell into further disrepair. The people looked haggard, hopeless. The sight of them tore at Emma's heart. Children, dressed in little more than rags, darted out from alleyways, running into the street and dashing in and out of buildings. Some of the younger ones, babies who couldn't be more than a few years old, sat propped against the rough stone buildings. A few cried out loudly for food.

The poverty surrounding them broke her heart. All of her life, she and her parents had struggled with money. One day, her father would insist they live like royalty, taking Emma to dressmakers and her mother to milliners. Within a week, they might be economizing by having only meat with their meals every few days. But never, no matter how desperate she'd felt their situation had become, had Emma seen something so close to verging on hopelessness.

"How do you stand it?" she whispered to Marcus.

When he turned to face her, Emma saw exactly how impacted he was by the sights around him. "I tell myself that someday it will be better for them," he said just as softly.

Feeling tears clogging her throat, she managed to get out, "Will it?"

This time, he turned his focus outward. Marcus took in all their surroundings with a single glance. "I hope so. I pray so."

Emma thought she understood better what he was facing in the House of Lords. How difficult must it be to convince people who knew nothing of true poverty the necessity of making reforms for the suffering and downtrodden?

"I think you're doing a brave thing," she told him as they continued to walk.

This earned her a smile, although one still tinged with sadness. "I'm just doing what I think God wants me to do."

Because Emma didn't trust her voice not to break, she said nothing else. And within a few more blocks, they'd reached the outside of a foreboding gray-stone building.

"It's not too late, Emma," Marcus said. "If you would rather not go in, I can still take you back home."

While she didn't want to see what was on the other side of the door—because she was afraid she might lose control over her emotions at what lay inside—Emma shook her head. "I'm made of sterner stuff than that, Lord Westin." She hoped so, at least.

His answering smile made Emma feel that she'd passed some unspoken test. And she couldn't help but offer him one in return.

"And in here, Emma," he said as he pushed open the heavy door, "I'm just Mr. Fairfax."

Nodding her understanding, Emma thought it explained why the constable hadn't referred to him by his title on the night they met. And why she'd been so surprised later to find he was a peer of the realm.

Within moments, there was no more opportunity for reminiscing. As soon as it became clear that Marcus had come by, the children in the house erupted in something very much like a riot. Each one was scrambling over the others in an attempt to get to him.

"I've candies with me," he whispered to her in an aside. And when he grinned at her, Emma felt a moment pass between the two of them.

Or perhaps that was just her wishful thinking.

"All right," he said to the children, holding up his hands in surrender. "Everyone calm down. I think I've enough treats for all. But lessons first."

This elicited some good-natured groans from his audience, but within minutes, Marcus had them situated in a room that looked remarkably like a schoolhouse.

"Did you do all this?" she asked when the kids were taking their seats. Emma had difficulty believing that the owner of the workhouse would fund something most people would find fanciful. Teaching orphans and workhouse children to read and do mathematics wasn't a high priority, she didn't think.

Marcus looked embarrassed. "They needed someplace to learn" was all the explanation he'd provide.

And when Emma took a seat to the side, ready to watch Marcus begin his instruction, she thought she'd never seen the earl look as happy. He'd crouch beside a student's desk, helping with an admirable amount of patience as the child tried to write the number four correctly. He lavished praise on the ones who blurted out their correct answers and would heap encouragement on the ones still struggling.

While she didn't think it was possible to care for Marcus

more than she already did, Emma was surprised to find that she loved him even more than she had only an hour earlier.

Marcus tried not to let himself be distracted, but he couldn't help but cast the occasional furtive glance at Emma. They'd been with the children for nearly two hours. And at some point after their studies, the girls had decided they wanted to play with the "pretty lady." Then, with the kind of enthusiasm only children are truly capable of, about ten little girls mobbed her, hopping in her lap, pulling her hair out of its pins in an effort to style it themselves and clinging to her skirts.

He'd wondered how she would take the attention. Of course, she'd been a governess. But neither of them had talked about whether she'd enjoyed dealing with children. But his Emma was laughing with genuine delight, moving her head to the side so that her makeshift maids could fashion an updo. She cuddled the youngest child, a girl of no more than three years, who had promptly climbed into Emma's lap and stuck her thumb in her mouth.

Smiling at the beatific picture before him, Marcus had to force his eyes away and back to the young boys demanding his attention.

Not surprisingly, the subject they all wanted to discuss was the "pretty lady" who had come with him.

"Is she your lady-love, Mr. Fairfax?" Timmy, one of the older boys, at twelve, asked.

How to answer that question?

"She's a friend," Marcus settled for.

"She's too pretty to be just a friend," Timmy continued.

"What would you know about pretty girls, Timmy?" Horace, who was about Timmy's age, called out.

Timmy crossed his too-thin arms over his chest. "I know enough," he defended.

"He don't know nothing," Horace whispered confidentially to Marcus.

"I heard that!" Timmy cried with outrage.

"Leave Timmy alone." One of the other kids came to the boy's defense. "After all, he's sweet on Eustace. And she ain't too ugly."

Marcus groaned, wishing that the defense hadn't been quite so loud, because Eustace stormed forward, ready to do battle.

"Who said I ain't too ugly?" the girl, also about twelve, demanded.

Timmy puffed out his chest. Clearly, he saw this as his moment to win her affections. "Michael did," he tattled.

Eustace looked ready to throttle Michael. The boy, having gained a bit of sense in the past thirty seconds, was edging his way closer to Marcus.

"I think Eustace is beautiful," Emma said, rising from her seat—hangers-on in tow—and coming to take Eustace's hand.

This was met with a chorus of "Do you think *I'm* beautiful, too?" from the girls. And once Eustace had been declared a nonpareil by Marcus's "pretty lady," the other boys looked at her with new respect.

While Emma was assuring the children that she thought they were *all* exceptional, Marcus noticed the clock against the wall. The hours had passed by more quickly than usual. Was it because Emma was with him and kept unintentionally distracting him, so he lost track of the time? Or was it simply even more enjoyable—and thus quicker passing—than usual with her here?

As he and Emma made their goodbyes, Marcus couldn't help but fight the stab of disappointment he felt at leaving. Nor could he fight the sense of guilt about not being able to do more, financially, to help the children right now.

It was one of the things he regretted most about his circumstances.

The other would be not being able to convince Emma to marry him.

Because as much as he loved her, Marcus wasn't selfish enough to jeopardize the security of her entire family because he didn't want Emma with anyone else.

"They want you to come back with me next time," Marcus said as they walked back out onto the street.

Emma cast a look back at the closed door to the house. He didn't think it was his imagination making her expression seem wistful. "I would like that. Would you bring me?"

He weighed his words carefully. Forgetting the potential hazards of bringing Emma back to this part of town, Marcus had to admit that he didn't think it would be the same without her there now. The children would likely lock him in a closet if he returned alone. Besides, Emma had brought a light, a joy, to the dark halls that he hadn't thought he'd ever see there. It was as though her very presence brightened everything.

Or perhaps he was being maudlin.

"We'll see" was what he said, rather than having to give her a definite answer. Because while she'd done the children an immeasurable amount of good—mostly by proving that people did care about them—Marcus didn't know if he could stand it himself.

Could he watch her playing with the children and not wonder what it might be like to see her with *their* children one day?

Impulsively, Emma grabbed his hand. "I just wanted to thank you for letting me come with you."

Because he wasn't certain he had words to say back to her, Marcus only nodded.

"I've never met a man like you before."

"What?" he asked, almost missing a step in their walk.

She repeated herself, the words even more unsure and vulnerable than they'd been moments before.

"Don't say that, Emma," he said harshly.

But she tugged his hand, pulling him to a stop. "No," she said with more resolve, "I mean it, Marcus. I knew you were doing a good work. But I had no idea…"

Shaking his head, as though he could shed the compliments she was trying to heap on him, Marcus continued walking. He also took special care to remove her hand from his, not wanting the intimate connection. There was only so much a man could withstand before he'd be bound for Bedlam.

"Why won't you let me—?" Emma began, no doubt to ask him why he kept barking at her.

"Because I'm not perfect, Emma." His voice was hoarse.

She laughed, probably in an effort to lighten the sudden seriousness of the mood. "Well, I know you well enough not to suggest *that*," she teased.

He nodded brusquely rather than answer.

At least that much, they were in perfect agreement upon. But while he might not be strong enough to deny her effect on him, neither was he rogue enough to act on the emotions she'd stirred in him that afternoon. Marcus most likely would have refused to take Emma back to Olivia's until she agreed to marry him.

Perhaps, if he'd been desperate enough, he'd have turned his phaeton out of London and toward Gretna Green.

As it was, once he handed her up to the empty seat, Marcus clicked the reins, steering the horses resignedly back to Mayfair.

Chapter Eighteen

Two days later, and Reverend Jacobs's words kept coming back to Emma. *Go to him.*

But the minister obviously didn't understand the way things worked. She couldn't possibly do that. Assuming that she could even work up the courage to do such a risky thing, what would Marcus say if she showed up on his doorstep? Likely, he wouldn't even see her. And then there would be no telling what he would think about her. What if someone else saw her making her way to the Earl of Westin's? She knew that would create a scandal that would set all of London atwitter.

Once the idea took root, however, it was nearly impossible to dislodge it.

So what if Marcus thought the worst of her? If the expression on his face when he was leaving was any indication, Emma doubted his opinion of her could sink much lower.

As for the rest of London…let them think what they would.

Am I really considering this?

What would I even say to him?

What if he sends me away?

But in some dim, distant corner of her mind, Emma had already decided. Now that Marcus knew the truth about her, was there really anything stopping her? And he already knew the worst about her…

Turning abruptly on her heel and heading back up the stairs, Emma tried to formulate a plan. Remembering the way he had trembled as he held her earlier, and the way that his eyes had softened when he looked at her gave her hope that her refusal hadn't dampened his desire to marry her.

That was the only excuse she had for leaving the house, once again hiring a hack and heading across town. It might have made her thirteen different kinds of foolish, but when she thought about their time together at the workhouse, about the powerful and noble lord who had more concern and compassion than she'd ever expected to see from a member of the nobility, well…she'd never forgive herself if she let a man like Marcus walk out of her life without fighting for him.

In what seemed like too little time, now that her nerves were rioting in her, Emma raised her hand to knock on the door to the Earl of Westin's home and prayed that no one saw her standing outside, without a chaperone and seeking entrance into a gentleman's house. She might have convinced herself that the threat of a scandal wasn't sufficient deterrence, but that didn't mean Emma would be pleased by one.

But she didn't even have an opportunity to rap on the door. Marcus's butler, Gibbons, opened the door with a flourish and a bow.

After stepping inside, Emma warred with what the appropriate thing to do was. Well, if anything about the venture could be appropriate. Finally, she settled for introducing herself to the butler.

"Miss Mercer," he greeted warmly. "I am Gibbons, and I am humbly at your service." His eyes twinkled with delight.

Well, at least *he* wasn't judging her for her unorthodox behavior.

"I— Is Lord Westin in?"

"Are you sure you wish to see him, dear lady?" the butler joked. "I'm not certain he deserves the pleasure of your call."

The observation made her brighten and helped to dull some of the nerves she felt. "Thank you, Gibbons. I'm fairly sure," she said with a smile.

"Charity work is such a noble pursuit, Miss Mercer," he said with another smile.

Gibbons showed her into a beautiful parlor, but as soon as he left the room, Emma's nerves returned. The brilliance of her plan seemed to dim with each second that passed without the door opening.

Would he be so angry that he'd refuse to see her? Or maybe he'd be disgusted by the fact that she'd ignored every social convention by coming to see him. Had she made a colossal mistake in coming? Perhaps she could turn and leave with no one but Gibbons being the wiser.

There wasn't any time to continue being afraid of the earl's reaction, because Lord Westin was opening the door to the room. He stepped inside and closed the door—save for a small crack to maintain propriety—behind him. She couldn't believe how awkward she felt standing in front of Marcus.

His handsome face was impassive, which was no surprise, but still wrenched at her heart. It would have been easier to speak, to apologize if he still looked angry. While it might not make any sense, Emma needed him to rail at her so she'd feel better about what she'd done.

"What is it, Emma?" Marcus asked, his voice more weary, more haggard than she'd ever heard it. The sound of it bothered her.

"No 'good afternoon'?" she joked. Her laugh sounded strained and forced—because it was.

"Good afternoon, Miss Mercer," he said, still sounding put out by her presence. "What is it?"

She wrung her hands, twisting them and twining them

until she had to force herself to stop. "Can we talk for a moment?" Emma finally asked.

"About what?" She couldn't blame him for his guarded expression or manner, but Lord Westin wasn't exactly making this very easy for her.

This was where her time rehearsing should have taken over, where her words should have come—if not naturally—at least more easily than before. Instead, Emma found herself grasping for what to say to him.

Time to be brave, she thought.

Now that the moment was staring her in the face, though, her mouth was dry. Her tongue felt thick and unwieldy.

"Y-you asked me to marry you," Emma said quietly. "A-and I said no," she finished.

Marcus tightened his jaw. "I know. I was there."

Well, this wasn't coming out nearly the way she wanted it to. "I'm sorry for that."

He said nothing.

Taking a deep breath, Emma decided it was time. Time to open her heart and see if she could mend the breach between them. If she was successful, the reward would be worth all the embarrassment and discomfort she felt now. She would get to spend the rest of her life with Marcus.

If she wasn't successful…

Well, that would be that, she supposed.

"I didn't want to say no," Emma began.

Dimly, she was aware of Marcus sucking in a hard breath, but she couldn't let his reaction affect her. She needed to say the words without worrying about how he might react to them.

"I couldn't say yes then. You didn't know about my family. And I was worried and afraid of losing myself. But I know that's rubbish now." Emma clasped and unclasped her hands together. She needed to do something with them, before the urge to run forward and embrace him, touch his face, smooth out the hard lines of his expression became too much to withstand.

Nothing had ever been so painful as the moment of silence when she waited to see what Marcus would say. Short of asking *him* to marry *her,* there wasn't really anything else she could do to get him to renew his proposal.

Would he think that she was only coming after him because of his money? Of course she was concerned Marcus would think so in light of her earlier confession...but surely he'd realize that if that were her aim, she would have accepted his proposal the first time.

There was no indication of what he was thinking. The Earl of Westin was silent and tight-lipped.

"Say something, please," Emma whispered.

His eyes closed, and he breathed heavily. "We shouldn't be talking about this," he said. His voice was quiet, but still steely.

Emma shivered at the implication. "Why?"

"Some things are better left in the past, Em—Miss Mercer."

Each word was a fresh stab of pain. She had her answer. And it was a no. The best thing for her to do would be to gather up the tattered pieces of her pride and go home.

Yet she didn't move. Maybe she figured that leaving without a shred of dignity was preferable to leaving without fighting for what she wanted.

"Do you love me?" she asked, the last possible question she intended to pose, and yet the first one out of her mouth.

"Do I love you?" he repeated.

Praying for courage to see it through, since she'd already stepped this far out, Emma nodded.

His silence was deafening, and the weight of it oppressive.

"I…wh…" He paused as though regaining his composure. "Why?"

Emma blinked. This wasn't exactly a question she'd been anticipating. Of course, it would have been too much to hope that Marcus would, at the slightest prompting, declare his undying love. And she should probably face the distinct possibility that she'd killed whatever affection he had for her.

At that thought, tears welled in her eyes.

"Can you not just answer the question?" she asked, hating the pleading note in her voice. This meeting, while she'd not been expecting a fairy-tale ending, was certainly not going as she hoped.

Every second that ticked by without him responding was like an extra lead weight in the pit of her stomach.

"Say something," she begged. *Say you love me still,* but she dared not ask that aloud.

"Circumstances have changed since we last discussed that," Lord Westin said finally.

Her throat constricted at the implications in his words. "Oh?" was all she managed to squeeze out.

He looked *almost* as uncomfortable as she felt. "Yes. Circumstances have…"

"Changed," she supplied for him. "I assure you, I've taken hold of your meaning." Her hands tightened into little, unimpressive fists.

She'd been a fool. As much as he might have protested otherwise, the information she'd shared about her parents must have been what had *changed* for him. Nothing else of any import had happened between then and now. Anger and disappointment warred with each other for domination of her emotions. The resulting internal struggle made her feel tired and even more miserable.

"And I can assure you as well that we'll have no revisiting of this conversation."

"Emma," he began.

But she cut him off. "Perhaps I should protest over your familiarity. As your sister says—"

"Olivia knows nothing. At least not half so much as she thinks she does. And she certainly has no idea of my own circumstances."

"*Circumstances*… That word again," she snapped. "Can you not speak plainly without blaming the capriciousness of your affections on something so vague?"

"I've explained it well enough," he said firmly.

"You tell me nothing, except that you have changed your mind. When *I* was equally vague about my reasons for visiting Cheapside, I was betraying our friendship by not being honest and forthright. But when your *circumstances* change, clearly I have no right to question you any further. Forgive me, but I thought men always claimed it was women who were the fickle sex. I see, in your case at least, they would be mistaken."

"Careful, Miss Mercer," he warned in a low, almost chilling voice.

But she was well past heeding any warnings from him. "What? One day, you talk of forever, and yet, when I mention it, you claim only a change in climate. I suppose I should be grateful to have said no, since you are more changeable than the weather."

"Enough!" he roared. "You know nothing about me. Nothing! Do you hear me?"

Emma gaped, hardly knowing what to say. She confessed as much to Lord Westin.

"Say nothing. The deed is done."

"And things have changed," she said quietly, noticing that he'd used the past tense in his rant. Her anger had given way to just sadness.

He nodded.

But how? she wanted to ask. How could things have altered so drastically? Had she killed any tender feelings he had for her?

It would seem she had.

"Let's forget this conversation. It will do neither of us any good," he said.

What choice did she have but to agree?

Lord Westin could not have looked more relieved than if he'd danced about the room singing a hymn of jubilation.

Emma didn't know how, at this point, to extricate herself from the conversation. She wanted nothing more than to run out of the room with her face buried in her hands.

But there was still too much dignity, too much within her that wouldn't allow her to lose it completely. When she turned to leave, however, Emma couldn't let a strained agreement to forget the "whole mess" be the last note of the subject.

"I really am sorry," she whispered to him. Waiting for a response would have been pointless, as it didn't appear that Lord Westin was even going to acknowledge her remark, so she excused herself.

"Miss Mercer has left, my lord," Gibbons announced, coming into the parlor about five minutes after Emma had breezed out the door.

Marcus hadn't moved. His hands were clamped firmly behind his back...he was afraid that if they weren't he might throw a punch at the wall.

"Thank you, Gibbons," he said shortly, hoping his brusque tone discouraged any further conversation.

Gibbons didn't say anything else...but nor did he leave. Marcus watched the clock on the mantel, silently wondering which one of them would crack first.

"She was crying, my lord," Gibbons said after three and a half minutes.

He was glad his back was to his servant because Marcus didn't want to have to explain the grimace that crossed his face. Tipping his head back slightly, he closed his eyes. When Marcus realized that only made it easier to visualize Emma's brokenhearted expression, however, he opened them.

"It is not unusual for a woman to cry," he said, fully aware that he sounded like a cad.

"How long have I been in your employ, my lord?" Gibbons asked.

Marcus was surprised by the question, so much so that he spun to face the butler, searching the older man's countenance for evidence of mischief. But his expression was as subdued and stoic as Marcus had ever seen it. "Since I inherited the title. And you were with my father before that."

Gibbons nodded. "I have been in the service of the family for a long time."

"What would your point be?" Marcus asked. Couldn't his servant see that he preferred to wallow in his grief by himself?

"Not only have I worked for you for years, but I've watched you grow up, become a man, assume the responsibility you were born to."

"Yes?"

The butler took a deep breath, shaking his head sadly as he exhaled. "And I've never been more disappointed."

Chapter Nineteen

Marcus had no rational explanation for what he was doing.

Some would maybe call him a glutton for pain and punishment.

Perhaps he was.

Surely, that had to be the best explanation for why he was attending his sister's dinner party that had been arranged with the sole intention of feting Emma's remaining suitors to urge them to propose. He should have told Olivia he was sick or injured. He should have thrown himself down his staircase and *made* himself injured, just to avoid this.

The evening promised to be filled with inane conversation and foolishness—and a lot of painful hours watching Emma with a succession of men who weren't him. His enterprising little sister had even been canny enough to prearrange for Madame Julienne de Luc—London's current operatic sensation—to come entertain the guests, which would drag the occasion out unbearably.

He was a fool. A fool to think that there would be any way for him to escape the evening unscathed with Emma in attendance. Marcus didn't know how well he'd be able to maintain his composure.

Thinking about her was enough to send his mind into a

spiral. Because Marcus couldn't think about her without remembering the shattered and broken expression on her face when he sent her away. The memory of it nagged at him... invading his dreams and plaguing his waking thoughts. No matter what he tried to do, how he attempted to distract himself, Emma was always there, a niggling reminder that had him crazed enough for Bedlam.

More than anything, he wanted to banish the image of her sorrow from his mind.

Her face, the bleakness she tried to hide but shone through her eyes anyway, haunted him. And whenever the image of her popped into his mind, Marcus ruthlessly pushed it aside. Those thoughts were better left buried, mostly because thinking of her would derail all of his attempts, all his better intentions at leaving her alone.

Already, he'd begun by limiting his frequent visits to his sister's. In the past two weeks, Marcus had been only once. His absence had precipitated Olivia's visit, and her convincing him to attend the soiree.

Marcus knew the moment the lady of his thoughts entered the room. Since she'd yet to look over and notice his presence, Marcus allowed himself the temporary pleasure of watching her. Emma was stunning, as usual. Watching her as she glided around the drawing room, he couldn't help but notice her inherent grace. His mind urged him to go to her, and even his feet seemed in on the conspiracy, as they began to move in that direction.

His better sense won out, however, and he stayed put.

The object of his attentions must have felt his stare, because she turned to look at him then.

Their eyes touched for the barest of seconds.

Marcus was transfixed.

Even from the other side of the room, he could see the storm of emotions in her eyes. And without looking in the mirror, he knew his matched hers. He prayed she didn't see it. Perhaps Emma wouldn't notice. Foolish though it may be, he didn't want her to realize how vulnerable he was.

How incredibly lost and adrift he was, knowing he'd have to spend the rest of his life without her.

"It's turning out to be quite a crush," Olivia said with satisfaction as she came forward to embrace him.

Murmuring his agreement, Marcus forced his eyes away from Emma, who had already turned her back to him and was conversing with another gentleman.

Barnwell.

With something that sounded very much like a growl, he turned to his sister. "What is Mr. Barnwell doing here?"

"I invited him," she said with a sunny smile.

Marcus had somehow hoped that Mr. Barnwell would be left off the guest list—though he acknowledged that that had always been an unrealistic wish. The man was wealthy, courteous and utterly intractable in his determination to woo Emma. None of Marcus's usual tricks had been able to fully drive him away...though they *had* made him considerably more wary of paying his calls while Marcus was in attendance. At this stage, he was probably the most promising suitor Emma had. Of course Olivia had invited him. She'd likely even accorded him the seat of honor right at Emma's side during dinner.

It was probably a battle he should stay out of. Not probably, he amended, it was one he should most certainly leave alone. But that knowledge didn't stop him from casting glances toward the unlikely pair every time he thought no one was looking. And he wondered how close they had grown in the two weeks that Marcus had been in hiding.

Sometime right before dinner was announced, Mr. Barnwell disappeared. Because he was essentially staring in that direction, Marcus noticed it immediately. And when a footman came out to call everyone into the dining room, the merchant had still not returned.

Marcus escorted Emma to dinner. Not by choice, but because everyone else had already paired up...one of the other ladies in attendance must have been temporarily missing, as Marcus and Emma were the only two left.

Reluctantly, as though he were afraid her touch might burn him, Marcus extended his arm to her. "May I?" he asked.

Emma looked just as wary as he felt. "But Mr. Barnwell," she said, pointing off in the direction of the hall.

"He's not here," Marcus said with a shrug.

"But he only stepped out for a moment. What will he do when he comes back and everyone's gone?" She wouldn't meet his eyes.

"If he comes back, I'm sure your Mr. Barnwell can figure out where we are." He took her arm, wrapping it around his. "Come on. Everyone else has already walked in."

She still didn't seem convinced, but with their arms linked, Emma couldn't get free of him.

Touching her was a mistake. His heart rejoiced at the simple contact, even while logic told him to stop it. Did she feel the same as he did? Chancing a look at her face, Marcus couldn't discern anything from the tightness in her features. She could just as easily be moved by emotion as he was...or she could be repulsed by his presence and looking for a ready escape.

Much like the last dinner party his sister had arranged, Marcus had been seated beside Emma. He groaned at the realization.

"What?" Emma asked, her voice hushed, as he helped her into her seat.

"Nothing. Nothing," he said with a bit more fervency. The very last thing he wanted was for the other guests to pick up on their conversation.

Wordlessly, he sank into the seat beside her. Barnwell stumbled in then, looking around the table—undoubtedly for Emma—with a bemused expression on his face. The man even looked as though he might protest the location of his seat.

Marcus was ready to defend the changes, if only to thwart Mr. Barnwell. Because truly, the only thing he wanted less than having to sit beside her was to have to watch Barnwell sit beside her.

If Emma had been going to say something, it was lost in the ensuing din of conversation.

Which meant she couldn't argue.

And that was perfectly fine by him.

Dinner was a raucous affair. Fortunately, so many people were in attendance that Emma was able to eat her food without feeling the need to entertain Marcus. Which couldn't have been anything other than a blessing because she had no idea what to say to him.

Once the meal was completed, Emma retreated to the far corners of the parlor, content to stand as the opera singer took the raised podium in the center of the room.

It didn't have a single thing to do with being afraid the Earl of Westin might come and sit beside her. Although, in all fairness to him, after dinner he had all but leaped from the table—seemingly in his haste to get away from her. Even now, he had taken a position against the far wall, as far from Emma as he could get without going to another room. And while there was the length of the room separating them, from the way Emma's skin prickled with awareness, he could have been standing no more than a breath away.

Madame de Luc had moved to the front of the room, and most of the guests had fallen silent in preparation for the woman's operatic genius. Was it Emma's imagination, or was Madame taking great pains to smile in Marcus's direction?

A couple of furtive glances at the Earl of Westin revealed that he seemed to be returning the smiles.

The singing was beautiful. Even Emma in her ill temper had to admit that. Everyone, including Lord Westin, seemed enraptured. Madame was singing high, soaring notes that rang out over the low din of murmured conversations.

"Beautiful, isn't it?" Olivia asked, coming to stand beside Emma.

Emma mumbled something noncommittal and hoped that Olivia wouldn't press her on it.

"Where did your Mr. Barnwell go?"

"He's not *my* Mr. Barnwell," Emma answered, her voice more than a little shrill.

Olivia didn't debate the issue. "Well, where did he go? I can't believe he would leave you unattended."

"I believe he left for home. He was feeling unwell." His departure had been reluctant, but when the gentleman couldn't stop reaching for his kerchief and sniffling loudly, Emma had advised him to go nurse his burgeoning cold at home.

By this point, Madame had finished her performance. The woman made her way through her adoring audience. She stopped along the way to exchange pleasantries for compliments. Emma watched with the pricking of envy as the beautiful woman glided through the crowd. It was as though she floated through her enraptured fans, gathering smiles and accolades with a gracious smile and nod. Stiffening, Emma realized the woman was homing in on Marcus.

"Emma?" Olivia asked, and from the tone of her voice, it was clear it wasn't the first time she'd said her name.

"I'm sorry, Olivia," she answered immediately. "What were you saying?"

But her friend only surveyed her with unblinking eyes,

before asking, "What could possibly be more interesting than my riveting description of what Lady Turnbridge said to Henri?" she asked—her voice definitely more amused than irritated.

Emma, shaking her head with equal parts regret and relief, wrenched her gaze away from both Madame de Luc and Marcus. "I'm sorry, Olivia," she said again.

"No apologies, Emma." The marchioness's gaze was becoming less amused and more concerned. "Is there anything you would like to talk about?" she asked in a quiet voice.

"Just what Lady Turnbridge said to Henri," Emma prompted, hoping to distract Olivia with the question.

For a long moment of silence, Emma didn't think her overly simple plan had worked. But then Olivia sighed and launched into a story of how the baroness had the audacity to call Nick's aunt a deficient rainbow. While she knew it wasn't the behavior a good friend would admit to, Emma found her attention wandering again. And now it was Marcus who kept pulling her reluctant gaze.

He had been standing by himself, propped against the wall with the negligent grace that Emma found inexplicably appealing. But in the few short minutes that she had been distracted, the slim, blonde, enticingly beautiful Madame de Luc had sought to alleviate his loneliness.

Marcus didn't appear to feel the weight of her stare. Or if he did, he had determined to ignore her. Not once did his attention so much as flick away from his overly attractive partner. Not that Emma *wanted* him to notice her, of course.

"Emma, please tell me if something's wrong," Olivia entreated, pausing in the midst of her story.

Emma shook her head, noticing too late that her hands were fisted at her sides.

Whether Olivia believed her or not, Emma didn't know. Their conversation, however, stalled. For several minutes, the two of them just stood silently, listening to the ambient buzz of conversations around them.

How easy it would be to tell Olivia everything in her heart…all the confusion and distress that she felt about Marcus. It would be such a welcome relief to be able to share her pain with her friend. In the end, however, she said nothing.

Madame de Luc must have said something that Lord Westin found exceedingly humorous, because he threw back his head and laughed loudly. Without being able to stop herself, Emma stiffened at the booming sound of his merriment.

Despite her efforts to hide her irritation, Emma must have not been as fantastic an actress as she thought. Seconds after Marcus's laughter could be heard from across the room, Olivia looked over at her brother.

And wordlessly, Olivia slipped down her hand to squeeze Emma's own.

Tears sprang to Emma's eyes.

"I must go greet Madame de Luc," the marchioness said, her voice tinged with remorse.

Emma could only nod. She was afraid if she tried to speak, only sobs would come forth.

But Olivia was obviously unconvinced by the nonverbal agreement. "Are you certain?" Her friend chewed the inside of her cheek. "Because if you're not…well, then my hostess duties can go hang."

The vehemently spoken sentiment made Emma chuckle. "No, please, go be a gracious hostess," she said with the first genuine smile of the evening…it might have been a small one, but it was at least the first sincere one she'd felt inspired to all day.

Olivia studied Emma's face for a moment, clearly looking for any signs of distress that would make her snub the singer in favor of looking after her friend.

"Truly," Emma affirmed.

Olivia must have been satisfied by what she saw, because she nodded in return. With a brief squeeze, the marchioness moved away. Emma was left standing alone on the fringes of the crowd. No one in particular seemed to notice her... Marcus certainly wouldn't have been any wiser if Emma were on fire and flailing her arms wildly in the corner.

Emma finally escaped into the hallway and leaned against the wall. The guests were far enough away that their mingled conversations were a low hum in the background.

The sounds of muffled footsteps in the hall didn't immediately draw Emma's attention. There were enough maids and footmen scouring the hallways and rooms of the house to not warrant much notice. And this portion of the hall was rather dimly lit. Only a few candles burned in a candelabrum on a side table. Were the other person prowling the dark corridor with her a servant, Emma doubted her presence would be anything noteworthy.

As the footsteps—and the person they belonged to—drew closer, however, Emma's attention piqued. And when she saw who was coming right toward her, she didn't know whether she wished she could slink back into the paneling on the wall, or whether she was looking for a confrontation.

Lord Westin strode toward her with purpose...as though he had left the parlor intent on finding her and had known exactly where she'd be.

"What are you doing?" he demanded when he drew alongside her.

"I need fresh air. It's quite a crush in there," she answered. Keeping her voice level—and emotionless—was harder than she would have imagined. But she didn't want to show any sign that his presence so close to her was affecting her in the slightest. His face, his scent, his voice were precious commodities, ones she'd missed during the days of their estrangement.

"You came to the hallway for fresh air?" he asked, raising an eyebrow.

"That's what I said," she snapped.

But then Emma took a breath. No matter what, she wasn't going to cause an uproar. Olivia would be most distressed to come upon them and find her friend and brother near to tearing out the other's hair. And no matter how restrained she tried to be, whenever they began arguing, it was like a meeting of gunpowder and fire. Combustible.

Lord Westin took a deep breath, and for a moment Emma wondered if he was giving himself the same lecture to remain calm. What a pair the two of them were.

For seconds, Marcus stared at her, indecision clearly written on his face. Finally, he heaved a ragged sigh. "Emma," he said, his voice low.

"What?" she whispered back.

"I can't—"

She didn't know what Marcus might have been preparing to say because before he could finish, a loud feminine-sounding laugh that could belong to no one but Madame de Luc rang above all of the other noises in the house.

Marcus cringed at the noise.

"We should go back in there," he said.

Emma nodded.

Still, neither of them moved.

"What do you want me to say?" he asked quietly.

"I didn't ask you to say anything," she returned. But the rejoinder had no bite to it. Looking back, she might regret how low her voice was, how intimate their conversation sounded. But right in the moment, Emma couldn't regret the vulnerability she knew was exposed in her face, in her words, in the way she swayed the slightest bit toward him.

She held her heart out to him again—something that was becoming much too frequent of an occurrence.

"I can't stand that look in your eyes," he said, mostly to himself.

Of course, she hadn't been aware there was a *look* in her eyes. Although she shouldn't be surprised. He held everything of her heart, and yet would give her nothing in return. Emma would have been more surprised to learn that she was able to control the emotions raging through her.

"I'm sorry." And she was. He had given her an answer, and while it certainly wasn't the one she would have preferred, Emma had to abide by his decision. And the knowledge and reminder that she had been the one to reject him first was a bitter draught.

Marcus turned away from her.

Did she so disturb him that he couldn't stand to look at her?

Did he think she condemned him? Judged him? Did anything but loved him?

Before Emma could stop herself, and before she could think of any number of reasons why she shouldn't, she reached her hand out to his.

His grip was firm, his fingers intertwining with hers.

For a moment, Emma's heart thrilled that he wasn't trying to pull away from her. And while he may still not have turned to face her, Emma could feel the tension thrumming through him.

How long did they stay in that dark hallway, with no contact other than the simple touch of hands?

Emma knew that she should break the hold, should return to the parlor. But she couldn't give up the contact.

After several moments, Marcus must have come to the same conclusion. However, he had much more willpower than she did. After a second, their hands slipped apart.

"We must return," he said. This time there was no hesitation. And before Emma could say anything else to him, he'd disappeared back inside.

Chapter Twenty

Marcus hadn't seen Emma for nearly a week. The dinner party had been the last time they'd been forced into close proximity, and as much as he missed the sight of her, Marcus had been so busy between meetings at the bank and meetings with his solicitor that he hadn't had too much opportunity to dwell.

In spite of how diligent he was being, however, the unfortunate truth was that nothing much had changed. There had been no miraculous restoration of his fortune...nor had there been any definitive word on what had happened with the ship. And until the lost ship either pulled into harbor, or someone turned up with some additional information, Marcus had to assume that his finances would remain severely depressed.

So he certainly had other things to be doing than standing outside, under the white tents, watching the other luncheon attendees stroll by on the Wrights' lawn. He'd been there only an hour, and Marcus was beginning to remember how much he detested these functions when he didn't have Emma by his side.

It was for the best. That's what he kept telling himself. Nothing could happen between the two of them. It didn't matter how irresistibly lovely he found her...how charming and intelligent she was…or even exactly how incomplete he felt without her.

Cursing the wretched timing of his financial ruin was no use. He'd done that many a time but to no avail. Nor had his prayers for restoration been particularly effective. Oh, yes, Marcus believed that God would provide for him. He'd never starve to death or be forced to sleep on the streets. But he also couldn't say with any certainty that this wasn't some measure of divine punishment…a penance he had to pay for the sin of taking his wealth and comfort for granted.

No, he was forced to endure it. Alone.

That was the bitterest part of it all.

Part of him wished that he could tell Emma. What would she say if he was to confess that the only thing keeping him from pursuit of her was the fact that it was looking very likely that he'd not have any money to support her?

Or her family?

Yes, that would surely be an excellent way to win her affections.

Honesty couldn't hurt anything now. But Marcus pushed the thought away. He'd had perfectly sound reasons for withholding information. Some things were better kept as secrets.

But you wouldn't accept secrets from Emma…why should she expect less from you?

Again, he couldn't let the thought take root. Yes, he'd pursued and questioned until Emma had confessed to him, but his reasons for pursuing truthfulness from her was different. He'd only wanted to know if any danger plagued her. If there was something he could do for her.

And while telling Emma his own problems might be cathartic for him, it would be painful for her to hear…to hear that a lifetime of happiness had been destroyed by matters beyond the ability of either of them to fix.

Deciding not to waste any more time pining for things that

wouldn't come to pass, Marcus watched the people milling about.

It was a beautiful day; the sun was high overhead, and a breeze blew across the lawn. Every bit of cheer disgusted Marcus even more.

"I'm leaving," he muttered to himself, turning and preparing to walk back to his coach.

The sight of *her* stopped him.

Of course she was here. Olivia had told him earlier in the week that she and Emma were coming to the luncheon. That wasn't why he came, of course. He came because…well, Lord Wright, host of the luncheon, was one of Marcus's major supporters in the House of Lords. And Marcus had spent too much time in his study poring over ledgers that weren't going to change no matter how much he wished or how hard he willed it to.

And he'd come because Emma was going to be…

"Doesn't matter," he huffed under his breath. "I'm still leaving." If Miss Mercer had any plans to come and talk to him, she would have already done so.

If she was eager to search Marcus out, Emma certainly wouldn't be all but cuddling on the back lawn with that idiotic Barnwell.

The sight of the man's arm wrapped with Emma's was one of those things that Marcus noticed with only a cursory glance. He even walked several paces past before something registered in his mind as "not right." But then the unnaturalness of it was so impacting that when the full report hit Marcus, he halted in midstep.

And he strode the short distance to be by her side.

"Miss Mercer, good day," he said, flicking only a small glance at her. "Barnwell," he said with no more enthusiasm than he would show greeting the hangman at the gallows.

"Lord Westin," Barnwell returned in a monotone.

For a second, Marcus wondered if the other man disliked him. Of course, he'd never done anything to gain Barnwell's ire.

Except to be in love with the woman the merchant was obviously interested in making his bride. And then the minor incident of beating him down to the ground at the ball where they'd first made each other's acquaintance.

Little things.

"Miss Mercer," Marcus said again, bowing his head in her direction. The fact that she'd yet to say anything to him was vexing. "You're looking well."

"She is, isn't she?" Barnwell replied when Emma showed no inclination to respond.

Marcus schooled his face into a bland expression. Mr. Barnwell wouldn't get the satisfaction of seeing Marcus lose his temper.

Which was a fine thought, but was rather hard to carry out.

"You weren't at church Sunday," he said, in an effort to force her to say something.

With no graceful way to continue to ignore him, she mumbled something in reply. It was so low, however, that Marcus had problems making it out.

Barnwell didn't seem to have the same difficulty. Immediately, the man was the soul of solicitousness, patting her shoulder. "I hope you are feeling better, my dear Miss Mercer," he said.

"I'm fine, Mr. Barnwell," she said in clipped tones.

Marcus wanted to smile at the shortness of her tone. So she wasn't so infatuated with her suitor that she couldn't think straight?

"My sister didn't tell me you were ill, Emma," he said as he studied her face.

"It was nothing but a cold," she returned.

"Must have caught the one I had at the dinner party," Barnwell supplied helpfully.

Marcus didn't have to ponder over the insinuation there. He narrowed his eyes at the other man, while trying to suppress the surge of anger.

"Olivia's talking to Aunt Henri by the pond," Emma said after a few seconds of quiet.

"Wonderful," Marcus said with the disinterested tone of a man who had absolutely no intention of putting that information to use. He knew what she was trying to do. And he wasn't a fool…or in the mood to be accommodating.

His lovely Emma frowned—or perhaps her expression was closer to a scowl. "I'm sure she and Henri would both love to see you." This was said not quite as nicely.

"I saw both of them yesterday at church, so I'm certain the reunion could hold for a short while." He smiled at her. "You, on the other hand, weren't at service, so I've missed the pleasure of your presence."

She blushed—he loved that he could make her do that so easily.

"I wasn't feeling well," she reiterated.

"Barnwell's contagious cold," Marcus said, his voice tight.

"But as you can see, she is now the picture of perfect health. Good company can work wonders. I've always said so. Haven't I, dear?" Barnwell's statements might have been directed to Emma, but it was the earl he was glaring at.

"I wouldn't know if you've always said so, Mr. Barnwell. I've only known you a short time."

The man laughed, the sound high-pitched and shrill. Marcus decided in less than two seconds that it was a sound that should never come out of a gentleman.

"Miss Mercer is such a delightful wit," Barnwell said, his hand reaching out to pat her shoulder again, but this time resting there, as if staking a claim.

The sight of it made Marcus's temper flare. Briefly, he thought about removing Barnwell's arm for him but then figured that would cause more of a scene than he wanted to deal with. At least Emma looked as surprised as Marcus was furious.

"Miss Mercer," he said, trying to fight the impulse to knock Barnwell in the jaw. "Would you take a stroll with me?"

For once, Emma didn't look ready to refuse him outright. Barnwell, on the other hand, opened his mouth—undoubtedly to protest.

"Emma has agreed to come look at the ducks with me," the merchant retorted.

This reminder made the lady in question hesitate to take Marcus's hand. But at least she moved out of Barnwell's grasp. That was enough for the moment.

"I wouldn't advise that," Marcus said, just to nettle Barnwell. "Ducks carry diseases."

Barnwell narrowed his eyes. "Where did you hear something that preposterous?"

"I read it in a book."

There was nothing he could say to argue with that.

"Well, I believe Emma and I can stand far enough away not to get the plague."

"I believe the plague died out years ago," Emma finally said, obviously through with listening to Marcus and Mr. Barnwell.

"So will you come and take a walk with me, Miss Mercer?" Marcus asked in spite of his better judgment. He should stay far, far away from her. And when that wasn't an option, he should at least be wise enough not to invite more trouble into his life—or hers. And yet he found he couldn't walk away and leave her with her ardent suitor.

Marcus held his breath to see what she would say. Emma

looked torn with indecision. She worried her lip with her teeth and cast surreptitious glances between both him and the merchant.

"I did promise—" she began, only to stop rather abruptly. As her half-finished sentence hung on the air, Marcus tried to follow her gaze because she was suddenly staring off in the distance.

And when he realized whom she was looking at, the ashen color of her face came as no surprise. The Viscountess Roth was walking close by. It didn't appear as though Lady Roth had caught sight of them yet, but that didn't seem to make any difference for Emma, who looked as though she wanted to hide behind a tree.

"Yes, Lord Westin. Let's walk," she said and then lunged forward, grabbing his arm.

Barnwell was clearly not going to let an opportunity to protest pass him by. "But—"

Emma's anxiety must have been so great that she didn't care about being rude, because she tugged on Marcus's arm. Hard. "Please, Lord Westin. I find myself in dire need of a brisk walk."

"I am ever at your command, Miss Mercer," he said with a little bow.

"Now?" she prompted.

Marcus tossed a farewell to Barnwell over his shoulder and tried not to look too triumphant. Besides, he wasn't a big enough fool to delude himself into thinking that Emma's sudden and vehement change of heart had anything to do with him.

"Why were you so afraid of Lady Roth seeing you?" Marcus asked once he and Emma had reached a secluded portion of the garden.

"I wasn't afraid," Emma said, not as believably as she probably intended.

Marcus was a gentleman, who would have normally let such a distraction tactic go unremarked upon. But at the moment, with the image of Emma and the simpering fool Barnwell all but embracing in his mind…well, he wasn't feeling very gentlemanly.

"If that's so," he said, advancing closer to her, almost like a predator about to pounce on his prey, "then why did you beg me to take you away?"

"I hardly begged," she began to argue.

But he wouldn't let her finish. "And why not solicit Mr. Barnwell to play the knight chevalier?"

"I was trying to save you as much as myself," Emma snapped. "I hardly think the viscountess has forgotten your rather memorable cutting of her."

Marcus shrugged. "But that's the brilliance of providing someone the cut direct. I wouldn't have even had to acknowledge she was standing there."

Emma crossed her arms over her chest. "Well, now neither of us has to worry about her, Marcus."

When he might have pressed the issue, just to reassure her that she never had anything to fear from Lady Roth ever again, Marcus was distracted by the fact that she'd used his given name. The thrill of the triumph was probably foolish but he felt it anyway.

"Why are you looking at me like that?" Emma asked, eyeing him warily and taking several steps backward.

"Like what?"

She blushed. "Never mind." And with a few clever side steps, she edged around him.

Marcus instinctively moved to block her. "Like what?" he said more quietly, but no less demanding.

She swallowed hard. "Like you might want to kiss me."

Involuntarily, his gaze moved to her lips. "I always want

to kiss you, Emma," he murmured. Well, that was frank…
too much so. But it was also honest.

For nothing more than a second, Marcus saw something
in her eyes…longing? Regret? Whatever it was, it was gone
before he could conclusively name it. Was she thinking about
how he'd turned her away?

Marcus knew that incident occupied most of *his* waking
thoughts. There'd been no other choice but for him to do what
he did. But that didn't mean he didn't feel the pain of his rejection of her keenly.

"Mr. Barnwell will be looking for me," she said in an obvious attempt to force him to escort her back.

But Marcus had eschewed his duty as gentleman already,
so refusing to bow to her unasked request was surprisingly
easy. Besides, he wasn't done yet. Recklessness that could
have only been the direct result of seeing *his* Emma with Mr.
Barnwell drove him on.

"And what of our precious Mr. Barnwell?"

She frowned. "What do you mean?"

"He is quite…attentive," he finally settled on because he
couldn't think of anything else that wouldn't seem like he
was bitter or jealous.

Emma looked away from him. "Don't mock him, Marcus,"
she warned, still looking off at the hedgerows of the maze
behind him. "He's a kind man. And he…admires me."

"So I noticed." Marcus ground his teeth together. And the
words came out harsh and clipped.

Immediately, her hands went to settle on her hips. "What
is your problem now?"

"You didn't want him nearby if Lady Roth caught sight of
you—have you not told him of your background?"

She flushed but did not back down. "He already knows.
Everybody knows. And yet, Mr. Barnwell seems to have honorable intentions."

Marcus didn't miss her sarcasm…or perhaps the veiled accusation that knowing about her situation had changed things for him.

"Yes, he's made his intentions abundantly clear, hasn't he? Barnwell's all but pasted himself to your side. It's scandalous." The words were out of his mouth before he had the foresight to think about what a jealous fool they made him sound like.

"How dare you?" she demanded, stepping forward and jabbing her finger into his chest to punctuate her thought. "He's been nothing but proper. And you…" She paused, obviously rethinking whatever it was she'd been about to say.

"Me, what?"

"You…" Her hand dipped back to her side. "I can't begin to understand why you're acting this way." Her voice had softened. Less angry, more confused. The sound of it twisted his gut.

Denying that he was acting any particular way was ridiculous. Marcus was self-aware enough to admit he was being an idiot, although he wouldn't give voice to that observation.

Emma obviously mistook his silence for contrition, however. And he knew this because she felt comfortable enough to lose her disapproving expression. She even reached for his arm, as though she might stroke it in consolation. But he didn't want to be placated. Marcus wanted whatever madness that had seized him to subside. He jerked away from her touch.

Emma's face went blank. Her eyes, however, held something that Marcus didn't want to look at too long.

"You don't get to do this, Marcus," she whispered.

He started to say something, but Emma shook her head. "No. No, you don't get to do this. You turned me away, so you don't get to act like I'm doing something wrong because I'm interested in someone else."

"So now you're interested in him?" He seized on the statement because it was much, much easier than confronting the other and trying to answer her questions. Besides, Marcus couldn't give her any answers.

"Any right you might have had to ask these questions, Marcus, you gave up. So just stop."

When he might have been going to press the issue further, one look at her eyes, at the pain there, made him stop. Her words were strong, but Marcus knew her well enough to see the vulnerability and sadness underneath the bravado.

She moved away from him, walking—or, perhaps more accurately, running—back to the other guests.

"Emma, please wait…" he said, hating himself for his outburst, for his lack of control. He used to be so disciplined. Now…

She stopped, staring at him. And again her eyes brimmed with some emotion that almost brought Marcus to his knees. She looked so bleak, so broken that he wanted nothing more than to crush her to his chest. To stroke her hair, to kiss her cheek, to whisper reassurances to her that there was nothing the two of them couldn't overcome together.

But there was no *them,* and Marcus couldn't see any time in the near future that they would ever be together.

So he let her go.

Chapter Twenty-One

"Be my wife, Miss Mercer...Emma..."

Emma looked down at Mr. Barnwell, who had maneuvered himself down on one knee. She looked at the ring that he held out for her inspection. She looked at his smiling, hopeful face.

She took all of this in...and none of it touched her.

Of course, she didn't expect to feel the same passion, the same twisting of emotions that she felt with Marcus. Besides the fact that she wasn't that delusional, Emma was also trying to be responsible.

And the responsible side of her was currently embroiled with the emotional, definitely not so responsible side of her. Her feet itched to stand up and walk out of the room, to leave Mr. Barnwell and his perfectly nice, perfectly sweet, perfectly boring offer behind. Her mind cautioned her not to lose sight of her priorities. Clearly, she was woefully unprepared when it came to matters of the heart—considering how she had given hers away and had received nothing in return. Addressing Barnwell's proposal should be done with a simple weighing of the benefits and drawbacks...an analysis of how this marriage would change her life.

Of how she would work to change his for the better. Such a frank appraisal would make it so simple.

So simple to hold out her hand, obediently allowing him to push the ring of promise onto her finger. It would solve most of her problems. She had told him all about her family's situation, and Mr. Barnwell had already agreed that he would see to the comfort of Emma's parents if they married. The gentleman also didn't mind that she had no dowry—why would he when he was as rich as Croesus? And while he might not make her stomach flutter or her heart race, he was a gentle, unassuming man.

Why then was she hesitating?

Because while marriage to Mr. Barnwell would solve most of her problems, it wouldn't solve them *all*.

Marcus was the biggest obstacle of all. Could she really marry another man when she loved the earl?

Has he left you any other choice? the logical part of her demanded.

She had no answer to that.

"My dear Emma," Barnwell said, his voice a little more insistent. Clearly, waiting for an answer was taking a toll on him.

"Mr. Barnwell, you honor me with your proposal…." The words came out effortlessly, as though she'd been practicing this speech her whole life. But what was she going to say next? That part didn't trip right off her tongue.

Mr. Barnwell, bless him, sensed her hesitation. And where another man might have pushed to press his advantage, he seemed to understand her indecision.

"You are a beautiful woman," he said, not rising from his position on the floor. "And one who is very wise beyond her years. I know I might not be London's most desirable bachelor," he said with a self-deprecating smile, "but I would certainly see that you never lacked for anything."

"I know that, Mr. Barnwell. You are an exceedingly generous man...far more generous than I deserve."

He patted her hand. "Never that, my dear."

Taking a deep breath, Emma decided to give him the opportunity to rescind his offer. "But while I admire you greatly, and appreciate what you are willing to do for my family, I don't love you." She said the words quietly, as gently as she could. It was bad enough that she would be gaining so much more from this marriage than he. The least she could do was be honest with him.

The confession didn't break Barnwell's heart or composure. "I don't expect you to love me. At least not right away. Surely you can agree that's something that will grow through the years."

Still, she couldn't say yes. Her prospective husband seemed content with the silence, at least for the moment. No doubt he was giving her a few more moments of contemplation before he asked again for her answer.

Going through the reasons why she should say yes...why she should say no...was pointless. She knew them all and doubted any more time spent going through the list would give her more clarity. Emma was going to have to make a decision. Hopefully it would be one she could live with.

Marcus entered his sister's house only to find the place as silent as a tomb. Mathis was even more subdued than usual.

"Where is everyone, Mathis?" Marcus asked as he handed the man his greatcoat and gloves.

"His lordship is in his study, her ladyship is in the hallway and Miss Mercer is with a caller." This was said in between several covert glances to the closed doors of the yellow parlor.

"Thank you," Marcus said, turning on his heel to find his sister. Perhaps she would be able to shed some light on the sudden sickening feeling he had in his gut.

As Mathis had indicated, Olivia was pacing up and down the hallway. She stopped short at the sight of Marcus.

"How long have you been here?" she asked without any other greeting.

"Hello to you, as well," he grumbled. "I just arrived."

"Was…were the salon doors still closed?" Olivia wrung her hands together.

"Yes." The word was drawn out to the point of sounding more like a question than an answer.

"Mathis said Emma had a caller. Is something wrong?" he asked when Olivia said nothing else.

Olivia's answering smile was too bright to be authentic. "No, no, everything's fine."

"You're a terrible liar."

His sister looked offended. "I don't lie. Everything *is* fine…depending on how you look at it."

Marcus suddenly found himself not in the mood for playing word games with Olivia. "Who is in there with Emma?" he asked, his voice a bit sharper than he intended.

"Mr. Barnwell."

Why did that make him suddenly want to slam his fist into the wall?

"What did *he* want?" Marcus demanded. But he already knew. Barnwell had made his intentions clear.

His sister's mouth was drawn into a grim line, which did little to assuage Marcus's sudden agitation.

"I won't even begin to speculate," she said, although Marcus was sure she knew, as well.

"How long have they been in there?"

Olivia looked from the closed door down the hall to her brother. "Long enough."

When Marcus was preparing to ask what exactly she meant by that, the doors to the salon opened. Barnwell walked out first, and Marcus immediately narrowed his eyes, trying to discern from the man's expression how the meeting had gone.

He looked pleased.

Which only fueled Marcus's fury.

The merchant noticed him and Olivia in the hallway and called out a greeting to them as he walked to the front doors. Olivia's reply was halfhearted, and Marcus didn't even bother to make one.

Once Mathis had handed the gentleman his hat, gloves and greatcoat, Barnwell nodded a farewell to everyone.

Marcus was preparing to enter the salon, to check on Emma, when the lady herself came out. Her gaze was so narrowly focused, Marcus doubted that she saw him and Olivia standing less than ten feet away. Emma was holding something clenched tightly in her fist, and she ascended the stairs.

He was going to follow her. But before he could take even two steps to go after her, Olivia placed her hand on his arm.

"Maybe you should give her some time," she suggested.

"Time for what?"

"To think about whatever just happened."

"And what *did* just happen, Olivia?" he barked.

Olivia's distress was written plainly on her features. She twisted her hands together and then, when that became tiresome, smoothed down the skirts of her dress. "I can't say anything for certain."

"Can't or won't?"

"I wasn't in there, Marcus, so I'm not entirely sure what went on."

"Shouldn't you have been sitting in there? Or Emma's maid? Are we so lax in propriety now that we allow a young, unmarried woman to meet with a man, alone, with the doors closed?" he snapped.

Olivia drew a breath, no doubt to begin defending herself.

Marcus changed directions, heading now for the salon,

and Olivia gave up trying to explain to him. If he and Olivia were going to argue, he'd do it away from wherever the servants could hear.

His eyes instinctively scanned the interior of the room when he entered. Not quite sure what he was looking for, Marcus wanted some sign as to what might have happened with the two of them in there.

Nothing seemed amiss in the room. But then, what had Marcus really been expecting to find? A scrawled accounting of events on the wall? Overturned chairs that might indicate a struggle?

Unfortunately, there were no such helpful clues.

Nothing at all to indicate what might have really occurred between Emma and Barnwell.

But then he spied the box on the table.

Olivia was right on his heels as he marched over and plucked up the clue. His stomach sank as he realized the significance of what he was holding. The package was clearly from a jeweler's, and a man gave a respectable woman jewelry for only one reason.

The man's intentions had always been clear. What wasn't so certain was whether Emma had accepted the overture.

Only one way to find out.

When he began to flip the lid open, Olivia stopped him.

"Should we really invade her privacy like this, Marcus?"

Nothing short of a pistol aimed at his head was going to stop him from looking, so Marcus didn't even acknowledge her protest.

The ring box was empty.

Everyone knew the significance of that.

Marcus gripped the velvet box until his knuckles turned white. If he could have crushed the offensive thing into tiny pieces with sheer strength and willpower, he would have done so. His sister laid her hands on top of his and was probably trying to ease the box out of his grasp. But Marcus wasn't ready to relinquish his hold on it.

"What was she thinking?" he asked no one in particular.

Olivia answered anyway. "You know she needs this, Marcus. It doesn't make any of us happy that she must marry in this fashion, but those are the circumstances. At least we know Mr. Barnwell is a good man."

Marcus raised his eyebrows. "Do we? What can Emma say for certain about the merchant?" he sneered. "She hardly knows him. He could have a wife hidden in his wine cellar for all we know."

"I don't believe Mr. Barnwell has a wine cellar," Olivia said calmly.

Marcus tried to ignore the amused expression on her face. "Perhaps he's not even truly a successful businessman. Has anyone verified this?"

Olivia's expression changed to one that was a mix of concern and pity. "Can you hear yourself right now?"

He could. And while he knew he was being beyond irrational, he didn't much care.

"Our only concern," Olivia continued without waiting for him to answer, "should be Emma's happiness. As long as she's content, then we've accomplished what we set out to do."

Olivia's words sounded right, but her voice lacked conviction, as though not even she believed in what she was saying.

Marcus pointed out into the hallway. "Did that look like a woman who was happy to you?"

Marcus wasn't entirely sure how a woman was supposed to look after accepting an offer of marriage. But if Emma was truly happy, wouldn't she have wanted to share her joy with them? Why then did she immediately head to her room?

Or was he grasping for anything to support his theory that this was a grudgingly made match?

Olivia threw her hands in the air. "What do you want me to do, Marcus?"

"You should have stopped her!"

"Emma's family is in dire straits *now.* We don't have time to begin again with finding a solution for their care."

Marcus was good and angry now, even though he knew he deserved the brunt of the blame. Emma *had* come back to him, and he'd sent her away…right into Mr. Barnwell's arms.

"I would have thought better of her," he ranted. "If the money's so important, why don't we simply arrange an auction and marry her to the highest bidder? At least that way there'd be no confusion or deception as to her motives."

He regretted the words the moment he'd said them, both for the hollow pit his hatefulness created within him and for the look of outraged astonishment on his sister's face.

But most of all for the decidedly feminine gasp from the doorway.

Marcus knew who would be standing there. And because he didn't think he could bear to see her face, he didn't— couldn't—turn around.

"Emma!" Olivia cried, shooting Marcus a look of pure fury before rushing to the woman at the door.

"He's talking out of his head," he heard his sister say to Emma as the two of them moved out into the hall. "He didn't mean a word of that."

Marcus knew that as a gentleman, and as her friend, he should go to Emma. Go to her and apologize. But he found that instead of the grand mistake dampening his anger, it only fueled it. If she hadn't accepted Mr. Barnwell's proposal, then he wouldn't have been put in a position to hurt her feelings.

He was still clutching the ring box. And with a yell of pure fury, he threw it into the fireplace, watching as the flames licked at the velvet and then consumed it.

Chapter Twenty-Two

Marcus slammed open the door to Nick's study.

If his friend was surprised to see him standing there, Nick didn't show it. Instead, he arched an eyebrow and gestured for Marcus to take a seat.

Marcus did. Grudgingly.

"Should I assume you have a good reason for banging in here?" Nick asked mildly.

Punching his friend in the nose was becoming increasingly tempting, but Marcus held his temper in check long enough for them to have a conversation. He was willing to give Nick the benefit of the doubt, thinking perhaps Barnwell *hadn't* come to him first.

"Do you know who came by to see Emma today?" Marcus demanded.

Nick might have sat a little straighter and put down the papers he was reading, but there was no indication of guilt or foreknowledge otherwise.

"And don't even think about giving me some sarcastic answer," Marcus warned before Nick could say anything.

"Yes."

Marcus gaped. While he'd had the suspicion that Barnwell would have spoken to Nick about his plans for Emma, hearing the confirmation was difficult. For several moments, Marcus couldn't even formulate what to say back. And when he did finally voice his thoughts, they came out as a rather ineloquent "Why?"

Nick knew him well enough to sense the tension and anger brimming and bubbling right under the surface. Only a fool would miss the fact that Marcus was one wrong word away from losing control over his raging temper.

Marcus could tell Nick was giving this all a lot of thought because he took great pains to use his "rational and calm" voice.

"Marcus, Barnwell's request was perfectly reasonable. What would you have had me do?"

Marcus banged his fists on the arms of the chair. "Deny him!"

"Barnwell asked out of courtesy, and truly he owed me no such regard. I'm not Emma's guardian." Nick scratched at his chin. "I don't think my permission was really being sought in this situation."

That wasn't enough to satisfy Marcus. "Well, when did he come to you?"

"Yesterday."

"You should have told me then. You could have sent a messenger to Westin House with the news immediately."

"What would you have done, then?"

"I don't know, Nick. But it's better than just walking into your house this afternoon and finding out that Emma is engaged to be married."

"Emma has accepted him, then?" Nick said, of course seizing on the least helpful observation of the conversation.

"She took his ring."

Nick slouched back in his seat. He looked…defeated? Surprised? Well, whatever emotions his friend was experiencing, Marcus would daresay they paled in comparison to his own feelings of betrayal.

"You know once it's announced in the papers, there will be no going back for her," Marcus told Nick.

"I'm sure she understands that," Nick said, but his mind was clearly occupied somewhere else.

"Are you? Because I'm not so sure. Someone needs to tell her this isn't a game, and the decisions she makes have permanent consequences."

Nick straightened again. "You don't give Emma enough credit, Marcus. She knows better than anyone the sacrifices she is making in order to have security for her family."

But Marcus was a man barreling downhill without any foreseeable way to stop himself from crashing at the bottom. He knew the inanity of everything he was saying. His arguments made him sound unbelievably ignorant and petty…but they were the best ones he could manufacture at such short notice without having to fall back on the searing truth—that she couldn't marry Barnwell, because Marcus couldn't bear the thought of her marrying anyone but him.

No, he couldn't say that, but if Marcus could have thought of a hundred reasons why Emma shouldn't marry Mr. Barnwell, he wouldn't have rested until someone listened to every last one of them.

"You're just as bad as my sister," Marcus grumbled.

"That's because we all understand the situation, Marcus. Unlike you, who seems to have difficulty comprehending what a bad position Emma is in."

This time, Marcus slammed his hands down on Nick's desk. The resulting boom echoed through the room. "Do you not think I understand, Nick? Do you think I just don't care what happens to Emma?"

There was such a long moment of silence after the outburst that Marcus resumed his seat and was about to apologize for his uncharacteristic anger when Nick answered, "No, I think you understand better than any of us."

There wasn't really anything left for Marcus to say. He stood up from the chair and grunted out a terse farewell to his friend.

When he was preparing to open the study door, Nick called out after him. Frustration threaded through his words. "You know, Marcus, if you're having such a hard time with this, you should have just married her yourself."

Marcus didn't even bother explaining he'd already tried that.

Emma hadn't left her room all evening. Olivia had rapped on her door right before six o'clock, wondering if she would join them for dinner. Since her friend hadn't elaborated on who would be dining that evening, Emma had declined. She didn't want to risk running into Marcus. How many times could the man break her heart?

Whatever the number was, Lord Westin was doing an admirable job trying to achieve it.

So she'd paced the length of her bedroom, had attempted a hairstyle she'd seen on one of Henri's new fashion plates and had tried sketching the view out of her bedroom window. All of that restless energy needed more of an outlet than Emma had provided, so when the rest of the house had retired for the evening, Emma still couldn't sleep.

She moved to the library, planning on finding some dull book on agriculture to help lull her to sleep. But after plucking an appropriate volume from the shelf, Emma tucked her feet under her on the couch and stared off into the empty darkness of the room. The book lay open on her lap, unlooked at.

The door to the library opened, and the unexpected action was enough to pull Emma out of her semi-trance. Instinctively, she snapped the book on her lap shut, as though she'd been doing something wrong being in the library so late at night.

It was Marcus.

The earl didn't see her at first. He walked into the room, tugging slightly at his cravat as he did so. Emma watched as he, illuminated by the few candles in the room, walked with great purpose to the small table slid against the wall.

She didn't know if she should call out to him or if she should simply stay silent and let him leave without knowing she was there. Was she ready to see him? Ready to hear whatever excuse he had for his atrocious behavior?

But then again, a voice from inside prompted her, *It's every bit as much your right to be here as his. Why should you have to hide?*

"Why haven't you gone home yet?" she said, rising from her seat. In the relative dimness of the library, Emma moved toward the earl, who had been so startled by her abrupt announcement that he almost knocked the table over.

"What are you doing here?" he asked, his voice gruff.

"I wasn't ready to sleep." She cocked her head at him. "But you haven't answered *my* question."

"I was actually hoping to speak to you," he said, looking off somewhere past her shoulder—probably wanting to avoid direct eye contact.

"And you knew I was going to be coming to the library at this late hour?" She didn't know whether to be amused or irritated.

"No. I—I waited for you to come out of your room this evening. And when it grew late, I decided I would stay the night here so I might see you first thing in the morning." Finally, his eyes met hers. Neither of them blinked.

"I don't know what to say to that," Emma confessed. Her

voice was soft, hushed…ridiculous since there was no one else awake to hear her.

Marcus took a few paces toward her.

"I'm sorry, Emma," he said softly.

Emma hated the fact that her eyes misted with tears. Why did every conversation with Lord Westin have to be so emotionally exhausting? "I appreciate that, Lord Westin," she said with intentional formality.

"Mr. Barnwell's a good man. A very good man," she said when Marcus didn't answer her.

The earl's face shadowed at that comment. Emma couldn't even begin to fathom why that would bother him. When she was on the verge of pressing him about it, however, he replied.

"Yes. It's clear that you think so," he said, brushing past her and walking back toward the door as though he was going to leave her there.

If Marcus thought she was going to be brushed off or away so easily, then he obviously didn't know her well enough. Emma picked up her skirts, running slightly behind him in order to get in between him and the door.

"What is that supposed to mean?" she demanded.

"Forget I said anything, Emma. I'm just tired."

He *did* look tired. But he looked something else, as well. Irritated? Disappointed?

What had put the shadows under his eyes? Her curiosity made her keep pushing him when it was clear he'd rather say nothing else to her except "good night."

"Why don't you just say whatever it is you're thinking?" she asked. "Because otherwise I'm going to try to figure out what you meant by that little snide remark myself. And I'm sure whatever I could come up with is worse than what you meant."

At least she hoped so.

What was it making her so bold? Was it the dimness of the room? The knowledge that they were essentially the only ones awake in the house? The knowledge that he'd hurt her as much as a man possibly could hurt her?

Marcus's features hardened. Had she pushed him too far? Fine, she was ready for whatever was on his mind.

"All I was simply saying was that regardless of the man's complete lack of decorum and probably even good sense, you seem to be his most stalwart champion." A muscle ticked in his jaw, and as soon as he said the words, he clamped his mouth shut.

Emma's mouth hung open. "What are you talking about? Do you even *know* what you mean?"

"Yes, I know exactly what I mean. I know as soon as Barnwell comes and bows over your hand and slips a ring on it, everyone's celebrating your upcoming nuptials," he accused. "You included."

Emma opened and closed her mouth several times, searching for what to say to him. What he was saying was so ludicrous she wasn't entirely sure she had a defense.

"Nothing to say, am I right?" he pressed. Another few steps forward and Emma was against the wall, and Marcus was so close she wouldn't have to move her hand much to touch him.

Naturally, she resisted the impulse. "So, you would judge me for celebrating?" she asked, despite the fact that had he been paying attention, Marcus wouldn't have seen the slightest bit of jubilation from her. Emma took no pleasure in her circumstances or in the options she'd been presented.

"Ha. I suppose we should celebrate, all of us be grateful that the wealthy merchant took an interest, shouldn't we?"

"Marcus, stop it. You're being ridiculous." But her voice wasn't as strong nor as convincing as she'd hoped it would be.

"Am I?" he asked, taking just the tiniest step forward.

"Y-yes," she stammered.

"He's been everyone's hero since the moment he stepped foot in this house."

Emma saw through his rhetoric to what he was really trying to say, or at least she thought she did. "Everyone's?" she questioned.

"Well, yours."

Her own temper was beginning to flare. "What should I have done, Lord Westin? Slam the door in his face when he comes to call? Refuse to dance with him? Question his motives for having polite conversation with me?"

Refuse to marry him? Wasn't that the most important question—the one that neither of them would voice?

Marcus put one hand on the wall above her head, leaning toward her slightly. Emma had no room to make an escape if she decided she needed one.

"You don't know anything about this man. He could be after any number of things."

"What, Marcus? I don't have a fortune or an influential family—what could he possibly be after?" she asked on a huff of exasperation. "Since you find it necessary to educate me on matters I have absolutely no understanding of, what dire plans does Mr. Barnwell have…besides marriage, of course." She hoped he caught the sarcasm.

The earl's eyes swept across her face, seeming to absorb the lines and flaws in her expression.

"You have attributes that are far more attractive than family and fortune." He pushed himself back the tiniest bit, lowering one hand to his side and dropping the other to run his hand from her cheek to the side of her neck.

Emma couldn't prevent her eyes from fluttering shut at the contact. As wrong as it was, she wanted him to kiss her. Who could tell what even the next second would bring? All Emma knew was that she wanted one last memory of this.

"As a matter of fact," he continued, "I daresay when a man is with you, money and pedigree pale in comparison to your beauty." He studied her. "Yet you don't realize how appealing you are. I always notice, Emma... Men—your Mr. Barnwell, included, no doubt—always notice, as well. That's lesson one." Yet his words were gentle, a perfect accompaniment to the strange tenderness in his eyes.

Her breath caught in her throat.

"So very lovely," he whispered.

Emma couldn't think of what to say, even if she'd had the air to voice anything.

It didn't much matter, apparently, because Marcus was continuing without any encouragement from her.

"I would think," he said, "Mr. Barnwell constantly finds himself thinking about touching your cheek like this." He trailed his fingers across her cheek, pushing a lock of hair back behind her ear.

"And he probably considered brushing his thumb across your lips." Again, his actions mimicked his words.

Emma struggled to breathe.

"Or even..." Marcus hesitated, as though even he weren't sure what was going to happen next. Then he covered her mouth with his own.

His arms moved to wrap around her waist, pulling her closer. His touch was gentle. The muscles at his shoulder bunched and flexed. His hands worked their way up to her hair. The pins holding the precarious coiffure together began falling out, and Marcus wove his fingers in the tresses.

Emma didn't want to move. Didn't want to do anything that might break the moment. But finally, Marcus ended the kiss. Instead of moving away, however, he rested his forehead against hers. His hands dropped to her shoulders—a comfortable weight for Emma to bear.

Neither of them spoke for several minutes, and the only sounds in the room were of their breathing.

She waited, her heart anticipatory for whatever soft words he would speak next.

"Don't let a crazed man kiss you at night in a deserted library." Marcus sighed and then dropped a kiss on her forehead. "Consider that lesson number two."

Chapter Twenty-Three

What had he been thinking?

Marcus watched Emma all but flee from the room, and remorse washed over him.

Emma had been right to run away from him, but he had to admit he'd watched her trailing out of the room with a fear that stabbed at his heart. Did she hate him? Could he blame her if she did?

Marcus knew the only honorable thing to do would be to walk away from Emma...even if that meant separating himself from his sister and best friend until Emma said her vows to Barnwell. He'd attempted to leave her alone while still staying on the periphery of her life, working to be only a concerned friend.

Yes, that had worked well.

Marcus couldn't be near her and be satisfied by only that. No matter what his good intentions were, there was an invisible cord pulling him ever closer toward her. And the only way to fix things would be to sever the cord.

So why was he still resisting?

He loved her. But plenty of people had to live without the person they loved. It was unfortunate, but it happened. And the only way Marcus was going to be able to move on with his life was to abandon any suppressed desires he had to spend his life with her.

If nothing else, perhaps leaving her behind would allow him to regain hold of his wits and his decorum. Quite the gentleman he was turning out to be…accosting a young woman at night in a dark library. A young woman who was betrothed to someone else. It didn't matter that for several moments, Emma returned his attentions. She was probably feeling as confused and frustrated as he was.

Maybe more so. Emma didn't have any answers, any explanations for why he'd sent her away…why he'd sent her away, yet couldn't keep his hands off her. Marcus had no excuse for his behavior…except to say that he loved her and *not* being with her was painful.

No doubt the woman he loved hated him.

Lord, what am I supposed to do?

His sins against Emma were grievous and numerous. The responsibility was his, and instead of leading by example and helping both of them move forward, Marcus was continually dragging them backward.

The realization that he was only hurting her was crippling.

Because while she might have responded to him with equal enthusiasm, Emma was an innocent. Marcus didn't know if she loved him or not, but he imagined she felt *something,* and his continual pull and push would only be confusing for her.

It was confusing for *him*.

But none of that mattered, did it? Emma was engaged to another man.

Feeling like more of a disappointment than he ever had, Marcus stepped out of the library. For a few seconds, he considered just heading back to his house. At least there, he could brood in silence. He could mourn Emma's engagement to Barnwell in private. If he wanted to yell or storm around the house there would be no one to stop him, and no one to witness, either.

The hallway was dark. Marcus half hoped and half feared Emma might be waiting for him out in the shadows. But of course no one else was there. Emma had fled nearly half an hour before. It would be easy to head down the stairs, out the door, to his house and pretend his lapse in judgment hadn't happened. Probably simpler, as well.

But remorse and conviction weighed heavily on him.

Marcus should have endured his anger alone, without pulling her into the raging center of it.

Emma deserved an apology.

She should be preparing to start her new life without having to worry about him waltzing in and ruining her happiness.

Once he'd committed—albeit grimly—to keep out once and for all, Marcus had to go tell her immediately…had to let her know she no longer had to worry about his interference.

Which was the only partially acceptable reason he had for bounding out of the library and up the stairs instead of out the door. Emma's room was the last on the right. And it was far enough away from Nick and Olivia's that Marcus doubted either of them would hear him. All he wanted to do was to tell her he was sorry.

And the apology couldn't wait another day, another hour.

Because part of not tormenting her meant not tormenting himself, and that meant not being around her until he could get his emotions under control. Even now, with resolve running through his veins, Marcus felt his determination might fray at any minute and he would change his mind. So he needed to get as far away as possible.

Right after he told her how sorry he was.

They might not be able to spend their lives together, but he wouldn't have her living the rest of hers thinking the worst of him.

So without any concern for the proprieties, or what the woman he loved might think of him for doing so, Marcus walked toward the end of the hall with purpose and a grim determination.

Since banging on her door would have roused everyone on the floor, Marcus settled for a series of three quick taps. But long moments passed without any indication she was awake or had heard him.

Sighing heavily, Marcus decided he might as well go back home because she clearly was either asleep or ignoring him. When he turned around to head down the stairs, however, he heard the whine of creaking wood as Emma opened the door.

"Marcus?" she breathed in surprise when she saw him.

He drank in the sight of her, his eyes starving as though he hadn't seen her in months, never mind minutes.

How are you going to spend your life without her?

Marcus didn't know, exactly. But he was going to have to. As he looked into her face, however, he knew he couldn't let this be the end without explaining himself. Emma deserved to know that the fault was with him—never with her. Would it make it any easier for Emma knowing what kept them separated?

He wasn't certain, but it was infinitely better than having her think that his love wasn't true, that his affections were capricious and ephemeral. Maybe he was being selfish, confessing because he didn't want her to think the worst of him. But Marcus rationalized those thoughts away because he figured that if he was going to be denying himself for the rest of his life, the least he could do was indulge his urge now.

He could only pray the truth didn't make it worse for either of them.

* * *

"Marcus?" Emma asked again. She stood partially behind the door, both of her hands braced on the edge. The earl had yet to say anything to her, but instead he stared at her with an expression she thought looked rather wistful.

"Were you sleeping?" he asked quietly.

She shook her head. Her hair was unbound, and the tresses swished around her shoulders. The movement momentarily captured his attention.

"Oh," he said finally, "I was afraid I might have woken you." There was something heartbreakingly vulnerable in his voice, in the way his body unconsciously swayed toward her.

"No. I couldn't sleep," she confessed.

Her admission wrenched a sigh from him. And almost as though he was in pain, Marcus slammed his eyes closed and tilted his head back. Once he opened his eyes, leveling an enigmatic gaze on her, his hands reached out, grabbing hers and pulling her out into the hallway.

She followed him willingly. Because while he confused her with his conflicting actions, Emma realized, in that moment, that she would follow him wherever.

"I need to apologize to you," Marcus said solemnly.

Before Emma could make any protestations, he continued. "I need to apologize for several reasons," he elaborated. "First, I shouldn't have kissed you like I did tonight. Forgive me?"

Emma felt the pangs in her heart. How could she possibly endure the coming conversation? Her instinct was to tell him that it didn't matter…that it hadn't mattered to her at the time, either. But her lips wouldn't let her form the lies.

"Forgive you? I suppose next you're going to say that it doesn't mean anything…" She meant it to sound caustic and biting. Instead, it sounded sad.

Marcus's eyes searched hers. "No. I wasn't going to say

that." His smile was even more despondent than his eyes. "It's always meant something."

Marcus blurred. It took her several seconds to realize it was because she was looking at him through tears standing in her eyes. She *wasn't* going to cry. No matter what, she wouldn't give him the satisfaction of knowing he'd reduced her to that.

But her best intentions, her strongest resolve couldn't keep the tears from slipping down her cheeks. While she turned to hide them from him, Marcus wouldn't let her. When Emma would have stepped backward and retreated to the safety of her room, his hand reached out and grabbed hers.

"Don't cry," he begged.

Emma wanted to sound unaffected, brave, indifferent. But that was going to be hard to do with wet tracks down her face. Besides, she'd returned his embrace with equal affection…so it would be a lie to pretend that she wasn't just as confused and conflicted as he was.

"Why do you keep doing this?" she asked instead of offering up some meaningless bravado.

Marcus rubbed the back of his neck with his free hand, seeming to massage the tense muscles there.

"I don't know what to think when you keep doing this to me," Emma plunged ahead when he didn't answer immediately.

He squeezed her hand tighter. "I don't know what to think most of the time myself."

"So why, Marcus? Why torture both of us? Why can't you leave me alone?"

"Because I love you."

Emma didn't know which of them was more surprised at his confession. After his stunning declaration, the Earl of Westin stared at her. His steady gaze seemed almost a challenge.

Emma didn't know how to respond. More tears gathered in her eyes, and she felt her entire body start to tremble. In her most creative imaginings, she never would have envisioned the man she loved declaring his own feelings in a dim hallway.

"Y-you what?" she asked, needing to hear the words from him again.

"I love you," Marcus repeated.

He couldn't have sounded less enthusiastic.

"Then why won't you marry me?" She'd only meant to *think* the question, but it was out of her mouth before she could filter it.

His response was instant. "Circu—"

"Circumstances," Emma finished for him. "Yes, you've explained that already." At least her voice didn't sound quite as wobbly that time.

So he would profess his love, but he wouldn't open up about anything else? Emma could feel her irritation peaking.

"You're going to have to do better than that, Marcus. I think it's time to start explaining what you mean by 'circumstances.'"

He wasn't going to answer her. After nearly a minute passed—a minute that she watched tick by on the clock in the hall—Emma started to turn back to her bedroom. There was no use in continuing to have the same exhausting conversation with him.

"I don't have any money."

Apparently, it was the night for startling confessions.

"What?" Emma asked.

"I don't have any money." Marcus's gaze never left her face. "My income for this year—it's nearly gone. Barely enough for the living expenses of a bachelor. It will take time before rents on the estate help improve my situation. Even then, half of my fortune is irretrievably gone. Your family needs help now…help I cannot give."

With everything reeling around her, Emma managed to croak out, "How?"

"It was an investment that went bad."

Emma tensed at the word *investment*. How could she not? And now Marcus was telling her that his fortune was gone because of it… How reminiscent of her father. She had thought the earl was different. Apparently, she'd been wrong.

Her mouth was dry, so dry that she didn't think she would be able to work it to get any sound out.

"That's why I can't marry you, Emma. You were right about your parents changing things for me. But not in the way you thought. I won't marry you because you deserve a man who can provide for your family. You *deserve* that."

Her mind still reeling from the shock, Emma couldn't decide what to say. The irony wasn't lost on her. Marcus wouldn't marry her because he'd lost his fortune investing… which wouldn't have mattered if her father hadn't lost *their* money investing.

When the weight of it hit her, Emma thought she might be sick.

Marcus was oblivious to her inner turmoil—if he wasn't, then he would have noticed that she needed to lie down. He dropped her hand, trailing the back of his fingers along her cheek.

"I'm sorry I can't be what you deserve," he whispered.

Brushing up to the outside corner of her eye, Marcus caught a tear before it had the chance to fall. Then his hand moved to cup the back of her neck, bringing her face closer. He pressed a chaste kiss against her forehead.

"I just want you to be happy, Emma. And I'm sorry…for all of it. I won't interfere anymore." Pulling her into his arms, he held her. Time was suspended, and Emma didn't know how long they stood locked with each other.

However long it was, it wasn't long enough. Eventually, Marcus pulled away from her after he whispered another "I love you" into her hair.

Then he was striding down the hall, to the stairs and out the door.

"I love you, too," Emma whispered to the empty house.

Chapter Twenty-Four

Mr. Barnwell should be arriving at any moment.

Emma sat nervously in the parlor, waiting for the second that Mathis would open the door, announcing she had a caller. Every muscle in her body was tense with anticipation. What-ifs and could-be's tumbled around in her mind.

Was she about to make one of the biggest mistakes of her life?

Her stomach clenched in fear. She'd told Mr. Barnwell that she needed a day to consider his proposal and had promised him an answer when he next returned. And now the moment of truth had nearly arrived. Once she committed, there would be no possibility of turning back. No chance to alter her future.

Not getting a single minute of sleep the night before didn't help the onslaught of nerves. Once Marcus had left, Emma's mind had been too busy to let her rest. She had cried more tears than she had in her life—over what had been and what perhaps should have been.

But with the rising of the sun came a steely, grim determination that no matter the consequences, she was going to make the situation right. Enough tears had been shed, enough emotion wasted on things she couldn't possibly change.

What would Marcus have to say about what she was about to do?

Emma shoved aside the thought. It didn't matter anymore *what* Marcus would think about her decision. He'd made certain that he wasn't any part of her life.

The door to the parlor opened.

"Miss Mercer," Mathis said quietly.

She swung her eyes up to meet his.

"Yes?" Her mouth was dry.

"Mr. Barnwell is here, miss."

"A-all right. Send him in, I suppose."

Her life was about to completely change. Emma wanted to open her mouth and tell Mathis that she'd changed her mind, that she wanted him to send Mr. Barnwell away…anything to forestall what she was about to do.

But the butler was an astute man and had already read the lines of worry and fear in her face. Clearly, he'd interpreted them correctly, as well.

"Would you like me to wait a few moments before sending him in?" he asked.

Maybe you should send him home.

But she didn't take any kind of reprieve.

"No sense in stalling the inevitable, is there, Mathis?"

The old man shook his head, his expression a little woeful—which was shocking to see on the generally stoic face. "I suppose not, Miss Mercer."

With a quick nod of the head, the butler backed out of the room. Mr. Barnwell entered not seconds afterward.

Mr. Barnwell's face was so open and excited that Emma felt ill. But she couldn't put announcing her decision off a minute longer.

"Good day, Miss Mercer," he said, coming to take the chair beside her.

"Mr. Barnwell." Emma's voice trembled slightly.

Am I really about to do this?

There was no other decision she *could* make.

"You are ready with your answer for me today?" he asked gently.

As awkward and nervous as Emma felt, it took several deep breaths before she took the plunge.

Emma took Mr. Barnwell's hands in hers. "I can't tell you how honored I am by your proposal, Mr. Barnwell," Emma began.

"The honor is mine," he protested. But his demeanor was more subdued than the last time they'd discussed marriage. Perhaps he could sense her impending refusal.

"I can't marry you," she told him sadly. Releasing one of his hands, she retrieved his ring and handed it back to him.

And Emma *was* sad. Accepting Barnwell's proposal would have been the mature, logical thing to do. But after what had transpired last night, after Marcus's confession, how could she possibly have done any differently?

Mr. Barnwell seemed to handle her rejection with aplomb. He smiled rather sadly and nodded slowly. "That is my most unfortunate loss."

The merchant might have been a bumbling sort, but he could certainly turn a charming phrase. And while he didn't ask for one, Emma felt she owed him an explanation.

"I can't marry you because there's someone else," Emma said quietly.

Surprisingly, Mr. Barnwell grinned. "I thought perhaps it was something like that."

His easy smile made her feel about an inch tall. "I'm not refusing you because I'm marrying him," she continued. "I just didn't think it would be fair to you if we married when I loved someone else."

His nod was understanding and his face compassionate.

"I understand, my dear. But why not marry him if you love him?"

Wasn't that the unanswerable question? Oh, of course, now Emma had Marcus's reasoning for refusing to marry her. And his intentions were noble. Olivia's idea of the husband hunt had been orchestrated to find someone with enough money to support Emma's family. If Marcus's fortune was gone, marrying him would only mean more hardships and struggling for her parents.

And he admitted to losing his fortune on an investment. Wasn't that the same thing her father had done to the family for years…the reason they were in their predicament? If Marcus had still been offering to marry her, could Emma really have accepted, knowing that doing so would forever tie her to a man with the same proclivities as her father?

No, Emma thought, the word resounding and resolute. No matter how much she loved him, she wouldn't consign herself, or any future children, to living an unstable, uncertain life.

As Mr. Barnwell kept watching her expectantly, Emma realized that she hadn't answered the question.

"Just an insurmountable hurdle," she said with a shrug.

Well, that sounded dramatic.

The merchant's smile was knowing and wise. "There's no such thing."

"If only it were that simple," she responded.

"Who said it can't be?"

Emma could have argued, but Mr. Barnwell was only trying to be kind and it wouldn't have really been fair to keep protesting. There was no easy answer, no ready-made solution that could solve her problem. And how had they gone from discussing Barnwell's marriage proposal to talking about Marcus and her failed relationship?

It was a disconcertingly odd situation.

"Emma, if I may call you that?" He stopped, waiting for her permission.

She smiled. "Of course."

"Emma, I know I've seen more of the world than you have. And I don't mean to sound like I know everything…but I think you'd be surprised how simple things can be when you let God take care of them."

Unsure of what exactly to say to that, Emma stayed silent.

"Now, my dear," Mr. Barnwell said, rising from his seat, "I'm sure you would rather I leave you to your thoughts and plans."

Emma was going to protest that he didn't have to leave so suddenly, that the least she could do was call for a tea service, but the gentleman wouldn't brook her arguments. So she followed behind him as he led the way to the door.

Turning at the last second, he clasped both of her hands in his large ones. "I hope that you find what you're looking for, Emma dear."

Her eyes misted at the unexpected kindness of the man that she had just refused. "Me, too," she said.

Emma tensed when she heard soft footsteps coming down the stairs. Loosening her grip on her valise, she sighed. This was exactly what she hoped to avoid.

"I don't suppose you're only taking a walk?" Olivia's quiet voice was tinged with sadness.

"I left a note," Emma said, turning around. The excuse was awkward and undeserving of all of Olivia's friendship and trust.

But her friend didn't seem angry with her, only disappointed and of course confused. "Why are you…?" she asked, gesturing at the valise Emma had set on the floor.

"It was in my note," Emma said, her voice breaking and tears filling her eyes.

Olivia watched her for a moment. Her mouth turned down in a frown. "You weren't going to tell me yourself that you were leaving?"

Emma had been selfish and cowardly, thinking only of how hard it would be to say goodbye, and likely a permanent one, to her friends—two people who had given her much more than material gifts, but had opened their home and their hearts to her and had selflessly given their time, concern and love.

"I'm sorry, Olivia," Emma said instead of confessing her inner thoughts. That litany was too dark, too shameful to repeat aloud. And it only reinforced her conviction that she didn't recognize who she was letting herself become…but she certainly didn't like it.

In a subtle, shifting moment, Olivia's face smoothed out, and her manner became brisk and efficient as she walked down the stairs toward Emma. And Emma couldn't help but watch the change with a bit of surprised stupor.

Is she going to grab my things and lock me in? Emma thought when the marchioness was only steps away.

But Olivia smiled, a cheerful, disarming expression.

"Would you at least have tea with me first?" she asked.

Emma could have said no…but she didn't *want* to. She was going to miss Olivia terribly, and maybe with few minutes spent in conversation, she could explain—without explaining *everything,* of course—why she'd chosen to abandon the plan.

"Of course," Emma said.

Olivia couldn't have looked more relieved than if she'd just received a pardon from the gallows.

Odd.

After a maid brought the tea service, Olivia prepared the cups, during which time Emma held her breath, waiting for her friend to question whether she'd gone daft.

But when Olivia finally did speak, the words out of her mouth shocked Emma.

"I'm sorry," the marchioness said.

"What do you have to apologize for?" Emma asked, bewildered. "You've been gracious and generous and...well, you're my friend." Her voice broke slightly at the last word.

Olivia looked away, as though uncomfortable with the words of praise and appreciation. "No, I've been wrong," she argued.

"I agreed to the plan, Olivia..."

The marchioness shook her head. "No, it's not that."

"Then what?" Emma prompted after several seconds of silence.

"I've...I've... This is really hard to say." Olivia paused. "I've been sending your parents money."

"What?"

For probably the first time since they had met, Olivia looked like she didn't quite know what to say. She looked a cross between guilty and afraid.

"I knew your parents needed the money since you weren't working for the Roths anymore. And we'd never really talked about that."

"So, how did you find them?" Emma asked. "I mean, you must have found them if you sent money."

Olivia nodded. "Marcus said that he saw you in Cheapside several times, and when he told me that, combined with the fact that your parents were *somewhere*..." She looked sheepish. "I just assumed."

"Oh." Really, it was all she could think to say because her mind was preoccupied with another, burgeoning concern.

"So to see if my assumption was correct, I went to see them."

This momentarily distracted Emma. "*You* went to see them?"

Olivia's smile was genuine for the first time that afternoon. "Well, Nick and I went. A couple of weeks ago. I didn't tell you because I knew you'd try to stop me."

Emma didn't know whether to be touched that her friends cared enough to investigate her comings and goings, or if she should be mortified that her secret was out.

Her friend didn't give her much time to make a decision, however, because she'd begun her own confessional and continued on with admirable speed and detail.

"I love your parents," Olivia said with a smile.

"Did…" Emma swallowed, wondering how to ask her next question delicately. "Did my father happen to ask you to help…um…finance any ventures?" As soon as she made the connection between Olivia giving her parents money and then their actually spending time with her parents, she worried that her father had seen the opportunity and seized it.

Olivia laughed. "No, although he and Nick had quite an involved conversation about some speculations."

Emma groaned.

"Actually, Nick thinks that your father has some very good insight."

"His record of losses wouldn't suggest that," Emma muttered.

"Perhaps he's too trusting," Olivia allowed. "But I believe Nick has plans to meet with your father to discuss some viable possibilities in-depth."

Emma didn't know what to say. What had the potential to be a disaster—her friends meeting her slightly eccentric parents—might actually become something for her father that could better their financial position.

She sighed with relief and was yet again reminded of how little faith she had sometimes.

"Well, thank you and thank Nick. There's no need to apologize. In fact, I can't tell you how much—"

"That's not why I apologized," Olivia interrupted, fretting with her nail, picking and smoothing an imaginary piece of skin only she could see.

"All right…"

"Nick wanted to offer your father a job weeks ago."

Emma couldn't help it—she choked on her tea.

Olivia held up her hand, as though to stop Emma from saying anything yet. "But I begged him to wait to discuss it with your parents."

"Wh-what kind of job?" So many questions came to mind. That one just happened to be the first one out of her mouth.

"As a steward at one of our estates."

It was too much to comprehend. Not only were Nick and Olivia acquainted with her parents, but Nick planned to offer her father a position. It would be honest employment…a steady income…and it wouldn't matter that she'd yet to find another governessing opportunity, or that she'd refused Mr. Barnwell's proposal.

Everything was going to be fine. Better than fine, really. Only…

Why had Olivia told Nick not to go ahead and offer the job?

When Emma asked, Olivia looked away.

"I didn't want you to leave" was the whispered confession.

"Olivia," Emma said, rising from her seat and crossing the little tea-service table to take a seat beside her friend, whose eyes were full of tears. "I'll be your friend no matter where I go."

The regal marchioness sniffed and wiped at her eyes with a neatly folded piece of linen. "I never wanted you to marry for anything other than love," she said, veering slightly off the subject. "I thought if I gave you and M—" She halted. "I thought with enough time, you might find that in a husband."

And as quickly as Marcus's shadow had settled over the

conversation, it lifted. Olivia straightened her shoulders, shrugging them as though she were foisting off the sorrow and worry. "Now, if you're truly leaving, I demand ample time to say my goodbyes. Or else I'll tell Mathis not to let you out the door."

Laughing, Emma threw her arms around her friend. Happiness for a moment overshadowed the sorrow she knew she'd always carry with her. It might not have been the solution she had hoped for, but it would be good for her family. And maybe the pain she felt would lessen with time.

Emma could only hope so.

Chapter Twenty-Five

Marcus forced himself to stay away from Olivia's for two weeks.

Without question, it was the longest fortnight of his life.

By now, Emma and Barnwell would be busy making plans for their wedding. Olivia would have undoubtedly thrown herself into the melee with gusto. The house would be abuzz with activity, preparations and excitement.

Marcus would have only been in the way.

Over the past couple of weeks, he had tried to expunge Emma from his mind. She would always be the woman he loved. And for that very reason, he couldn't be around her right now. It had been difficult enough for him to confess to her, to explain himself and then to let her go. Why would he further torture himself by being around the happy nuptial planning?

It'd been two weeks since he'd slept…two weeks since he'd seen Emma…two weeks since he'd felt the ground tip underneath him.

He'd ignored letters from Grimshaw, shunned visits from Mr. Wilbanks, had refused to do anything or see anyone that might remind him of possibly one of the most stunning failures of his life.

She deserves better, has found better with Barnwell, became the running criticism whenever he thought about going after her. And he thought about going after her a lot.

And what would he do? Go to her with the honest admission that while he loved her, he couldn't give her a good life? Emma knew that already—he'd told her himself. And she hadn't stopped him from walking away…then she'd walked straight into another man's arms.

He hadn't read the paper for that long, either. Marcus wasn't foolish enough to believe that as long as he didn't see the betrothal announcement in the *Times* that it wasn't happening. He just didn't want to be reminded any more than absolutely necessary. He'd instructed Gibbons to ignore any missives that came to the house. No contact was better than hearing news he'd rather ignore.

"Lord Westin!"

Marcus's head swung up at the sound of his name being yelled through the halls. Abandoning the paperwork he hadn't really been paying attention to in his study, the earl pushed back his chair. In several quick steps, he was out in the hall, trying to figure out why it sounded like Grimshaw was making a ruckus downstairs.

The reason for that was because, apparently, his estate manager *was* making a ruckus downstairs. "My lord!" Grimshaw called out once he caught sight of Marcus, taking the stairs two at a time in his haste.

"Grimshaw?" he gaped.

When the manager finally came abreast of him, Marcus searched his employee's face for a sign of what had happened. Other than being a bit out of breath and having a ruddy complexion, no doubt due to his sprint, Mr. Grimshaw appeared otherwise fine.

But Marcus knew better than to be lulled into complacency by that. So his heart pounded a fast, heavy rhythm in his chest. Lately, the estate manager had not brought anything other than ill tidings.

"What is it?" Marcus asked, his voice unintentionally loud.

The manager bent over at the waist, placing his hands on his knees and gasping for air. Marcus forced himself to remain patient, but he did wonder if the man had run all the way to London.

"It's about the ship, my lord," the manager finally said.

"What about it now?" Marcus asked, thinking he never wanted to hear another word about the doomed ship.

"It pulled into harbor this morning."

Marcus felt as though his breath was knocked out of him. "It what?"

Grimshaw's face broke into a huge smile. "The ship pulled into harbor this morning. It's fine. Everything's fine. Better than fine, really."

In a situation like this, Marcus might have hoped to be the epitome of cool composure, but in reality, he found himself close to having to sit down right on the floor where he stood. It was a glorious, completely unexpected answer to prayer. And he couldn't even find the first word to ask another question.

"We had word that another merchant vessel had spotted our ship. Wilbanks and I have been trying to get in touch with you," Grimshaw explained.

So that had been the reason behind the constant missives and visits Marcus had been ignoring?

"You're an even richer man now than ever before, my lord," the estate manager said, looking no less relieved and discomposed than his employer.

"I don't care about that," Marcus said in a hoarse voice.

And he didn't.

Living on a drastically reduced income was not something Marcus had ever anticipated, but these past few weeks, where uncertainty had been his closest companion, he'd resolved himself to that fate. He'd adjust. If entrance into adulthood with the death of his parents had done anything for him, it had taught him the importance of adapting to the circumstances. So while he'd not relished having to scrape and losing the luxuries he'd taken for granted, Marcus had been resigned. His greatest concern had been the people who depended on him for their living.

But now all was right.

God, he prayed, *I don't even know how to thank You.* And he met the place in prayer where his words would have been ineffective, but where God could hear the desires of his heart, the gratitude, the amazement.

"Perhaps we should go in your study and talk a little bit more," Grimshaw said, looking a little concerned that his master had yet to say anything of substance.

But Marcus was still too flabbergasted to respond. So Grimshaw clapped Marcus on the back and made a move to help him to the room.

"Come, my lord," the older man said. "Perhaps you should sit and rest for a while. I can have a footman—"

"No," Marcus interrupted. "I'll be fine. You, however, have been making too many mad dashes to Town," he said with a grin. "I'll have Gibbons show you to a room."

Grimshaw smiled and inclined his head. "I'd be most grateful for a room. In truth, my ride over was rather furious, so I could use a bit of a rest before I head home myself."

Marcus was thrilled that his money was once again secure, that he wouldn't have to break the news to his tenants or his employees that money had become a pressing concern.

Grimshaw bowed, still watching Marcus closely as though he expected the man to fall over from shock at any moment. The surprise was slowly ebbing away, leaving in its place a gratitude Marcus hoped he would always feel. The only thing that could possibly make the moment better was having Emma by his side.

But she'd already made her decision. And as a man of honor, Marcus couldn't ask or expect her to cry off from her engagement to Barnwell and marry him instead.

Although, he had to admit, the thought was tempting.

Two days after the good news about his finances, Marcus was still avoiding Olivia's and Emma's wedding plans. He'd managed to stave off any visits from Nick and Olivia for the past couple of weeks by sending them a missive indicating that he was unwell.

But it would appear his sister was tired of waiting.

"Gibbons, you have exactly two minutes to produce my brother!" Olivia bellowed as she stomped up the stairs.

Marcus was in his study with the door shut, yet he could still hear Olivia's enraged voice ringing through the halls.

Gibbons said something in reply, but since the butler wasn't yelling—unlike Olivia—all Marcus could make out was a few words here and there. He thought he caught "indisposed."

The voices and steps stopped outside of the door to his study.

"Do you care to tell me why my brother is hiding?" Olivia asked Gibbons.

Gibbons mumbled something inaudible.

Heaving a sigh, Marcus rose from his chair. He might as well go ahead and let Olivia in. Otherwise, she would stand outside in the hall bellowing and berating Gibbons until he cracked. He wasn't ready for the upcoming confrontation.

It looked like he didn't have much choice, though.

"Good afternoon, Olivia," he said as he pulled open the door.

Whirling around, his sister almost stumbled in surprise

when she saw him. Just as quickly, however, her eyes narrowed. "You don't look sick," she accused.

That was because she couldn't see inside. His fortune might be restored, but his heart was still aching. Commenting on that would only make him seem maudlin, so Marcus just stepped aside to let her in the room. "Come in," he said. Perhaps his voice wasn't as gracious as it should have been, but he could easily blame that on his reluctance to hear about Emma.

Olivia leaped into his arms, squeezing him tightly. "I was worried about you."

He returned her hug. "Don't be worried about me," he said gruffly.

"Impossible," she said. Stepping back from him, his sister went and took a seat and then motioned imperiously for him to do so.

"How have you been?" Olivia asked. Her eyes raked over him, searching his face for any signs or answers.

"I've been…" Marcus didn't really have a word to describe it that wouldn't give himself away. When his mind refused to turn up an adjective, he simply shrugged his shoulders.

Olivia wouldn't be fooled. During the years when they had only each other to rely upon, their bond had been forged much deeper than usually found in siblings. And his sister was perceptive enough to read past the grasping for words.

Her gaze sharpened. Olivia knew the truth.

But surprisingly, she didn't say anything.

"We've missed you," his sister said simply.

Marcus shifted in his chair. "How has everyone been doing at your house?" He tried for a casual, uninterested tone.

"Nick's fine. I'm fine. Mathis seems to be doing well… although he rarely says much to the contrary."

That's not everyone in your house. "And Emma?" he asked. Marcus wished he could unask the question as soon as Olivia began fidgeting and fussing with a thread on her sleeve. Did he really want to know the answer to that?

No, he didn't.

Which is why it was completely inconceivable that he would press Olivia when she didn't answer. "How is Emma?"

After an audible inhale, she answered, "Emma's gone, Marcus."

"What?"

His sister's nod was sad. "She left nearly two weeks ago. I would have told you, but you weren't accepting visitors—"

"Where did she go?" Marcus interrupted before the conversation centered on his extended absence.

"Back to her parents."

Unable to help himself, Marcus slammed his chair backward. He was on his feet within a second. "What do you mean 'back to her parents'?"

Olivia gaped. Her eyes tracked his every step as he paced the length of the study.

"She packed her things and went home.... Well," Olivia amended, "not exactly home. Nick hired Mr. Mercer as steward to our Yorkshire estate."

Which part of that confession should he address first? The fact that she returned to her parents? That Nick offered Emma's father a job—thus taking Emma across the country? The complete lack of mention of Mr. Barnwell?

"Is she coming back?" Marcus asked, hating how hopeful the question sounded.

His sister shook her head.

"What about Barnwell?" Had he growled the name?

Olivia furrowed her brow. "I suppose Mr. Barnwell is doing fine..."

Marcus smacked his hand against the wall in frustration. "When are they getting married?" he barked. Perhaps he shouldn't be losing his temper with his sister, but couldn't he get a straight answer?

"You don't know?" she whispered.

"Clearly, I don't—"

"Emma said no," Olivia interrupted him.

"She said *no?*"

Olivia nodded.

"Why?"

Olivia's smile was so sad Marcus felt his heart breaking. "You'll have to ask her that."

How could he when she was so far away?

He cleared his throat and moved back toward his chair. "Well…well…as long as Emma's happy."

Olivia rose from her chair. "How long are you going to lie to yourself, Marcus?" She held up a hand to stop his almost automatic protest. "And don't pretend you don't know what I'm talking about."

Marcus said nothing. But he wouldn't meet her eyes.

"I know you have things going on right now. And no, I don't know what, exactly…because you won't open up. You won't let me help you with your burden. We should both know better by now."

Marcus didn't breathe. She was right. Yet he had no idea how to even begin to make his confession. And he wasn't even sure that if the words would come he'd be ready to say them. The secret had been his own private torment, and he wasn't sure how to share…even though the crisis was over.

"I thought the money was gone, Olivia," he said, surprising even himself with the utterance. "I thought everything in the investment accounts had been lost."

Her eyes widened. "What do you mean?" Her voice was almost a whisper. "You've always been so responsible. I've never known you to risk more money than you could afford to lose on an investment."

He nodded. "You're right. I don't risk more than I can afford to lose. But this wasn't completely my doing," Marcus explained.

"What do you mean?" Olivia asked slowly.

He explained the situation. The ship that was lost and then found. The monies he'd expected to survive without, and then finding that he was unaccountably richer than before.

She was silent for several moments. "You should have told me," she said finally.

He had no acceptable excuse. Not wanting her to have to worry about her older brother, knowing he was the one who had always taken care of *her,* was a thin reason for keeping the secret.

"So what about Emma?" Olivia asked next, changing the subject. As though she knew that he might stop her at any moment, the question was blurted out.

Had he not been thinking that very question since Olivia had told him Emma didn't accept Barnwell's offer? Really, how he'd been able to carry on the rest of the conversation with his sister was nothing short of astounding, so consumed was he with wondering whether Emma would have him back.

"What if she doesn't want me anymore?" Marcus asked, feeling more vulnerable than he ever had.

Olivia frowned. "She loves you, Marcus."

He brightened. "Emma told you that?"

A long, uncomfortable pause. "She didn't have to tell me," Olivia settled on, finally.

He thought of the night outside her room, when he'd promised her that he would stop interfering in her life. Thought about the confusion on her face when she'd asked him why he couldn't leave her alone. Had she fled to Nick's estate with her parents in an effort to avoid him?

And if so, why would he think she'd be agreeable to him renewing his proposal?

"But *you* most certainly love her," Olivia said, breaking into this thoughts.

Marcus nodded but remained unconvinced. Perhaps Emma was through with him—Barnwell or no. "Yes, I do. But sometimes that's not enough, Olivia."

"You're wrong, you know," his sister said with a surprising air of wisdom. "It's everything."

Olivia didn't say another thing about it. For the next half an hour, she stayed and chatted with him about various subjects, save the one that was the most important. And when the time came for her to leave, his sister hugged him tightly.

"Do the right thing, Marcus," she whispered in his ear.

He hugged her back. "As soon as I figure out what it is."

For long hours after his sister left, Marcus sat, nursing a headache, one borne from too many thoughts and possibilities tumbling through his mind.

Give Emma a chance to find happiness without showing up and making things worse for her.

But maybe you should try one last time before you give up.

What if she thinks you're coming only because the finances are sound? What if she doesn't realize you would have fought for her—as a pauper, even—were Barnwell not in the picture? If it weren't for the fact that you thought them engaged.

Give Emma a chance to decide for herself what she wants.

The thoughts came unbidden and unsought. But once they had passed through his mind, Marcus was unable to think of little else.

Could it be that all of his problems came from his inability to let go of the control long enough to actually pray about what he should do? That thought was crippling. But once it had crossed his mind, the niggling suspicion that he had ruined his own chances at happiness refused to disappear.

Lord. How can I make this right?

There was really only one way. And while Marcus couldn't begin to predict how Emma would receive him, the urge to go to her couldn't be denied. So with a rash impulsiveness that was rather foreign to him, Marcus prepared to ride to Yorkshire.

Chapter Twenty-Six

"There's someone coming up the road," Emma's mother called out through the house with the excitement of one who rarely saw visitors. They'd been in the country at Nick's estate for a couple of weeks, and they were all still adjusting to the change from London's busy streets.

There hadn't been any visitors except for Nick and Olivia. No Marcus, of course. Not that she expected him to come.

Emma didn't even bother to look up from her darning. It wasn't until she'd come home—after months without the chore—that she remembered how much she detested it. And that was mostly because she was so bad at it.

"He's still approaching." Her mother's voice began to sound worried, suddenly afraid of how they would entertain a mysterious traveler.

"I wouldn't worry overmuch, mother. He's likely to ride right past, or veer at the fork toward the Cranfords."

"I don't think so, Emma," her mother said, wringing her damp hand on her apron. "He didn't take the fork. And he's looking right at our house."

This was enough to finally pique Emma's curiosity. Besides, she was more than willing to lay aside her darning, especially if something—or more appropriately—some*one* interesting was on the horizon.

"Who is it, Mama?" Emma asked, coming to stand beside her mother at the window. "Is it Mr. Frank, the butcher's son?" She squinted against the sun that was cresting over the horizon.

"I think not," her mother returned. "But I can't make out who it might be."

Neither could Emma, with the sun shining so brightly in her eyes. "I can't imagine who would be by this early if not Mr. Frank's son." The young man, only a year or two older than Emma herself, had made visiting their cottage a frequent occurrence since their family had arrived.

"I tell you it's not him. That gentleman seats his mount too fine to be young Frank."

On that point, Emma agreed with her mother completely. The unexpected visitor, though riding at a breakneck pace, didn't appear to have the slightest trouble handling his horse.

"He does appear to be in a hurry," her mother fretted. "And the house isn't nearly ready for visitors."

Emma patted her mother's shoulder. "Don't fret. Everything is acceptable. And he, whoever he is, can surely expect no grand reception after showing up unannounced."

Her mother neither agreed nor disagreed with her, although it was probably quite a strain on her not to insist that regardless of any forewarning—or lack thereof—her home should always be adorned as though the Prince Regent himself might be coming to call.

"Go meet him outside," her mother ordered.

Emma hesitated. "Surely that's not proper," she argued.

"I must go get your father. Meet the gentleman outside and stall for time," her mother urged, giving her no more time to protest before she was scurrying up the stairs.

"Are you expecting someone?" Emma tried calling after her.

The only response that floated down the stairs was, "Try pinching some color into your cheeks, dear."

She ignored that last command.

One more quick look out of the window told her the rider was already near enough that he could no longer be seen through the glass panes. Sighing—a bit in resignation, a bit in frustration—Emma walked purposefully to the front door. Likely, this gentleman was a wayward traveler, seeking directions. So it was best to be done with him so she could return to her darning.

Shielding her eyes against the glaring sun, Emma watched the rider approaching. There was something familiar about his gait, about the way he held himself. But she couldn't tell enough about him from that to know who it was.

But obviously, the rider saw her. In two quick kicks, he had the horse flying across the distance separating them. Emma felt a moment of panic. Who was this man? And why did he suddenly seem as if he was being chased toward her by a pack of wild animals?

When he came to the place where a stand of trees blocked out the sun's glare, Emma's eyes had to adjust to the sudden absence of light.

After a few seconds, everything came into focus. The sky. The trees. The visitor.

And it felt like her heart slammed to a stop in her chest.

"Marcus?" she whispered.

He pulled his horse to a stop and slid down from the saddle in one fluid motion. Even when he was walking toward her, and she could clearly see his features, Emma had difficulty believing it was really him...at her home.

"Emma." He said her name like the softest caress. And then as though uncomfortable with the intimacy of the moment, he looked at the copse of trees before quirking a grin. "I'd imagine a place like this would appeal to the tree-climbing hoyden in you."

"So you came all the way out here to admire the landscape?" she asked, almost breathlessly.

Marcus shook his head.

"C-come inside, then," she managed, even though her stomach fluttered with nervousness.

Marcus followed after her. "You must forgive my dusty appearance," he said with an overly formal air. "I…I rode all day."

Her relief…her surprise…the mixture of emotions she felt upon seeing him again—when she'd all but given up hope of ever laying eyes on him—made her willing to forgive him anything.

Emma made no apologies for their simple abode. And she could tell he expected none. His praise of her home was modest and sincere.

Once they were in the little room off the foyer that doubled as their makeshift sitting room, Emma let her eyes drink their fill of him. He *was* dusty after a day spent pounding down the country roads. She wanted to tell him how badly she'd missed him, how she'd counted the days that they were apart, but to no purpose since there was never any understanding between them. She could have told him that she didn't care what his reason was for coming, she was only glad to see him. Instead, she said none of those things.

"Would you care for some tea?" she asked instead. "Or coffee?" she amended when she belatedly remembered that he didn't like tea.

Marcus shook his head. "No," he added as an afterthought.

"All right." Emma sat on the couch, watched as Marcus paced across the worn rug in the little room. She was out of courtesies to offer him. And if she weren't careful, before long, she'd be making inane comments on the brightness of the sun or the mildness of the weather.

"I'm surprised you came by to visit me," she said honestly. It perhaps wasn't the best thing she could have said, but it was at least more interesting than discussing winds and clouds.

He paused his pacing. "Oh. I'm not here to visit you."

Emma sat back against the couch, almost in a slump. "Oh," she said flatly…but still not understanding him.

"I apologize. That came out wrong," he said with a self-deprecating laugh. "I'm glad to see you, but I'm here to see your father. I sent a missive ahead of me since I was delayed by…*business*. Maybe it didn't arrive," he said with a frown.

"My father?" she repeated in confusion.

He didn't look confused, but he *did* look uncomfortable. "Yes…"

"Ah, you must be Lord Westin," her father said, coming down the stairs. "Welcome!"

"It is a pleasure to meet you, Mr. Mercer," Marcus said, moving forward to shake hands with her father.

Emma watched with a mixture of confusion and fascination as the Earl of Westin and her father, who looked better put together than she usually saw him—his hair wasn't sticking out in tufts everywhere and he was actually wearing a jacket—shook hands. It was as though they were old friends reuniting for the first time in years. And how did they even know each other? Emma looked around for her mother, hoping that she might be able to shed some light on the situation.

But if her mother were aware of anything unusual in this meeting, her face showed no signs of it. Instead, she was smiling as graciously as a grand lady of the manor as she entered the room.

"How delightful to meet you, Lord Westin," she said after Marcus introduced himself to her.

He bowed over her hand and then turned a dazzling smile on. Her mother nearly swooned into the nearest chair from the force of it.

"I don't understand what's going on here," Emma complained, no longer content to watch this strange tableau without trying to figure out what was happening. It was like being thrust right in the middle of a play where everyone knew their lines but her. Disconcerting.

"I've come to visit with your father," Marcus said again.

"Quite right, Lord Westin. Emma, would you see to a tea service?" her father asked, guiding the earl with a hand on the younger man's shoulder.

Emma was going to protest for Marcus's sake that she would bring coffee for him but then thought better of it. Since everyone thought it was acceptable to refuse to answer any of her questions, she certainly was not going to go out of her way to be helpful.

So it was with an almost wicked glee that she made the tea as strong as she possibly could. And when she went to deliver the tray to her father's study, she tried to step lightly so that she might overhear whatever was being said inside the closed room. What purpose could Marcus have in coming to see her father? To the best of her knowledge the two men had never met before. And unless Marcus was coming to try and talk to her father about some business matters…

But none of that made any sense whatsoever.

She supposed all she had to do was be patient. If it was something she was supposed to know about, she'd discover it eventually. Although she was overwhelmed with curiosity, Emma went to the parlor to sit and wait.

"I'm a fool." Marcus surprised her by walking into the sunny little parlor at the front of the house unannounced.

In spite of her resolve not to buckle easily, Emma felt the corners of her lips pull upward in a smile. She smothered it before Marcus mistook the expression to mean she was ready to capitulate.

"Go on," she said, turning around to face him.

Marcus sighed and pushed his hand through his hair. "I should have realized…should have thought…" He couldn't manage to finish his sentence.

Emma was about to stop him, to try to alleviate his suffering. Before she could manage anything, he kneeled at her feet.

"Emma," he whispered. "I was so wrong."

The catch in his voice, the sight of this powerful man on his knees before her brought tears to her eyes.

"Emma," Marcus said, peering into her eyes with such intensity she thought he could likely see the whole of her yearnings and desires. And surely he could see that each moment spent apart from him was agony to her.

"I've made so many mistakes. And I'm sure I'll make many more," he said. "But my biggest mistake was letting you walk out of my life. And if you're willing to forgive me, then I promise I'll never make that one again."

She said nothing. She couldn't. Tears lodged in her throat until she thought that even to part her lips would unleash a storm of weeping.

"Emma?" Marcus asked. His smile began to drop.

Putting her hands to her lips, she shook her head. She needed a few moments. This was all so wonderful and unexpected. She'd resigned herself to a life without love, but now, Emma didn't have to settle for that kind of half existence. God had provided for her in every way she needed… and wanted.

Marcus must have taken her reaction the wrong way because he rose from his knee and was moving away. As soon as she realized what he was doing, Emma jumped to her feet. His back was to her, but she spun him back around to face her.

"What—" he began.

But Emma silenced his protest with a kiss.

She must have really surprised him because it took at least two seconds for his arms to wrap around her and return the embrace. When the kiss ended, Marcus grinned.

"Is that a yes?" he asked.

"A yes, and an 'I love you.'"

Marcus dropped a kiss at the corner of her mouth. "I love you, too."

Emma rested her head against his shoulder. They could stay entwined like this forever, and she'd never complain again. But Marcus pulled slightly back. "I should probably tell you that you're going to be disgustingly wealthy," he said with a smile.

"What?"

"The ship came in," he said as though that explained everything.

"I'm so glad for you, Marcus."

"Be glad for *us,* love." And then, digging in his pocket, he produced a box. "I wouldn't have been delayed getting here, but I wanted to be optimistic. So I got you a gift."

Emma smiled at how nervous he sounded. And then gasped when she saw the beautiful ring twinkling up at her. "It's lovely," she said, tears springing to her eyes.

After he slipped it on her finger, he embraced her again. "Should I let you go?" he asked finally with a smile.

"Why?"

"Don't women usually want to go and tell everyone they're getting married? Surely my sister is dying to know…"

"My letter to her can wait," Emma said, burrowing her head into the curve of his shoulder.

"You know she never intended you to marry anyone but me," her future husband said with a chuckle.

"So I guess it was more of a Marcus-hunt than anything…" she said, hiding her face because she couldn't believe she'd let something that sappy out of her mouth.

He laughed. "I've heard that's the most dangerous prey to pursue. Because they're so elusive."

"And stupid," she contributed.

"No arguments here." This time he kissed the top of her head. "You might have been the better hunter," he said, "but I've won the better prize."

"No arguments here," she returned.

"I'm glad I have a lifetime to prove you made a good choice," Marcus said, sobering slightly.

"You don't need a lifetime to convince me of that," Emma said. The love she felt for him seemed so great she didn't know if her heart could hold it all. "But I'll give you one anyway."

* * * * *

Dear Reader,

I want to thank you for picking up *Engaging the Earl* and seeing it through to the end! You enable me to do what I love most—craft stories that hopefully warm the heart and lift the spirit.

I've been in love with Marcus since he waltzed into the drawing room in his sister's story. He was everything I felt a good brother should be…protective, loyal and perhaps comically aggravating. But in his own tale, he became a complex hero…more complex than I thought he would be. Little did I know in the beginning that Marcus would have a long list of faults and foibles. Crazily enough, I think it only made me love him more.

And then there's Emma. Forced to shoulder a heavy burden, she continually had to deny her own wishes and desires in order to serve the greater benefit of her family. But in spite of her strength and courage, she let fear govern her actions, even to the point where it separated her from the man she loved.

These two needed each other. And in a way, I needed them. Writing Marcus and Emma's story continually reminded me that God's provision is greater than my biggest imaginings and that there is no situation He can't redeem if only I let Him.

I hope you've been blessed by this love story. And I always look forward to hearing from my readers. I can be found online at www.mandygoff.com or can be reached via email at mandy@mandygoff.com.

Blessings,

Mandy Goff

Questions for Discussion

1. Emma is forced to work as a governess in order to bring money home to her impoverished family. In Regency England, women had few means of employment open to them. Have there been times, even in our modern society, where you've felt unfairly limited based on something you couldn't change (gender, race, age, etc.)?

2. Marcus, while certainly happy that his sister and best friend have found love with each other, cannot help but feel envious, as well. What are some situations that have caused strong—and conflicting—emotions for you? And in those situations, how do you allow the positive emotions to triumph over the negative?

3. Emma's decision not to tell her parents about her termination frequently weighs heavily on her. Are there ever times when withholding the truth really is "for someone's own good"? If so, when do you decide when to make your confession? If not, what are some ways to tell the truth without causing additional harm?

4. When Marcus's estate manager confesses the investment blunder that might have cost the earl his fortune, instead of dismissing his employee, Marcus shows mercy and compassion. How difficult would it be for you in a similar situation to immediately extend forgiveness?

5. Although she initially protests, Emma finally agrees with Olivia's proposal of launching a "husband hunt." What do you think of her motivations for wanting to find a husband?

6. After years spent caring for Olivia, Marcus finds that he is unable to refuse her anything—including her request to assist Emma with finding a spouse. But he certainly doesn't plan on being overly helpful...in fact, he goes out of his way to scare any potential suitors off. Have you ever agreed to do something, wishing all the while that you could say "no"? How do you extricate yourself from those kinds of situations?

7. Olivia quite clearly wants to see her friend and brother together. And her attempts at playing matchmaker show a concerted effort to push Marcus and Emma into love. Are you ever guilty of thinking that God needs your help? And have there been times when you've tried to help something along but have actually ended up causing harm?

8. Emma's father frequently lets his optimistic nature overrule his better sense when it comes to his favorite hobby—making financial investments. Where should we, as Christians, draw the line between being optimistic, yet realistic, and being staunchly pessimistic?

9. Emma, because of her background, struggles with fear. Fear of not having security, fear of losing her independence. Because of her fears, she turns down Marcus's proposal. Has fear ever kept you from seizing a blessing or gift God intended for you? Why should we, as Christians, live courageously and without fear?

10. While Marcus doesn't necessarily recognize it, he has a problem with control. Circumstances in his life that have been beyond his ability to change them have made Marcus cling tightly to his well-controlled existence. Are

there any events in your life that had long-lasting negative effects, such as spawning a desire to always be in control? How has God redeemed those qualities?

11. Emma is frequently disappointed and angry when she learns that her father has once again risked their financial security and lost. While she is justified in her frustrations, do Emma's reactions glorify God and adhere to the commandment to honor one's parents?

12. Marcus decides, once he finds out about Emma's parents and their situation, that it would be wrong to marry Emma, since he might not be able to provide for them financially. Yet he is unable to stay away from her. How does his longing to be near her override his desire for a better future for her? And by being noble, how does he hurt both of them?

13. On the surface, it appears Mr. Barnwell would make a good husband. Ultimately, however, Emma decides that she won't marry for anything but love, even though that means she won't have any money for her family. Have any decisions you've made in the past carried weighty consequences? Were you tempted to do something you didn't believe in to spare yourself or others from those consequences?

14. Matthew 6:26 highlights God's care for even birds, asking, "Are you not worth much more than they?" How does this promise of care and provision affect you when making important decisions? How does it apply in day-to-day life?

15. Both Emma and Marcus seem to be distrustful of good things. Because of their cynicism, they frequently dis-

count blessings in their lives, while fearing something terrible must be around the corner. Do you ever look for the "strings attached" to your blessings? How can cynicism steal our joy?

INSPIRATIONAL

Love Inspired HISTORICAL

celebrating 15 YEARS

COMING NEXT MONTH
AVAILABLE APRIL 10, 2012

THE WEDDING JOURNEY
Irish Brides
Cheryl St.John

BRIDES OF THE WEST
Victoria Bylin, Janet Dean & Pamela Nissen

SANCTUARY FOR A LADY
Naomi Rawlings

LOVE ON THE RANGE
Jessica Nelson

Look for these and other Love Inspired books wherever books are sold, including most bookstores, supermarkets, discount stores and drugstores.

LIHCNM0312

REQUEST YOUR FREE BOOKS!

2 FREE INSPIRATIONAL NOVELS
PLUS 2
FREE
MYSTERY GIFTS

Love Inspired
HISTORICAL
INSPIRATIONAL HISTORICAL ROMANCE

YES! Please send me 2 FREE Love Inspired® Historical novels and my 2 FREE mystery gifts (gifts are worth about $10). After receiving them, if I don't wish to receive any more books, I can return the shipping statement marked "cancel". If I don't cancel, I will receive 4 brand-new novels every month and be billed just $4.49 per book in the U.S. or $4.99 per book in Canada. That's a saving of at least 22% off the cover price. It's quite a bargain! Shipping and handling is just 50¢ per book in the U.S. and 75¢ per book in Canada.* I understand that accepting the 2 free books and gifts places me under no obligation to buy anything. I can always return a shipment and cancel at any time. Even if I never buy another book, the two free books and gifts are mine to keep forever.

102/302 IDN FEHF

Name _____ (PLEASE PRINT) _____

Address _____ Apt. #

City _____ State/Prov. _____ Zip/Postal Code

Signature (if under 18, a parent or guardian must sign)

Mail to the **Reader Service**:
IN U.S.A.: P.O. Box 1867, Buffalo, NY 14240-1867
IN CANADA: P.O. Box 609, Fort Erie, Ontario L2A 5X3

Not valid for current subscribers to Love Inspired Historical books.

Want to try two free books from another series?
Call 1-800-873-8635 or visit www.ReaderService.com.

* Terms and prices subject to change without notice. Prices do not include applicable taxes. Sales tax applicable in N.Y. Canadian residents will be charged applicable taxes. Offer not valid in Quebec. This offer is limited to one order per household. All orders subject to credit approval. Credit or debit balances in a customer's account(s) may be offset by any other outstanding balance owed by or to the customer. Please allow 4 to 6 weeks for delivery. Offer available while quantities last.

Your Privacy—The Reader Service is committed to protecting your privacy. Our Privacy Policy is available online at www.ReaderService.com or upon request from the Reader Service.

We make a portion of our mailing list available to reputable third parties that offer products we believe may interest you. If you prefer that we not exchange your name with third parties, or if you wish to clarify or modify your communication preferences, please visit us at www.ReaderService.com/consumerschoice or write to us at Reader Service Preference Service, P.O. Box 9062, Buffalo, NY 14269. Include your complete name and address.

LIH11B

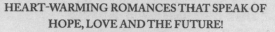

For a sneak peek of Shirlee McCoy's heart-stopping inspirational romantic suspense UNDERCOVER BODYGUARD, read on!

"It's okay," Ryder said, pulling Shelby into his arms.

But it wasn't okay, and they both knew it.

A woman was dead, and there was nothing either of them could do to change it.

"How can it be when Maureen is dead?" Shelby asked, looking up into his face as if he might have some way to fix things. He didn't, and he'd stopped believing in his own power and invincibility long ago.

"It will be. Eventually. Come on. You need to get the bump on your head looked at."

"I don't have time for that. I have to get back to the bakery. It's Friday. The busiest day of the week." Her teeth chattered on the last word, her body trembling. He draped his coat around her shoulders.

"Better?" he asked, and she nodded.

"I can't seem to stop shaking. I mean, one minute, I'm preparing to deliver pastries to my friend and the next she's gone. I just can't believe…." Her voice trailed off, her eyes widening as she caught sight of his gun holster.

"You've got a gun."

"Yes."

"Are you a police officer?"

"Security contractor."

"You're a bodyguard?"

"I'm a security contractor. I secure people and things."

"A bodyguard," she repeated, and he didn't argue.

Two fire trucks and an ambulance lined the curb in front of the house, and firefighters had already hooked a hose to the hydrant. Water streamed over the flames but did little to douse the fire.

Suddenly, an EMT ran toward them. "Is she okay?"

"She was knocked unconscious by the force of the explosion. She has a bad gash on her head."

"Let me take a look." The EMT edged him out of the way, and Ryder knew it was time to go talk to the fire marshal and the police officers who'd just arrived, and let the EMT take Shelby to the hospital.

But she grabbed his hand before he moved away, her grip surprisingly strong. "Are you leaving?"

"Do you want me to, Shelby Ann?" he asked.

"You can leave."

"I know that I can, but do you *want* me to?"

"I…haven't decided, yet."

Pick up UNDERCOVER BODYGUARD for the rest of Shelby and Ryder's exciting, suspenseful love story, available in April 2012, only from Love Inspired® Books Love Inspired® Suspense.